For Carolun,

MW00426990

The House on Ashbury Street

Susie Hara

MUMBLERS

Copyright © 2023 by Susie Hara

Cover photo © 2023 by the author

All rights reserved.

No part of this book may be reproduced in any form or by any electronic or mechanical means, including information storage and retrieval systems, without written permission from the author, except for the use of brief quotations in a book review.

Copyright promotes creativity, encourages diverse voices, supports free speech and creates a vibrant culture. Thank you for buying an authorized edition of this book and for complying with copyright laws.

This is a work of fiction. Names, characters, places and incidents either are the product of the author's imagination or are used fictitiously; any resemblance to actual persons, living or dead, businesses, companies, events or locales is entirely coincidental.

Published by Mumblers Press LLC, San Francisco CA USA

ISBN 978-1-7362444-8-7 (e-book) | 978-1-7362444-9-4 (paperback)

LCCN 2022921687

On the whole, human beings want to be good,
but not too good, and not quite all the
time.

— George Orwell, *All Art Is
Propaganda*

Contents

Prologue

Ron locked the door to his room, reached up to the top shelf of the closet, moved the decoy box aside, and grabbed the case. Ashbury House Rule: No guns. Which made him laugh. They had practiced the drill in basic training. Hold out your weapon: *This is my weapon.* Grab your dick: *This is my gun.* Hold out your weapon: *This one's for fighting.* Grab your dick: *This one's for fun.*

He set the case on his desk, opened it, and took out the Colt 1911. Once a month, he went through the ritual of cleaning it, even though it wasn't necessary. There was something about it that calmed him down.

But, he thought, if the housemates *did* find out about the pistol, they would freak out and have a big fucking house meeting. Supposedly the decision would be made by consensus, but really what would happen is Mama Linda would have her say, and then everyone else would agree, except maybe Che, and then after a while he'd give in too. They'd demand

1

that Ron get rid of it or move out. He'd try to explain—an unloaded weapon, with the ammunition hidden in a different spot—is completely safe. No one could ever get to it, especially not Nik-Knock. But they wouldn't understand.

He finished cleaning the weapon and held it in his hands. The weight of it was comforting. One of these days. But not today. He put it back in its case and stashed it in the closet.

The sound of voices drifted in and pulled him to his window. On the back deck, Willow and Mama Linda were talking, their heads together. Phoenix was in the garden, her small hands carefully pulling up the weeds from their roots and stacking them in a pile. With her lower lip stuck out, her brow wrinkled, and her curls gleaming in the sun, she was about as perfect a human being as you can get. She glanced up at his window—somehow she sensed he was there—and her gap-toothed grin lit her face. If not for her and Deb, he'd do it.

Chapter 1

Sand

2005

Phoenix "Nikki" Gold chose the less-comfortable chair in her office and focused on her client. The child, perched on an armchair, her ten-year-old form packed into jeans and a pink top, squirmed until she settled into the perfect spot. It was Nikki's sixth session with Hannah at the Brooklyn clinic. Maybe this time, she thought, I won't get triggered. A thin film of sweat formed on her upper lip.

Nikki waited. Nothing. Waited some more. Leaning forward, she said, "What did you play in PE today?"

Eyes darting, Hannah rhythmically patted the upholstery. "Soccer." Sniff. Pat, pat, pat.

"Nice. Which position?"

Hannah looked at her, expressionless. "Forward." She slid her eyes around the room, her gaze settling on the sand tray that sat on a table in the corner. She pointed at it. "Can I do that?"

"Of course." With a sweep of her arm, Nikki invited her to play.

3

First, Hannah smoothed out all the sand. Then she pushed it up into the center of the tray, creating a hill. From the shelf of miniature objects, she chose a bulldog toy, placing it on top of the mound. She tilted her head to the side, examining her creation. Then she placed a ring of miniature soldiers around the mound. With a plastic cup, she scooped up the sand and poured cup after cup over the bulldog until it was buried. When she was finished, she stood perfectly still.

"What did you build?" Nikki asked.

"A world."

"Where is it?"

"I don't know." She patted the sand. "Iraq."

"Where Sasha was a soldier?"

Hannah nodded, picking up the toy soldiers, one by one, gently placing each one back in the basket. But she left the bulldog where it was, buried. "I'm done," she said, moving back to the armchair.

Silence.

"I had that dream." Hannah stroked the cushion three times.

"Which one?"

"You know."

"About your sister?"

"Yeah."

"What did she do?"

"Same thing. Sasha waves to me. Not talking. Not nice! She left, gone away, never come back!" Hannah's lip trembled.

Nikki had never heard her use this baby voice before. But of course Hannah would regress, she thought, the trauma would send her back to a safer time—it made total sense. "It's sad that your sister died."

"But she didn't have to—she made herself died. No one died her!"

"You're right. She did that."

"Not fair!"

Nikki was finding it hard to breathe, and the familiar floating sensation threatened to take her away. Dissociating. What was it about Hannah that set her off? Come back, she told herself. With each breath, I am more calm and grounded. She is the client, and I am the therapist. I am thirty-seven years old. I am not a child.

Hannah peered at her. "Ms. Nikki?"

"Yes."

"Are you gonna go away?" Hannah asked.

"I'm not planning to."

"Not *planning*. But you might go away?"

"Sometimes things happen, like—let's say your mother decides it's best not to bring you anymore to see me. Then it might feel like I've gone away. Or if I got sick, I wouldn't be able to see you for a little while. But then I'd come back. So I can't promise you 100 percent, but I can say I have no plans to go anywhere." She smiled.

"Good. Would you come to my soccer game?"

She wanted to say yes, but would her supervisor, Susan, say this was too loose a boundary? An activity outside of the clinic, too friendly with the client and family, just like they'd discussed—out of bounds? Now Hannah was wrinkling her brow, and her lip was starting to tremble. Say something, quick. "I'll be there. I'd love to come to your soccer game." She couldn't let her client down. Besides, she would sit high up in the bleachers and just wave to Hannah at the end. No boundaries would be breached.

· · ·

After the session, she walked Hannah down the hall to the reception area. But instead of the teenage babysitter who usually picked her up, a forty-something blond woman, her hair pulled tightly in a bun, paced back and forth.

"Mama!" The child flew into the woman's arms.

This was the first time she had seen the mother. "Mrs. Stevanovich?" She extended her hand.

"Please, call me Yelena." The woman took her hand. Her accent was Eastern European, with a guttural tinge.

The vibes coming off Hannah's mother hit her—a wave of grief and an edge of anger. Of course, Nikki thought, it was the recent suicide of her older daughter. But it would be inappropriate to bring that up. She mentioned Hannah's invitation to the soccer game, and Yelena urged her to come.

On her way back to her office, Nikki ran into Susan.

"How was San Francisco?" Susan asked.

"It was good," she lied.

Susan responded with a tight half-smile and a nod.

When Nikki first got this job, nine years ago, she had lucked out. The clinic director back then was great—he always had her back. But then he left for another position and Susan replaced him. She was nice enough, Nikki thought, just not a good supervisor. She was so fixated on rules; everything had to be by the book. Susan didn't seem to get that therapy was more of a creative practice.

"I'm still waiting for you to give me the signed agreement," Susan said. "It's been almost two weeks."

Shit! Nikki'd left it at home. Again. "Sorry. I'll get it to you tomorrow."

Susan had spoken to her a few times over the last couple of years about what she called Nikki's "boundaries issue." Last month, she'd thrown a fit when she found out Nikki was tutoring Joey to help him with schoolwork. She said it was a "dual relationship," reminding Nikki that she had to keep relationships with clients within the confines of the clinic. Shortly after that, Susan had drawn up a sort of agreement that Nikki promise not to do that anymore. It wasn't a *sort of* agreement, she reminded herself, it was a real one. She had to remember to bring the damn thing back tomorrow. What was wrong with her? She kept forgetting to bring it to work.

Taking a deep breath, she opened the door to her office, planning on a moment of quiet to check in with her feelings. Shit. Her officemate, Victor, was getting some papers from their shared desk, stuffing them into his bag, resolutely not making eye contact. His stocky body and round face, which used to be full of warmth, were now stiff and guarded. They'd shared the office for a couple of years, but it was only in the last few months, ever since his divorce, that they'd become friends. "Good morning, Vic," she said, hoping he might magically shift into his old self.

"Hey," he said, coldly.

"Do you have a client?"

"No." He moved past her and out the door, closing it gently behind him.

Oh, for Chrissake, she thought. We agreed it was just a casual physical thing, so what was he getting his panties in a twist about? Last week, he said he didn't want to hang out anymore, and she'd said that was fine. But he was acting all weird about it, and she'd asked him if maybe his feelings were hurt, that maybe she'd misunderstood—did he want a different kind of relationship? But he'd said there was *nothing to talk about*. Ha ha, she thought: How many therapists does it take to talk about their feelings? None, because they only want to talk about other people's feelings.

Imani stuck her head in her office. "Come in, come in,"

Nikki said. They hugged and Nikki closed the door and said, "How was the big date? Tell me everything."

Her friend gave her a blow-by-blow on her date (not so good) her new client (super-challenging), and her mother—still in the hospital.

After Imani left, Nikki sank into the armchair and checked in on the sensations she'd put on hold from her session with Hannah. Ever since she'd started working with her, Nikki had had classic fight-or-flight reactions. Sweating, shortness of breath, quickened heart rate. But in today's session, the body sensations were stronger than ever. Had the trip kicked up her stuff? She'd chosen the conference partly because it was in San Francisco, and partly because it was on post-traumatic stress disorder, and PTSD was a big issue with so many of the children she worked with. She hadn't been back for ten years and thought maybe visiting would jog her memory and shed some light on what was going on in her own troubled psyche. She'd been in therapy on and off throughout her early twenties and then after the divorce. They'd gone over all her childhood shit: the lack of boundaries in the commune family, the hot-and-cold mother, the absent father. But a trauma, or any kind of PTSD symptoms, had never come up. Until a couple of months ago, when her sessions with Hannah had thrown her for a loop. When she'd tried to put a more specific name on her feelings, the closest cousin was a vague kind of dread. Anxiety? Even though she knew a trip back to the House (in her mind, it always had a capital H) wouldn't magically resolve her issue, she'd hoped it would at least give her some insight.

From the downtown hotel in San Francisco, she'd taken the N Judah train to the Upper Haight (which was now called "Cole Valley," probably a realtor's wet dream to separate it from the gritty Haight-Ashbury for a higher price tag). When the train came out of the tunnel, she got off at Cole and made her way down to Haight Street. The neighborhood had morphed from the seedy, crime-ridden scene of the seventies, when she'd lived there as a child, to a sort of reimagined, touristy summer-of-love site, with vintage clothing stores, a Ben and Jerry's ice cream shop, and upscale bars. The only remnants of the Haight from her childhood were a head shop, the anarchist bookstore, and the Blue Front Café. Even when she'd been there in the nineties, it hadn't seemed so spiffy.

She made her way diagonally across the Panhandle, to Ashbury Street and then up the half-block to the House. Her eyes traveled up to the third story of the sprawling Victorian to the tower, the round space that had been her room until she was twelve. Just standing there, looking, she felt a sort of emotional vertigo. A shiver ran down her spine. A somatic response, she observed silently, just as she would with a client. And then, as she continued looking at the tower room, a rush of sexual energy spread through her body, straight to her yoni. Okay, understandable, she'd had her first sexual experience there in that round room—by herself, of course. But still, getting turned on by looking up at her room was a little weird. What if she had been sexually abused? Was that what this was all about? But that made no sense. She'd worked with so many clients who'd been sexually assaulted—usually by a family member or a "friend." She'd spent countless hours with them, attempting to heal those wounds, and she'd never, not for an instant, been triggered.

No. It had to be something else. Something about her client Hannah was bringing up this feeling of dread. Her eyes moved to the rest of the third story. Next to the tower was her mother's bedroom, and behind that was the open attic space Mumma had called the "art studio."

She felt the hollow space of grief that started at her chest and made its way to her navel. But it was softer than before, without the sharp edges. It had been almost a year since her mother died. She had been gradually moving away from the tangle of guilt and anger. Now she was better able to let in the sadness at losing her lovely, complicated Mumma. She turned her gaze to the second floor. Mama Linda had had the giant master bedroom, with the big round window, a couch, TV, and fireplace. On the wall, the Angela Davis poster that Nikki had spent so much time staring at as a child. Finally, she examined the bottom floor, with its wraparound bay windows in the parlor and pseudo-classical arches framing the doorway. Back when they lived there, the House had an earthy, seventies look—brown and orange paint on the verge of peeling. Now it was upscale, freshly painted in three shades: a delicate forest green, a lighter gray-green, and soft, gold trim. Giant pots of blooming red geraniums lined the stairs.

What else had changed? Silky drapes masked the windows on the first floor, and upstairs there were shutters. Shutters to shut away the memories, shudders to bring them back, she thought.

The therapist voice in her head suggested she sit with her feelings. Unpack them. Just like she told her clients—except she'd say, we're going to make friends with your feelings. And the client would inevitably look at her, wide-eyed: What do you mean? So she'd walk them through it, one feeling at a time. She'd been raised to believe that feelings were something you had to work at producing for inspection. She'd basically imprinted on all the housemates—RJ, Mama Linda, Che, Stretch, and of course her mother, Willow. RJ's sister, Meadow, had stayed with them off and on for a few years. She was eleven years older, and Nikki had had a major crush on her. Meadow was still, in Nikki's eyes, a teen goddess.

Nikki surfaced from the memory and straightened up her

office in preparation for her next client. Was she overlooking the obvious? Was she getting these flashes and weird images about the House because she was still processing her mom's death? But she never had these sensations after her mother died. It was only after she started working with Hannah that they started coming up.

As she smoothed out the sand in the tray and put away the miniatures, she mentally prepared for LaMarr, an eight-year-old with a history of attention issues and depression. Fortunately, working with LaMarr didn't push her buttons. All she had to do was listen and guide, and as long as she gave the child plenty of space to move around during the session, he relaxed and opened up. She met LaMarr in the waiting room, and he flew down the hall and into the office. Beginning as they always did, she handed him a pack of playing cards, and he laid them out carefully, all the while telling the story of how he got in trouble on the playground again today, but it *wasn't his fault!*

After work, Nikki took the long way home so she could walk through Prospect Park. The sun was setting, and the light hit the water in a way that made the lake look surreal. Once in the lobby of her building, with its familiar scuffed black-and-white tiles and wide staircase, she made her way up to the second floor. She had a fleeting thought of finding another apartment, but she dismissed it. When she and Christopher had split up, she'd planned to move—too many memories of their life together in the South Slope. But then the neighborhood started to turn trendy, and the rents shot up, so she couldn't leave—she would *never* find a one-bedroom like this now for the rent she was paying. She was stuck with it.

Christopher. She still missed him. On the first day of grad school at Columbia, she'd arrived late to class and noticed him right away. Their eyes met as a shaft of light fell across his face, and she sensed a subliminal shift in the atmosphere. She had always thought that first moment between them was a flash of recognition, a love spark. But Christopher told her much later that the look on his face was, in fact, the pleasant surprise that he wasn't the only Black student in their program. They'd laughed about that, because back then she still thought she was a white Jewish girl. By the time she found out he was right after all, they had split up, and it didn't matter anyway. Still, she remembered what she saw in his face that first moment—a whole world of grace and sweetness and fire.

Nikki had replayed the gradual breakup so many times in her mind. "You're moving away from me, little by little," he'd said one night. She was washing the dishes and he was drying them and putting them away, slamming plates and cupboard doors.

"What a projection! You're never here, you're always with your friends!" she said.

"I like to unwind after work, is that a crime? But when I'm here, I'm completely present with you. But you—you're always on the phone, with a client's parent, or you're at your computer, or you stick your nose in a book. You're in a zone." He shook his head in frustration and his beaded braids went thwack-thwack-thwack.

"Yeah, you're 'present' with me as long as you smoke a little weed first," she snapped.

"You just don't get it," he said.

Marriage counseling went nowhere. Every time she brought up his weed habit, he said he didn't have a problem, *she* had a problem. He maintained she left him, but she was pretty sure he had already left her, emotionally. She finally kicked him out when she found out about his brief affair with his coworker. *We didn't do anything,* he kept saying.

Nikki unlocked the door to her apartment and inhaled the heady aroma of beef and wine. She checked the slow cooker. The boeuf bourguignon looked beautiful—the wine had reduced down to a perfect consistency. She stirred the stew. Meat! From the time she was little until they moved from the House, meals were mostly vegetarian, with the occasional fish or chicken dish, and fairly tasty. But when she was twelve, they left the collective and moved up to Petaluma, and her mother was the sole cook, making bland vegetarian meals. That was when Nikki started cooking. Her mother encouraged her and didn't even mind when she added red meat to their menu. Even now, with so many reasons to go vegetarian, Nikki couldn't help it; she was still a carnivore. It always felt like she was getting away with something.

She heated up the leftover rice and grabbed her book, *Harry Potter and the Order of the Phoenix.* The next book was coming out in a few months, and she wanted to be caught up. She spooned the stew over the rice. It was her first time using this recipe. She took the first bite. Not bad.

After dinner, she went to her desk and pulled out her laptop from the bottom drawer. The desktop computer was for work and other projects. The dedicated laptop was just for her thing. First she checked craigslist. Nothing. Then she went to Nerve.com. But the more she looked, the less she felt like getting dressed in real clothes, taking the train to Manhattan, and going through the motions of the obligatory drink or cup of coffee. She looked away from the screen and out the window, resting her eyes on her favorite tree, an ancient sycamore. Never mind. She wouldn't fuck anyone tonight. She closed the laptop and put it back in the drawer.

Chapter 2

Death Valley

Deb Travis opened her eyes to the darkness of the trailer, hoping it was morning. Today was the thirtieth anniversary of Ron's death. She switched on the bedside lamp and squinted at the clock. A few minutes before four. Better if it were five—she could call it morning and get up. Or, say, three, which everybody knows is officially nighttime, then she could lull herself back to sleep. But the hours between were murder.

She sat up in bed. It was freezing. She got back under the covers. She drifted off, and then there was her brother's voice in her head, calling her by her house name. "Meadow, you should call your website project *Soldiers with Invisible Wounds*." Wait, was that a dream? Or just his voice? Her belly hurt. Get up, Deb, your stomach will feel better after you walk around a bit; it always does.

She pushed herself out of bed and, naked and shivering, pulled on sweatpants and a T-shirt. Barefoot, she stepped over the cold linoleum to open the trailer door. The desert floor of Death Valley stretched out in all directions, lit by a sliver of moon above the Panamint Mountains.

She closed the door and went directly to the mini-fridge. There was one cookie left in the freezer compartment. She'd rather smoke a joint, but it was too big a risk to keep a baggie of weed in her trailer. Even with the medical marijuana card, she was still on federal land. Like her boss said, when you work for the National Park Service, even if you're a volunteer ranger, you have to be squeaky clean.

She took out the cookie. The drawback of eating rather than smoking was that the buzz stayed in your system so much longer, and she had to be at work in a few hours. She cut it into quarters and put one in the toaster oven, then remembered that the last time she'd done that, the trailer was permeated with a distinct sugary cannabis smell. She took it out right away. Sitting in the cramped breakfast nook, she nibbled at the frozen cookie, looking up at the pictures on her shelf. She plucked a photo off the shelf. She and her two brothers were smiling, frozen in time. She blew the dust off the frame and set it on the table. Then she got a candle and a beer from the fridge and placed them next to the picture to complete the tableau. Almost. From the box on her dresser, she took out the beaded bracelet, now barely held together by a tattered string that Nik-Knock had given her so many years ago.

The memory came rushing back to her—it was the end of her first summer at Ashbury House, the day she had to go back home to Michigan. She didn't want to leave but her parents had thrown a fit at the very idea that she might drop out of high school and stay in San Francisco. Her bags packed, she paced the parlor, waiting for Ron to come downstairs and take her to the airport. Phoenix came running down the stairs and into the room, with Mama Linda close behind. The child's eyes wide with excitement, she handed Deb a small box, wrapped in orange tissue paper. "It's a go-away present."

15

"Going-away," Mama Linda said.

"I know what you mean," Deb said. She opened it quickly. Inside was an orange and blue bracelet. "Thank you, Phoenix. It's beautiful."

"I made it myself," the child said.

Sliding the elastic bracelet on her wrist, Deb gazed at the perfectly strung beads, in awe that a five-year-old had made something so lovely. "Far out." She crouched down to her friend's level and opened her arms for a hug.

Phoenix hugged her quickly, then stepped back. "I love you, Meadow."

"I love you too, Nik-Knock," she said, using the child's house name. "I'll be back next summer."

"Good. When you come back, we can be lovers."

Mama Linda, frowning, pulled the child into the hallway and whispered something angrily to her.

Phoenix shook her head. "Not what I meant," she stammered.

Of course that wasn't what she meant, Deb thought. She was a little kid; she didn't know. Linda continued to talk to her in a stern whisper.

Finally, Phoenix nodded in defeat, glaring at Linda from underneath her puckered brow. They came back into the living room, and Phoenix said, "Meadow, when you come back, we'll *love you*." Glancing sideways at Mama Linda, she lifted her chin.

Deb closed her hand around the circle of beads as the memory receded, then slipped the bracelet over the framed photo. She went outside and down the path to the mesquite tree, where she picked a sprig for the altar. Coming back, she relished the sight of the Airstream, its silver shell an apparition in the moonlight. The only way she'd managed to get out of living in a park service dormitory with other rangers was to bring her own mobile housing. Adding the mesquite sprig to her kitchen-table shrine, she lit the candle. She traced her fingers along the edge of the picture frame. She and her brothers were on a camping trip, the weekend before Ron went off to recruit training. Ron was eighteen, she was thirteen, and Matt was about eleven. She was in the middle, her arm hanging loosely around Matt's shoulders. Ron's arms were slung around her, gripping her in a side hug. She would give anything to have just one more of those bear hugs. Matt was grinning ear to ear, but she and Ron were only half smiling.

She would never forget all the times Ron had stood by her when she was little. She would argue with her mother about the injustice of having to do housework while her brothers did nothing, or how they got to do the fun stuff like shoveling snow or raking leaves. He would volunteer to help out in the kitchen alongside Deb, even when their mom tried to shoo him out. He would sneak her out with him to do the lawn chores, or show her how to fix her bicycle, or even how to change the oil on the car—any number of things her parents said she "didn't need to know how to do" because she was a girl. The day he left for boot camp, when they hugged goodbye, he was holding back tears. "Little sister, I will miss you so much."

She shook her head. As much as she had loved his taking care of her and standing up for her, he had gone overboard with the protective older brother thing, especially with giving her boyfriends the third degree. It was the only thing that had ever driven her nuts about him.

She usually called Matt on the anniversary, or he called her—it was their tradition. But there was no cell phone service out here; it would have to wait until she got to the ranger station. It was almost seven a.m. in Evanston now. She pictured her brother and his wife rushing around, preparing for work and getting the kids off to school, in a perfectly choreographed ballet of domestic teamwork. Deb's brief foray into couplehood was a distant memory. She had been a tourist once in the land of married people and had vowed to herself she'd never go back.

She put on the coffee pot. Gazing out the window at the Panamint Range in the distance, she let her eyes rest on the burnished gold of the Mojave Desert, the mountains a deep violet, the sky an inverted bowl of midnight blue. The desert was a mirror, and today its reflective surface was covered by a film of grief.

An hour later, she put on her ranger uniform and headed to the truck. Driving slowly on the dirt road, she scanned for creatures. When she reached the National Park road, she was about to turn toward the ranger station but instead kept going straight, toward the Mesquite Dunes. She still had a couple of hours before work.

The road was peaceful in the early morning, not many people out yet, and she had to admit it did look like the middle of nowhere, the phrase Matt had used to describe Death Valley. She heard her brother's voice in her head, with its sarcastic undertone: "You're leaving the Bay Area, your secure library job at the university with a *pension*, your cottage with a view of the bay—to live *in the middle of nowhere*—in the Mojave Desert, for fuck's sake? For a volunteer thing? Why?"

"It's only a year," she had countered, "and I didn't resign from my job; I took a sabbatical. I told my boss I love being a librarian and I'm coming back. Which is sort of true—I might go back. But you know what? *You* live in the middle of nowhere." Matt had responded that Evanston was near Chicago, which was *somewhere*. Then he said yeah, he knew what was happening, she was having a midlife crisis, plus she was an empty nester.

Empty nester. She hated that expression. But yeah. When her daughter Andy went off to college, it *had* thrown her. And now that Andy had settled in Philadelphia with a new job as a junior trader at a boutique brokerage (What exactly *was* a boutique brokerage, and why did she have to move clear across the country? Surely there were those kinds of jobs in LA or San Francisco), she was still getting used to the idea that her daughter was not coming home. Okay, yes, she accepted that Andy had her own life, and Deb needed to "let go," as the self-help books said. Except no one ever lets go of shit, really, they just put it in deep storage. She turned into the parking lot. The Mesquite Dunes lay before her like a velvet pelt, illuminated by the early morning sunlight. She wanted to leap in and roll around in their lush softness.

Hiking over the dunes, her boots sinking into the sand, she looked for familiar landmarks, but of course there weren't any. The dunes were constantly shifting, and there was no going back to the same place. She sat down on a ridge and carved out a spot in the sand with her butt, breathing a sigh of relief. This was why she came here, for the calming sight of endless nothing. A movement in the distance caught her eye. She took out her binoculars. A coyote, yes, but was it Buddy? She looked for the nicked ear, but didn't see it. So it wasn't him. The animal was moving slowly, barely visible, his fur almost blending into the dunes. Sifting the cool sand through her fingers, she gazed out at the loping, sloping expanse. It goes farther and longer than any of us, she thought. But today, instead of washing over her with a wave of comforting peace, the view out over the dunes only compounded the empty place inside, the reminder of the anniversary and all its unfixable sorrow.

The first couple of years after Ron died, she would call her parents on the anniversary. Her mother's voice would break and she'd say she couldn't talk about it and would hand the phone to Deb's father. Her dad would say something like it was "in God's hands" and then there'd be a long silence and he, too, would get off the phone.

Whenever she got to know a potential new friend, she used to say up front, "My brother committed suicide when I was eighteen years old." That was before she found out the value of saying "died by suicide," to signify that it wasn't a crime. Telling someone about Ron was like lifting up your shirt and showing your scar. Except there was no scar, it was all inside, never getting enough sunlight to dry out and heal. But after a while, she learned to hold back from telling new people about it so she wouldn't have to deal with the inevitable reaction: the blank look, the silence, followed by the changing of the subject. Or, almost as bad, they would initiate The Conversation, in which they would ask: 1) Why did he do it? and/or 2) How did he do it?

The only problem with *not* showing a potential friend your invisible scar was that then you might never know if they were part of The Club, an exclusive organization of people who had lost a loved one to suicide. With members of The Club, The Conversation didn't happen because they knew that question number one, *why*, was unanswerable, and question number two, *how*, was asked solely to satisfy the asker's curiosity. She'd met members of The Club everywhere. All she had to do was mention that her brother died by suicide, and, if someone *was* a Club member, it was like opening the floodgates. Among those she'd met over the years: a coworker whose husband had taken his life; a stranger she'd met on the train whose aunt had shot herself; the mother of one of Andy's classmates who had lost her older daughter to suicide.

She shook off the feelings, brushed the sand off her uniform, and headed back to the truck. Time to go to work. Hiking through the dunes, she tried to feel her feet on the earth, to get grounded. But she kept spacing out.

In the parking lot, she picked up the trash bags from the Park Service bins and heaved them into the back of the truck. She hadn't realized when she first signed up that a huge part of her job would be picking up garbage. Two or three times a day. At first she was repelled by the smelly bags, but by now she just laughed it off; all the rangers did.

Climbing into the truck, she wiped her hands on a paper towel, telling herself, stay focused, Deb. It's just a slight buzz. Only a little piece of cookie. And her stomach felt much better. Turning onto the road, she tried to piece together the sort of half-dream from Ron in the early morning hours. It was a good name for her website—Soldiers with Invisible Wounds. She had thought about Suicide Wall, but then she found another website with that name. Besides, she wanted to focus on the veterans themselves more than the virtual wall.

Coming around a bend, she spotted a shape in the road. A creature, low to the ground, yellow eyes glinting. A coyote? She swerved and the animal darted away. But something was wrong. The truck kept swerving, not straightening out. She clenched the wheel and her stomach tightened. She made a strangled gasp as she tried to wrest control of the jeep. She steadied her hands on the wheel and braked. The jeep came to a stop and she sat, in the middle of the road, taking deep breaths and scanning the desert for the coyote. But she didn't see him. Or her. Trickster creature, what are you telling me? You don't need a coyote to answer that, she told herself. You've been putting it off for three years. It was one of the reasons you took this sabbatical. Stop procrastinating, Deb. Do it. For Ron.

Chapter 3

Running

I t was drizzling when Nikki left the apartment at six a.m. A couple of times a week, she and Ira met and ran around the Prospect Park lake loop. As she approached, the familiar sight of her best friend buoyed her, his barrel-shaped body in coordinated sweats, circling his arms vigorously. She reached him and they hugged. It always surprised her that she was taller than him. At 5'7", he was three inches shorter, but she always remembered him as being taller than her, like he had been when they first met in junior high.

They started off on the trail at a slow jog.

"If you're going to San Francisco, be sure to wear some flowers in your hair," Ira sang. "How was it?"

"The conference was good."

"What about the hippie house—did you go back down memory lane? Did you have a big, dramatic flashback, like in the movies? Should I not joke about it? Am I being an asshole?"

She laughed and smacked his butt. "Yes, I went down memory lane. No, I didn't have a flashback. Yes, it's okay to joke about it. And yeah, you're being an asshole. But I still love you."

"Well. But. Okay. What about your client and the anxiety you've been having—those weird feelings?"

"I still have them. I don't know."

They ran in silence for a while. "Don't forget," he said, "the seder is Thursday."

"I know. I still want to come, even though now I have proof I'm only half-Jew."

"You didn't know if you were all-Jew before, and you came anyway. Besides, try telling the neo-Nazis you're only half. You're a Jew as far as they're concerned. They have lists, believe me. But you—bingo! A Black Jew, you get double points for that. Maybe triple."

"Great, I'm thrilled." Nikki slowed down for Ira's sake. He was breathing heavily but would never admit the pace was too fast. "You know I wouldn't miss it. It was the only Jewish holiday we had at the House, and I always liked it. Maybe it was the wine, but still. We did all kinds of rituals, Kwanzaa and Christmas and Winter Solstice and Spring Equinox—the whole multicultural thing. What stayed with me about Passover was the liberation stuff."

"It's not 'liberation stuff.' It's a universal story of liberation. It's the cornerstone of our people's humanitarian tradition."

"What, are you getting all Jewish on me? Do your parents know you go to mass with Javier?"

"No, for Chrissake, and don't tell them."

"Yeah, like I'm gonna call them up: 'Mr. and Mrs. Feldman? It's Nikki, the girl you used to hope your son would go steady with, praying he wasn't queer? I have to tell you something. Your son goes to *mass* at a *Catholic church* every Sunday.'" Nikki added a drag-queen "ta-da" gesture, arms extended, "'With his *gay, homosexual lover*.' Your parents don't have a problem with you being gay, right? It's that going-to-church-on-Sunday thing, now *that* would be an issue."

He laughed. "Not every Sunday, just once in a while." They lapsed into silence again, concentrating on running. "Are you still seeing Vic? Sounded like it was fizzling."

"Yeah, it was, and then he ended it. Which was fine, but now he seems all pissed off," she said, wiping the sweat from her face with her T-shirt.

"Probably not a good idea to bonk someone you work with, anyway."

"Yeah, I guess," Nikki said. "What can I say?"

"Are you doing your online adventures?"

"Now and then. But don't tell anyone about that, okay? Like I said before. Not even Javier."

"I haven't. I won't. But it's not such big a deal. Unless. You know."

"No, I don't know."

"Unless it interferes with you connecting with a man on a deeper level. Like finding a real boyfriend."

"I'm not looking for a relationship right now."

A woman runner, passing them from the opposite direction, smiled at Ira and said hello.

"Who was that?" Nikki asked.

"I met her at a party. A birthday party for one of the attorneys at my firm."

"Okay, what?"

"What do you mean, *what?*"

"I mean—I know that tone of voice. And your body language. What are you *not* telling me about that party or that woman?"

Ira sighed. "Shit. I wasn't going to say anything."

"Now you're starting to freak me out."

"Christopher was there—turns out he's a friend of a friend of the birthday guy."

"Why didn't you tell me you saw him?"

"Because you obsess on what coulda, shoulda, woulda been. It's better this way—he's moved on and you've moved on. They say it takes two years to get past a divorce, so now's the time."

"Wait a minute. Back up, back up. When you say he's 'moved on,' does that mean he was there with someone?"

Ira didn't respond.

"Well?"

"Yes," he said resignedly.

"What was she like? Wait, let me guess. Nordic. Straight blond hair. Thin. Buff. Petite," she said, speeding up.

"So you saw them somewhere?"

"No. I just knew he'd find someone who was my complete opposite. Was she hot?"

"I didn't notice."

"Oh, come on, don't give me that—you've got a rating system for women that's worse than any straight guy's."

"Okay, fine. She was, in a way. But you're hotter."

"So is she an attorney, this woman?"

"No, worse."

"What do you mean, *worse*?"

"Worse, as in—she has a cool job. She works for Amnesty International."

"Fuck me."

"We tried that in high school and it didn't work, remember? We couldn't stop laughing."

"Ha ha. Don't try to change the subject. The girlfriend. Was she nice?"

"She was okay, but really, what's the point of this?"

"How did Christopher seem?"

"He seemed pretty good. He told me he's doing NA."

Nikki stopped in the middle of the path. "He's doing Narcotics Anonymous? Are you fucking kidding me?"

"Yeah," Ira said, jogging in place. "That's a good thing, right?"

"Yes, it's a good thing. But why wouldn't he do it when I asked him to? Why is he doing it now that we're divorced?"

"Nikki, I know you don't want to hear this, but you need to move on."

He started running again and she joined him. "But I *have* moved on. Sort of."

As they neared the end of the loop, they slowed down to a walk. He put his hand on her shoulder lightly. "Look. I know it's hard to hear about Christopher. But it's cleaner this way. Remember how unhappy you were?"

She shook her head. "No. I wasn't."

After work, she stopped at the bodega. Her father was coming over, and she had to pick up something to drink. She stood in front of the drinks cooler, looking for the ginger ale, her mind drifting back to her earliest memory of wondering who her father was.

She was in the first grade. Her new friend Juanita had come back to the House with her after school, and they went out to the backyard and climbed up the eucalyptus tree. RJ came out on the back deck and looked at them, said, "Don't climb up any higher," and went back inside. She saw him sitting at the table inside by the window, watching them.

"How come you and your mama live with all these white people?" Juanita asked.

Nikki got a funny feeling in her stomach. "Not everyone's white. Mama Linda's Black."

"Yeah, I know. She's your mother."

"No, she's my auntie."

"Then why you call her Mama Linda?"

"Everyone calls her that."

"Well, who *is* your mama, then?" Juanita wrinkled her forehead.

Nikki climbed down the tree. "My mom is—you know— she picks me up from the bus." She pulled out a weed and threw it in the corner of the garden.

"The white lady with the blond hair?"

"Yeah. What's wrong with that?"

"Nothing," Juanita said. "But why come you're brown, then? Your daddy must be Mexican. Like me."

"I guess." Nikki looked down at her arms. They were light brown. Her mom always said, *We are all one color, the color of love*, but she was pretty sure her friend would make fun of her if she said that now.

Juanita jumped down from the tree and walked up and down the rows of seedlings that Nikki and her family had planted and took turns watering every other day.

"Hey, wait!" Nikki yelled, jumping down, a pain shooting through her ankle. "You're crushing the plants."

"There's nothing here. It's just dirt."

"Those little green things—they're plants."

"Okay," Juanita said, sitting down on the back steps. "So. What are you: brown or white?"

Nikki knelt down, patting the soil around the tender green shoots, thinking. What was the right answer? Her friend was waiting. "Brown," she said.

Juanita grinned and nodded. *"Bueno.* So where's your papa?"

"He lives in New York." Nikki didn't know that for sure, but one night, when she pretended to be asleep on the couch, she heard the adults whispering about her father, and they kept saying the words "New York."

Juanita nodded. "Nueva York! That's cool. That's where you get your brown skin from. Your papa."

Nikki grinned. Juanita will still be my friend, she thought. And my dad is brown. In New York.

Nikki buzzed Charles into the building and waited for him in the hallway. Her father came up the stairs and down the hall with an uncertain tread, almost like he didn't belong there. A tall, mahogany-colored man with close-cut hair, he exuded a subtle smell of Ivory soap that almost, but not completely, masked the underlying scent of paint.

"Phoenix," her father said. He was the only person who still called her by her real name.

"Charles." They hugged. "How's business?"

"Same old, same old. Painting houses, making a living."

She handed him a bottle of ginger ale, part of their recently established ritual.

Ten months ago, there had been a message on her answering machine from a man named Charles. "This is a message for Phoenix." He said he was an old friend of her mother's and was so sorry to hear she'd died. He'd gotten her number from Mama Linda, and could they meet for coffee sometime? It had been two months since Willow had died, and Nikki was curious—she'd never heard of him before from her mother or Mama Linda, so she called the man back and agreed to meet in Brooklyn.

When he walked up to the café table where Nikki was waiting, she wasn't surprised he was Black. She'd detected something in the voice on the phone—the whisper of a southern cadence strong-armed by New York vowels. Charles was a tall man, wiry and energetic, radiating an undertone of insecurity. Nikki was picking up on something more, though. The man was anxious as hell.

After they'd ordered coffee and exchanged pleasantries, Charles cleared his throat. "I'm sorry about your mother, that she passed."

She felt the tears starting to gather but blinked them away. She didn't even know this man. "Thank you," she said.

Charles seemed to be bracing himself. "If you're wondering why I wanted to see you, I'll—I'm going to say it, now. Why. I've been clean and sober for five years, eleven months, and five days. You're familiar with the twelve-step program?"

Nikki nodded, thinking, Oh shit, what is this?

"I'm on the eighth step. Making amends. I've come to tell you that I am . . . oh, man . . . that I'm . . ." He took a deep breath and blew it out. "Your father."

The surfaces around Nikki tilted. She was in a café in Park Slope, at a sidewalk table, but this was not her world—it was someone else's. "Father unknown," it was right there on her birth certificate. Her mother had said it was wild times, free love, all that. She'd asked her many times if her dad lived in New York, but her mother always said she didn't know. It flashed through her mind—how often someone would ask Nikki if she was Iranian, or Indian, or Puerto Rican. If this really *was* her father, how could her mother keep such an important piece of her identity from her? She swallowed and tried to speak. Finally, she said, "I don't know what to say."

"Yeah, I understand. I didn't expect you to be excited about it."

"But—my mother said she didn't know. Who the father was." She took a gulp of coffee.

"Willow lived in San Francisco, and I lived here. It was a

long-distance thing, and we didn't have the money to fly back and forth. I wanted to move out there. But she cut me off. Wouldn't come to the phone when I called. The housemates would say she was 'unavailable.' She returned all my letters unopened. She wrote me, said she didn't want me in her life or yours. Said it was better that way." He seemed to be waiting for Nikki to say something, and when she didn't, Charles said, "I know this must be—strange."

"Yeah, it is." She didn't even know this person; she wasn't about to open up to him. The questions tumbled out of her mouth: "Where do you live? Are you married? Kids?"

"Queens. We have a house in St. Albans. I'm married to a wonderful lady, Bernice. No, never had kids. Except . . ." he gestured at Nikki.

She exhaled, and it came out an exasperated sound. "How can you be sure that you're my—birth father?" She didn't know why she used that term. Or maybe she did, because this man wasn't and would never be her real father. Just the sperm donor. But even as the thought passed through, she saw: the almond shape of his eyes; the wide forehead; his mouth, just like hers; and even something in the way he looked at her, like he could see right through her.

"You were born March 14, 1969—nine months after I stayed with Willow in San Francisco. She refused to list me as the father on the birth certificate, but she did give you a small part of me. Your middle name. Phoenix Charlene Gold." Charles sat back in his chair and waited.

She didn't believe it. Just because he knew her real name and birthday. Anyone could find that information on the internet if they really tried. When she'd asked her mother about her middle name, Willow always said it was a family name.

He continued. "Besides, I see you—even though you're

light-skinned, your looks are a combination of me and Willow, and you have the build of the women in my family."

Nikki took a deep breath. The "build"? She was big and curvy. Was that what he was getting at? "If this . . . if this is true," she sputtered. "All this time—they never told me? Not Willow, not Mama Linda, that you were—interested in seeing me? That I'm mixed-race? Jesus! I *knew* there was something. I knew it." And then she found herself standing, gathering her bag and blurting, "I don't—I don't think I can talk to you right now." People in the café were staring. Was she yelling?

"Look," he said softly. "I appear out of nowhere, and you probably think, where the—where has this jerk been all these years? I understand. But I'm asking you, please—just hear me out, and then I'll go away. I promise."

She stayed standing. "I'll try."

"I was in New York when Willow wrote me that she was pregnant. I called her on the phone—which was a big deal back then because long-distance was so expensive. I said I was going to move to San Francisco to be with you all. But she told me not to, because of—the drinking. And it was true, I was drinking all the time, couldn't hold down a job, and . . . I figured I'd clean up my act, and I did. Stopped drinking, worked hard, got into the carpenters' union. Wrote to Willow, told her I was six months clean and sober. But she said she still didn't trust me, and besides, she didn't want to be with a man. She had the 'family,' you know, the collective. I felt like a failure and I went back to drinking then—I'm not proud of it, that I wasted all those years."

She sat down again. He was being so open with her; she should at least hear him out.

"And then," he said, "nine years ago, I met Bernice. It changed my life. I joined AA, went back to working steady, got my contractor's license, and started my own business.

31

With the twelve steps, I knew I'd have to do the making-amends step at some point, and that you'd be the most important person. 'Cause I should have kept on, I should have said to Willow, let me into my daughter's life. But I was in touch with Linda, and she always said Willow had dug her heels in, and nothing would change her mind." He stopped talking and swallowed, seeming to pull himself up, saying, "Anyway, when I heard Willow passed, I thought, now's the time. So, I'm here. I would like to—be in your life. If you would be willing. And you don't have to decide now."

The therapist in her would have said, I understand, and I appreciate what you went through to come here today, and I'll have to think about it. But this wasn't therapy. She had heard him out and now she was done. She found herself on her feet, throwing a few dollars on the table, mumbling a goodbye, and bolting. Weaving her way down Fifth Avenue, she stepped through the stream of twenty-somethings out for brunch, alongside the older Brooklyn residents doing errands or taking a walk, everyone out and about on an ordinary Saturday. They had normal lives, unlike her. They didn't have a father— real or fake— popping up out of nowhere. An image stuck in her mind—the look on Charles's face when she left the table: unsurprised, his eyes full of sadness and resignation.

That was almost a year ago. She'd contacted him a few weeks later, and they'd gradually formed a tentative connection, getting together about once a month. Now they took their bottles of ginger ale and went up to the roof. They sat in rickety chairs, looking out at the river and farther, to the panoply of Manhattan lights.

"I've been meaning to ask you," she said, "When you got my number from Mama Linda, did she seem—I don't know— like she'd want to talk to me?"

"Definitely. She said she wrote you and didn't hear back,

so she was going to give you some space. But she also said too much time had gone by and she was going to get in touch again soon. There's a lot of love there."

"Maybe I'll call her. I can't believe she never told me about you, though."

"Willow said not to ever tell you, and she honored your mother's wishes, even though she disagreed."

She nodded slowly. "Okay. I've been thinking about the House lately. Are you in touch with anyone besides her?"

"I didn't get to know the others as well as Linda. The only other housemate I dug, though, was RJ. It was such a shame."

"What was such a shame?"

"That he died the way he did. A terrible thing."

A prickling sensation rippled down her spine. "He died?"

"Yeah, you know," he said, a puzzled look on his face.

"No, he didn't. He moved away. I still remember that guy. I loved him—" she was about to say "like a father," but stopped. That might hurt Charles's feelings. She took a breath. "When he took off, he didn't stay in touch. It was weird."

Charles was staring at her, examining her face closely.

"Why are you looking at me like that?"

He shook his head, took a sip of his ginger ale, then tilted his head back and finished the bottle. "No reason," he said. He stared out at the view quietly. When he turned back to her, something was different. A tenderness settled lightly over his features.

Fatherly, she thought. He looks fatherly.

"I guess I was mistaken. He—moved away." Charles moved his gaze back to the water, the bridge, and beyond.

Chapter 4

A Message from the Universe

Deb paced the back room of the ranger station, talking softly into her phone. She had a headache that had started in her temples and was now wrapping around her skull. "Ming. We have to finish the website in the next month."

Her friend chuckled. "Okay. What's the rush, after you've been putting it off for so long?"

"I had this sort of dream or vision. Ron asked me to finish it and to call the site Soldiers with Invisible Wounds."

"Wow. An invisible vision."

"And I think maybe I've been holding back, kind of like if I finish it, I'll lose a piece of my brother, but that's crazy, right? Because it's probably the opposite."

"I hear you. Let's do it," Ming said. "I'm halfway done with the design; I was just waiting for you. It'll be beautiful. I'll finish it and send you a mockup."

"Thanks." Deb rubbed her temples and the back of her neck. "How's Duncan?"

"He's still a bit pissed off that he has to live at my house, but every day when John gets home from work, he holds him on his lap and pets him and scratches under his chin, and from the sound of the purring, I'd say Duncan is pretty good with that."

Deb laughed. "I appreciate you and John taking care of him. I owe you."

"You don't owe me anything. Tell me more about your vision to finish the website; maybe it'll give me more ideas."

"Yesterday, I was driving on a Park road, and this coyote darted out. I avoided him and then the jeep swerved, and I almost lost control of it, and it was scary but then it was all okay. And I'm pretty sure that was a sign too. To finish the project."

There was silence on the other end of the line. "Are you sure it wasn't a sign to not get high and drive?"

Deb laughed. "Very funny." Another stab of pain hit her temples. "No, seriously. It was a message from the universe."

Chapter 5

House Family

Nikki pulled out the two cartons from the back of the closet. "Phoenix" was scrawled in Willow's handwriting on both. Seeing her mother's handwriting, knowing her mom had saved the boxes in her garage in Petaluma, brought up a whisper of guilt. If only she had known how little time they had left, she would've flown out to visit her more often. But the part of her that had wanted to be free of her mother's intense, clingy energy had won out. Her mother had visited her in Brooklyn several times, and it often seemed like an intrusion, but now all she could do was wish her mom had visited more.

She sliced through the packing tape with a knife. She'd brought the boxes back home with her after her mom's memorial in Petaluma and had opened them briefly, then closed them up again and stashed them in the back of her closet. Now she cracked open the first box, the ripping sound of the tape a satisfying accompaniment. A packet of incense sat on top, smelling of patchouli and bringing with it a whiff of the entryway of the House, with its burnished wood floors and broad staircase. On top of a stack of papers was a family photo, a snapshot from the House. Mama Linda, with a big Afro and a red-and-yellow jumpsuit that set off the rich tones of her umber brown skin, her arm around five-year-old Nikki. Jesus, she thought, looking at herself in the photo, I really was pudgy. She looked closer. Her hair was curly and dark with lighter streaks, and her skin was tawny. Did she look mixed-race? She didn't know. Looking at the photo, she thought, But it would've been nice to know, especially with Mama Linda as a role model, right there in her world. On the other side of Nikki was Stretch, her long, straight hair parted in the middle, wearing giant hoop earrings, a polka-dot halter top, and a miniskirt. Then there was RJ, bearded, with soulful eyes, wearing a plaid flannel shirt and jeans. Wow. He was drop-dead gorgeous. She'd never noticed it as a child, but now it was so clear. It wasn't just his looks. Even in the snapshot, you could see it, a kind of loving vibe that shone through his features. Next to him was her mom in a long, Indian-print dress. She looked so young and blond and slender. Nikki felt a familiar ache—the longing for that girl-woman who was her mother, who gradually became the tough single mom as the years went by. She never stopped smoking. Her voice got huskier and her breath got shorter until she had had a heart attack a year ago. A band of grief wrapped around Nikki's chest. She took a deep breath and, as she exhaled, pushed the sadness away. In the picture, her mom's arms were crossed, her shoulders hunched. What was she protecting herself from? On her other side was Che, smiling, with a sprawling, bushy mustache and wire-rimmed glasses. Nikki peered at the image. Even though it was hard to see his eyes clearly, she was pretty sure he was stoned. But he also had a stiffness about him, too, like he was doing his best not to touch Willow. She nodded at the realization. Of course. Her mother and Che had had a really weird thing going—the photo made it clear.

She'd known about it, everyone did, but back then, to her child self, it had seemed normal. Holding the snapshot in her hand, she had a flash of a House meeting when she was around six years old, when the collective had tried to get her mother and Che to mend their differences.

She'd always liked House meetings because the family would gather together around the big dining room table and she got to be with them while they talked about grown-up things. That night, Stretch said she had an agenda item to discuss. "It's a bummer," Stretch said, "that Willow and Che are always fighting, and the rest of us have to deal with the bad vibes."

Her mother crossed her arms. "We've tried talking it through many times. You're all just going to have to accept that Che and I don't get along. We avoid each other, and it works."

"That's right," Che said. "It's a beautiful arrangement."

The housemates laughed, and she didn't understand that. It wasn't funny and it wasn't beautiful. Che and her mother often yelled at each other and it was ugly.

The family talked some more, and they kept saying Willow and Che should process and do conflict resolution.

"You know," Stretch said, "It's probably just blocked sexual energy. If you two would just fuck for, say, a week, I think it would solve everything. "

"Jesus Christ!" RJ said. "You think if they sleep together that will magically make them get along?"

Then everyone started yelling at once. Mama Linda got the serious look on her face, the one where her lips were pressed tight together, and everyone stopped talking. "Someone should take Nik-Knock upstairs for this discussion."

"I agree," Mumma said.

"I'll take her," RJ said. "But I'm going to put it out there that I don't agree with this as a solution."

She didn't want to leave the meeting, but RJ said they could play cards, so she agreed to come with him. He took her hand and, along the way, made a stop in the pantry. "Shh, top secret," he said with a grin, reaching for a cookie tin hidden on a back shelf.

They went up to his room and ate the cookies. "These are the best chocolate chip cookies ever," she said. "Who made them?"

"I did. It was easy. I'll show you how."

"When?"

"Tomorrow, after school."

They played Crazy Eights and Go Fish, and then he let her tickle him, and they laughed until they got tears in their eyes, like always, and then she said he could tickle *her*, but he said he wouldn't, that it wasn't right. After a while, Mumma came upstairs to get them. The housemates had all agreed with Stretch's idea, she said, but they still needed RJ to come back to the meeting and add his input, for consensus.

After that night, sometimes she got to sleep with Mama Linda in her big bed, which was really nice, because Mama Linda let her watch TV, and Mumma would never have let her do that. One time she wanted to talk to Mumma before bed, but Mama Linda said no, Mumma was in Che's room having a slumber party. The next day she asked Mumma if the sleeping was helping, and Mumma smiled and said maybe.

Nikki laughed to herself, putting the photo back in the box and shaking her head. Conflict resolution through fucking. In the seventies, in the alternative universe of the collective, it must have made some sort of sense. Now, the mainstream culture had gone back to monogamy as the norm, and if you weren't married or living with someone, there was something wrong with you. Digging through the box, filled with her old comic books, school papers, and more photos, she found another snapshot of the family. This one included several men in drag, dressed up as nuns, with theatrical makeup. She smiled. They'd lived in a big house across the street, and they did street theater. The Sisters of Perpetual Indulgence. They each had a stage name—her favorite was Sister Missionary Position, a parody she hadn't understood back then. All those things had seemed so normal to her, growing up—men in lipstick dressed as nuns, roommates instructed to have sex. She shuffled through more photos and stopped at a picture of her and RJ, working in the garden. She turned it over. March 1975 was penciled on the back. In the image, RJ was grinning, but there was something in his eyes— a kind of haunted look. Funny, she didn't remember him that way, not at all, but she could see it now in the picture. She got a panicky feeling in her chest and put her hand on her breast-bone. Was this about RJ? Why did he leave? Did something happen, and that's why he split? Why didn't he keep in touch?

Nikki went over to the window. Resting her eyes on the sycamore tree, she saw the leaves were starting to come in, one by one. She'd read somewhere that when you look at patterns in nature, the brain relaxes. What had happened that made the collective fall apart? She was twelve when her mom had announced the two of them were moving to Petaluma, in Sonoma County. Willow said she wanted to get Nikki away from the heavy drug scene in the Haight-Ashbury. But Nikki wasn't interested in drugs. She didn't run with a bad crowd and she didn't hang out on Haight Street.

She'd heard Willow and Mama Linda talking quietly one night in the parlor when they didn't know she was listening from the hallway. Willow said something about how she had to "get away from him," but she never said who *him* was. When she asked her mother about it, Willow said she didn't know what Nikki was talking about. But Nikki wondered if it was Che, because she knew they'd continued to sleep together, on and off, for years. She hadn't thought much about it as a kid, but now she thought it was kind of dysfunctional to keep having sex with someone you didn't even like.

When they moved to Petaluma, it was hard to get used to living in a little one-bedroom house with just her and her mother. There was a sort of downtown but mostly it was rural, with the smell of manure on the quiet country roads. And it was *way* too quiet. Even though it was a beautiful place—surrounded by trees and green meadows—it was hard to get around; there were no buses or trains, and you had to ride your bike for miles and miles to get anywhere. She'd met Ira her first day of junior high, in science class, when the teacher paired them up to work on an experiment. Ira didn't have any friends and lived in his own secret world of comic books and video games, trying to escape the bullies who taunted him and called him a faggot. Nikki was the gawky new girl with the frizzy hair. When they started eating lunch together every day, the bullies backed off. She and Ira had been friends ever since.

At the top of the second carton was a stack of sympathy cards. They were all opened, so she must've read them before packing them away. She spotted Mama Linda's handwriting on one of the envelopes and opened it.

Dear Phoenix,
My heart goes out to you for losing your mother.

41

After you called to tell me she had passed, I just sat down and wept for all that lost time from when she and I had drifted apart. We never know when our time will come. I'm so sorry that she died, and that it was so sudden.

I'm sorry I couldn't come to the memorial, but I had some health issues and it wasn't possible.

Things are good with me. I retired and got a decent pension, moved to Santa Fe, and actually went back to school and got a BA in Art. My partner Gena and I separated a couple of years ago, which was hard, but I'm starting to date again.

There are so many things I want to talk to you about. You should come and visit me in Santa Fe. I have lots of room; you can stay with me anytime. I love you, Nik-Knock.

Love and blessings,

Mama Linda

Nikki stroked the paper, thinking how nice it was to get a real letter in the mail. She was pretty sure she'd responded to Mama Linda's card with an email. She opened up her computer and found the email she'd sent. It was full of reassurances that she'd come visit Mama Linda soon. But she hadn't.

She got up from her desk and headed for the kitchen. Staring into the refrigerator, hoping there might be something interesting in there that she'd overlooked, she scanned the shelves and opened the bins. Nothing except a loaf of bread. She had to go grocery shopping. She made toast, slathered it with butter, and ate it slowly. Each of her pseudo-parents at the House had a particular snack they used to make for her. With Che it was a quesadilla. Stretch would give her carrot sticks, and her mother, a fruit smoothie. RJ would fix her a peanut butter and honey sandwich, which she loved, but her favorite snack of all was from Mama Linda—buttered toast.

Finishing the toast, she braced herself to make the call. Just thinking about the House always brought up a whole set of conflicted feelings. Longing, layered with regret and confusion. Come on, do it, she told herself. She tapped the numbers on her phone. The line rang and rang, and she waited to hear an answering machine.

And then the sound of her voice—her real voice, not a recording.

"Mama Linda? It's Nikki. I mean, Phoenix."

A slight pause, then a chuckle, "How're you, Nik-Knock? I was just thinking of you this morning."

"You must've felt me getting ready to call you."

"That's right. And I was remembering your mother's passing. It seems like last month but it's been a little over a year. Sugar, I'm so sorry you lost your Mumma. Even after a year—a year goes by so fast. How are you doing? Must be hard."

Tears sprang to her eyes when she heard "Mumma." She swallowed. "I'm doing okay." Her voice in her ears sounded so small, like a child's. She sat down on the couch, then stood up again and paced the room. "I'm sorry it's taken me this long to finally get in touch with you."

"I was going to call you, but I thought maybe you—"

She waited for Mama Linda to finish. The silence stretched on.

Linda continued, "Maybe you didn't want to be in touch."

43

The hurt in her voice was palpable.

"I really did—really do," Nikki said. "Want to be in touch. It's just been a hard time."

Linda sighed and when she spoke again, her voice had changed, and it was layered with love. "I thought maybe you were mad that I didn't tell you about Charles. I made a promise to your mother to never tell you. I had decided I was going to break that promise though, after all, when Willow passed. But then Charles said he wanted to be the one to tell you, and that seemed right. I know it must be hard, losing your mother and then finding out about your true racial identity."

"I love you, Mama Linda." The words came out of her mouth, surprising her. Mama Linda was her only link to her House family, and now they were further linked by race and culture.

"I love you too."

They fell into a conversation, as if no time had passed from when they were still in touch, before she went to graduate school and got together with Christopher and time spun away. As they talked, the shadows lengthened in the apartment, and she closed the blinds and turned on the lamp, its glow creating a pool of golden light that made her living room, with its secondhand furniture, look deceptively artful. A feeling settled in and around her like a warm comforter on a cold night, a sense of peace she hadn't even realized she'd been missing.

There was a lull in the conversation, and she had a strange sensation in her midsection—it was the same alert she'd get with her clients when they weren't telling her something. "Linda? Is everything okay with you?"

"Yes, fine. Why do you ask?" But she'd paused a bit too long before she responded.

"Just a feeling."

"Maybe you're just picking up on—I'm a little tired, that's all."

"No," Nikki said, "I have a sense there's something you've left out."

Linda sighed and then laughed sadly. "You always were so intuitive. I had a touch of breast cancer—not a big deal; didn't even have to get chemo—just radiation and then tamoxifen. I've been taking it for close to five years. Almost done. I'm fine, really."

The news hit Nikki like a punch in the stomach. It took her a moment to catch her breath. Five years. She should have been there for Mama Linda, and she would have been if she'd stayed in touch. "I'm so sorry. How are you doing now?"

"I feel great. I'm close to being done with the medication, and in two months they'll declare me officially cancer-free."

Nikki shook her head. "I'm sorry I haven't stayed in touch with you. I should have, and then I could've been there for you."

"No, it's fine. You didn't know—how could you have known?"

They talked some more, and Mama Linda urged her to come visit her in Santa Fe. Nikki promised she'd get time off work and come to see her soon. After they hung up, she paced the length of her apartment. It hadn't seemed right to bring up her stuff, once she'd learned about the cancer and all Mama Linda been through. It would have to wait until she visited. Mama Linda could tell her then if something had happened to her when she was a child at the House.

The next evening, Nikki plodded up the stairs to Ira and Javier's Park Slope apartment. She'd been looking forward to the seder, but now she felt a sense of dread. Her memories of Passover at the House were mixed: anxiety, laughter, discussion, pleasure, and boredom. The bland flavor of vegetarian matzo ball soup, the bitter taste of herbs, and the sweetness of a raisin-date spread that she used to load onto her matzo. Her family had friendly arguments, like about whether the quote from Ho Chi Minh should be cut from the seder script, or whether they should keep it because they needed a revolutionary version of the traditional ceremony. Some of the memories were sweet, like the time she drank too much Manischewitz wine. She was what, around eight years old, and was supposed to take only one or two sips from her mom's glass for ritual purposes, but she kept sneaking more when her mother wasn't looking. Tipsy, she'd crawled under the table and Meadow had joined her, giggling among the grown-ups' feet. But along with those recollections, she had a brush of a sensation she'd had lately, a disoriented sense of the world and the whisper of a memory she couldn't unearth, no matter how hard she tried.

She rang the doorbell. Javier let her in and immediately showed off the seder table, covered with an embroidered linen tablecloth, adorned with place settings in coordinated colors. The seder plate was at the center, with its symbolic hard-boiled egg, lamb shank, and greens. No one ate the lamb, it was just a prop. Javier stored the lamb shank in the freezer every year, until the day before the seder, when he did the ritual defrosting. A practicing Catholic, Javier had fervently adopted the ritual aspects of the Passover meal and was more exacting about it than his Jewish boyfriend or Nikki's hippie family had ever been. He presided over the seating arrangements like a nervous balabusta. Nikki tried to switch her place card to sit in another spot, but Javier fussily put it back. They had seated her next to a new guest, Adam, not one of the usual crowd. She was fairly sure it was a setup—the two single heteros seated next to each other. She was not happy about it, but it was probably Ira's doing. He was set on getting Nikki to "move on."

As they all took their places, Adam, a white thirty-something therapist with black-rimmed designer glasses and a multicolored yarmulke, started his conversation opener with their common profession: what was her specialty? His was couples counseling. When she didn't show much interest in talking shop, he kept talking and didn't stop—he covered the Yankees, then the war, then the book everyone was reading, *The Da Vinci Code*. If it weren't for his nonstop monologue, he seemed like a nice enough person and he was good looking, but from the moment she'd met him, she just wasn't interested. She couldn't find an edge to him—something to bump up against. No traction. She tried to keep up her end of the conversation, but she was tired of talking. Tired of drawing boundaries between her, her clients, her coworkers, her friends.

Across the table was a couple, Todd and Phil, with their young daughter, Emily, who were also new to the yearly seder. Ira had whispered to Nikki earlier that they were *Buddhists*. Nikki looked around at the group. It was only in the last year, since finding out she was mixed race, that she started doing the color math. She was the only Black person in the room, although half the guests probably didn't realize it. Javier was brown and Emily, with her gay white fathers, was Asian American.

Ira led the seder, directing each person at the table to take their turn reading from the Haggadah, the ceremonial script. When it came time to read the four questions, he said, "Emily, as the youngest person here, you get to ask the questions."

"Why is this night different from all others?" she read

aloud.

"On all other nights, we'd still be working at this hour. Tonight we're actually eating dinner like normal people," Ira's brother quipped.

"What's 'normal'?" Nikki asked.

Everyone laughed and lifted their glasses.

"It's not time to drink yet," Javier said. "Stick to the script."

The child read the three remaining questions aloud and the group answered in unison to each one. When they said, "We were slaves to Pharaoh in Egypt, and God brought us out with a strong hand and an outstretched arm," Nikki had the same sense of excitement she'd had as a child. They got away —they escaped and were free. No longer in bondage. When everyone recited, "The seder reminds us that we can never truly be free until all people everywhere can celebrate their freedom with us," she thought, That's the best part.

Emily piped up: "I have a question of my own."

Ira raised his eyebrows at Nikki, the message clear: you take it, you're the child therapist.

"Questions are good," Nikki said. "Go ahead."

"How come it's called Passover?"

With a nervous tickle in her throat, she tried to assess Emily's age. She looked to be about nine going on thirty. She forged ahead, hoping for the best. "The Jews were slaves in Egypt. No human being should ever be enslaved by another," she said.

"Yeah, I got that."

"And, to free the slaves, God sent a series of plagues."

"Like the locusts," the child said.

"Right. The final and the worst plague was to kill the first-born children, but the Angel of Death *passed over* the houses of the Jewish families because they were marked with the blood of the lamb, and that's where the name 'Passover' comes from."

"What?" Emily said, her eyes wide. "They *killed* the children? And a lamb, too? That's so violent." The table was deathly quiet. The child looked over at both her fathers, who glared at Nikki.

Right, they're Buddhists, Nikki thought. Maybe they'd never been to a seder before. Asking questions was at the heart of the ceremony, and the child deserved the truth. "Yes, it was a terrible thing," she said. "So terrible, in fact, that the pharaoh finally got the point: he had to let the slaves—the Jews—go free. And so, we gather on the same day every year, to remember that we were freed, but also to acknowledge the tragic loss for the Egyptian families. And to remember that even today, people are still enslaved."

Emily frowned. "I have another question."

"Yes?" Ira cut in, clearly determined to take the discussion in another direction.

"Is killing children a good method for conflict resolution?" she asked.

"Oy vey," Ira said.

"That," Nikki said, "is a very good question."

The table erupted in discussion—an eye for an eye versus turning the other cheek, Old Testament or New, Martin Luther King Jr. or Malcolm X, Judeo-Christian or Buddhist traditions? And that led to another inquiry: Was it important to preserve traditions if they have become outmoded or if the community changes its beliefs, and if so, should rituals be adapted? Finally, they agreed that next year they would revise their Haggadah for a script that embraced both the old and new traditions.

After dinner, everyone retired to the living room with

their wine glasses. Adam planted himself next to Nikki on the couch.

"Where are you from?" he asked.

"Originally? San Francisco."

He said, "No, I meant, your family. Are they from Latin America or the Middle East—or—are you Italian?"

"Black. I'm from Black."

He stuttered, "I—I didn't mean to offend you. You're very pretty, and I was just curious about your—"

"I'm mixed. My dad is Black and my mom is—was—white. Jewish." She knew she could be nicer to him, but she really didn't feel like it. All those years of people asking her about her ethnicity and she didn't know. Now she knew, and it was still annoying.

Javier came in to the room with dessert, announcing, "Flourless chocolate cake!"

"Excuse me," she said to Adam, "I promised Ira I'd help with the dishes." Which wasn't exactly true.

Ira was loading the dishwasher, and she joined him.

He squinted at her. "What's wrong?"

"Why do you ask that?"

"You have that dazed look."

"I guess the seder makes me miss the House and my mother and everything. I feel just sort of, I don't know. Homesick."

Ira nodded. "That makes sense, of course."

Javier appeared in the doorway, frowning. "What are you —oh." His look turned to one of pleasure. "You're doing the dishes. That's nice. But join us for cake when you're done." He departed, giving Ira a raised-eyebrow glance before leaving.

"What was that look?" Nikki asked.

"Me doing the dishes—it's foreplay. You were saying—about the seders when you were a kid."

The exchange between Ira and Javier—all those things couples have—private jokes and nonverbal cues. She missed that.

"Earth to Nikki," Ira said.

"I don't know. It's like I keep getting triggered by something I don't even remember."

Ira nodded and said gently, "Maybe it will come back to you."

They finished cleaning up and joined the others in the living room, but Nikki begged off, saying she had an early meeting the next day.

Adam followed her to the door, handing her his card, saying, "We should get together sometime and talk shop." Nikki said yes, they should get together for coffee sometime, reassuring him with a smile, thinking, No way.

Once on the sidewalk, she took in a deep breath of the spring night air and let it out it in a satisfying rush. She walked home, looking in shop windows, considering stopping at a bar for a drink. But of course she didn't want a drink. She knew what she wanted, and the urgency rushed through her whole body, pounding through her, driving her. She *could* read a book or draw in her sketchbook. But she didn't want to.

When she opened the door to her apartment, the drive that had been building up inside her through the long walk home took over and pushed her forward. No time to waste. She took out her laptop and checked craigslist. They either sounded too sleazy or too first-date-ish. She checked Nerve.com and found a hit. She emailed him and got a response back right away. She had three rules: safe sex, meet in public first, and always meet in Manhattan. She didn't want to run into one of her Brooklyn coworkers and then have them asking about her new "boyfriend."

It was a long ride to Washington Heights, but she didn't mind. When she got off the train and came up the stairs to the street, a thrum of anticipation ran through her.

They met in a bar and she checked him out. She trusted her intuition to suss out a violent man; this guy was okay. On the walk to his place, he peppered her with questions about her job, where she lived, what she liked to do on the weekends. "I don't like to talk," she said.

Once in his apartment, it was quiet except for occasional street noise. It was no-talk, it was listen, wait-touch, touch-wait. They joined their bodies in a gentle push-pull, and she was going to guide his hand but he got there first, sucking on her nipples and circling her clit slowly until she came. She pushed away for a moment, surprised, relieved that she hadn't had to tell him exactly what to do. She reached for the condom on the bed stand, and they were moving, moving; he slid it on and went in, and they were underwater.

Afterward, she got dressed and as he sat up in bed, watching her. "Reverse striptease," he said. She smiled with her eyes and waved goodbye. Walking out into the cool night air, she felt good, whole, comforted. As she made her way to the station, another feeling crept in. Loneliness.

When she got to the 181st Street station, she stopped in her tracks. Somehow, she'd never been to this entrance. The cavernous entryway had a distinct Art Deco vibe, with a vine-like pattern snaking around the peaked archway and SUBWAY stenciled in pale green glass letters on a vertical post. She stood in awe, taking it in, while others, blind to the mysteries of Gotham, brushed past her quickly and made their way into the station. Taking one last look at the facade, she went inside, descending into the station and the familiar damp hum, smelling the muggy grit. The subway system, with its tiled walls, station names elegantly lettered in classical fonts, grimy overlay, and guarantee of anonymity had always, for her, captured the essence of New York. It was at once comforting and alienating.

On the platform, waiting for the train, she thought about how different it was before the internet. She used to pick up men in cafés, bars, and grocery stores. Once she met Christopher, she stopped. It wasn't worth jeopardizing their relationship. For the eight years she was with him, she never did it. And she proved to herself that she didn't *have* to do it.

She liked all kinds of men. A Black man with a whisper of a southern drawl, a Caribbean lilt, or an African way around his vowels. A white guy from Eastern Europe or the Midwest, a transplant who'd come to make it in the big city. A Latino guy with soulful eyes, an Asian American man with a broad New York accent, or a kinky-haired Jewish guy with glasses. Working-class guys who worked with their hands, nerdy software programmers, medical students, or community activists on bicycles. She was an equal opportunity fucker. No talking, no analyzing, no thinking, just skin against skin.

The clattering sound of the A train brought with it the comfort of anonymous transport. Alone in the crowd, she stepped onto the train.

Chapter 6

Virtual Wall

Deb settled into the breakfast nook of the trailer to work on her project. She still had a neck ache from the whiplash of almost crashing the jeep. Opening up the web-building program, the usual error message popped up: *The connection failed. Try again.*

"Yes, I know I'm in the middle of the Mojave Desert," she snapped. She selected the Work Offline option and glanced through her mockup of the home page.

Suicide Veterans Memorial Wall
    A virtual wall to honor wounded veterans of the Vietnam, Iraq, and Afghanistan wars who took their own lives. Suicide is often treated as a shameful act, kept in secret, in the dark. With this memorial, we shine the light on these men and women, casualties of war, whose invisible war wounds resulted in suicide.

Was it the right tone? She tweaked the words, then clicked over to the "Virtual Wall" page. Ming's graphic was beautiful—a granite wall, triangular in shape, with shades of

silver and gold. Deb had been clear she didn't want an imita-
tion of the Memorial Wall in Washington. This virtual wall
would be the background image for the names of the soldiers
with invisible wounds. Her hope was that once she put up the
website, people would send in the names of their loved ones,
and she could post them on the "Virtual Wall" page. All these
years she'd wanted to do something to vindicate her brother—
to put his suicide in context and share it with all the people
like her who'd lost their loved ones because of a fucking war.
Now she was so close to finishing. She couldn't put it off any
longer.

She checked the page she had set up for Ron. It was the
prototype for posting individual memorials. She included
three photos: the first of her brother before the war, a smile in
his eyes, a skinny boy-man, with his hair just touching his
collar. The second was from boot camp, a tougher version of
the same young man, with muscles and a buzz cut. The last
one was post-war, a long-haired, barefoot hippie in the back
garden of the house on Ashbury Street, holding hands with
little Nik-Knock, back when Ron was RJ, his lips stretched
into a smile, but his eyes haunted. Under the photos, she had
included a brief tribute:

> We remember and honor his generous heart, his big smile,
> his keen mind, his ability to take apart anything and put it
> back together, his green thumb. He was always good with
> children, he knew everything about plants and wildlife and
> the mountains. He always stood up to volunteer if there
> was a difficult task at hand. He was our big brother, the
> best. We miss you, Ron.

She knew it was supposed to be good to express your feelings, let it out, all that. But if it was such a good thing, why

was it so damn hard? Her physical urge was to just get up and walk away, go anywhere but here. But instead she told herself: This is nonnegotiable. If she didn't finish it now she might never do it. She clicked the tab for the "About" page—should she write something about how this all began? She thought back to her first inkling of it.

Eighteen years ago, she'd flown to DC to visit the Vietnam Veterans Memorial. She had recently discovered that large numbers of Vietnam Vets had died by suicide, putting Ron's death in a whole new light. When she arrived, it was late afternoon. She checked into her hotel room, put on her coat, hat, scarf, and mittens, and walked to the National Mall. As she approached the Memorial Wall, the skin on her arms prickled. She'd seen photographs of it, lots of images, but nothing had prepared her for what she saw before her. Making her way slowly along the curving expanse of black granite, she picked a place at random and stopped. She gazed into the polished surface—taking in the names, the lack of glory, the absence of figures. Instead of a towering phallic column of men raising a flag, marking their territory, the Wall was a mirror. Observing her own reflection, she wondered if the Wall asked, How are you involved? How are you implicated? No, Deb thought—not implicated. It didn't judge, it simply *gave back* an image of the loss. Of course the architect was a woman.

She moved down the Wall a few feet, finding her way to another place. It was then she realized what she was doing. Looking for his name. A fury rose up in her—why the hell wasn't Ron's name there? He had died from inner wounds from the Vietnam War just as surely as these soldiers had died from outer wounds. She clenched her fists, wanting to hit something, but there was nowhere and nothing to strike.

"Do you have someone here?" a voice asked.

Deb hadn't noticed the lady beside her. She was in her seventies, wearing one of those clear plastic rain bonnets over her hair, her blue eyes alight with intelligence.

Deb shook her head. "No. Well, yes. Not here exactly, but . . . It's hard to explain."

"I understand, honey," the lady said.

"You do?"

"We've all lost someone—maybe not in this war, but . . ." the woman said, with a faint southern twang.

"My brother. He served in the war. But he died afterward."

"There's all kind of wars, not all of them on the battle-field," the woman said softly.

"Thank you," Deb said, tears filling her eyes. "You are so kind. And you—do you have someone here?"

The woman didn't answer, but instead crouched and began to spread out a tarp over the wet pavement. Deb bent down and helped her with it. Then the woman placed a narrow yellow foam pad on the tarp and knelt down on it, saying, "There's room for both of us on this thing." Deb got down on her knees and knelt beside her.

Pointing to a name in the last row, the woman said, "Here. My daughter. Karen Louise Roberts."

"That is so sad," Deb said, and her voice broke. She put her hand on the woman's arm. The longer she gazed into the lustrous surface of the Wall, the more she saw that the memorial was a container for collective grief. Her anger dissipated and gave way to a well of sorrow. The silvery wall blurred and shimmered in the lightly falling snow.

"What's your brother's name?" her companion asked.

"Ronald James Travis."

Gazing down, lips moving slightly, the woman was silent

for a few moments. Then she looked up. "I said a prayer for him. And one for you, too, dear."

Deb wiped her eyes, thanked the woman, and helped her fold the tarp. It was then she noticed the others, people up and down the Wall, some leaving keepsakes, some polishing the granite with a handkerchief, and some just gazing into the reflective stone.

Coming back to the present, Deb stared at the computer screen. When she'd visited the Wall that first time, in 1987, the internet hadn't even existed. But in the last few years, when everyone started making their own websites for every conceivable project, she realized an online memorial was the perfect way to honor Ron and others like him. She'd started and dropped the project more than once, but when Andy went off to college and Deb had more time, it loomed over her as a constant reminder of her failure to find justice for Ron.

She had taken the sabbatical from her job to try out being a volunteer ranger. But she also knew it was time away from her regular life—time to focus on the website memorial project and finish it. No more procrastinating.

She clicked through her new web pages. She still had to add a sidebar about the In Memory plaque in Washington. In 2000, after repeated pressure to add to the Wall the names of veterans who'd died *after* the war from the effects of Agent Orange and the refusal of the Department of Defense to allow it, Congress authorized the In Memory plaque instead. Four years later, it was dedicated. The inscription reads: "In memory of the men and women who served in the Vietnam War and later died as a result of their service. We honor and remember their sacrifice." The veiled reference was to veterans who died from the aftereffects of Agent Orange and *possibly* vets who'd died from suicide. But who would even notice the plaque, which, instead of being next to the Wall, was hidden in a corner near the other Vietnam memorial, a statue of three soldiers, erected (Deb stopped in her thoughts —yeah, *erected* was the phallocentric word) after protests that the Wall wasn't heroic enough. The irony was that most visitors bypassed the heroic statue altogether and went straight to the Wall instead.

The In Memory plaque was set flat in the ground in a corner, blocked off by a chain. When Deb had visited it a few years ago, she'd swept off the leaves and crouched beside it. She read the inscription aloud. "Died as a result of their service." That was a euphemism if she'd ever heard one. Why not tell it like it was—died as a result of the effects of Agent Orange, of PTSD, or of suicide related to all of the above? "Fuck," she'd muttered, or maybe said it louder than she intended, but the people passing by on their way to the Wall glanced at her and then ignored her.

That was four years ago, and she was still furious about that insipid plaque. She stood up from the computer, knocking over her chair in the process. She banged through the door and went outside, surprising a desert cottontail, who took off into the brush. After a few circles around the trailer, she calmed down. *Deb, it's okay. You're finally funneling your grief into a project. You're creating something. It'll work, you'll see.* She went back inside.

Chapter 7

Out of Bounds

T he Saturday after the seder, Nikki walked to the parade ground in the park and settled into a spot high up in the bleachers. The last time she and Susan had the boundaries discussion, her boss had said it was okay to go to a client's school play or game as long as you stayed in the background and made a quick exit afterward. So Nikki had deliberately chosen her remote seat, avoiding the small group of Hannah's mother and family members.

"You came!" Yelena said, appearing out of nowhere and sitting down on the bleachers next to her, giving her a kiss on the cheek.

Fuck. Sitting by her client's mother was not part of the plan. She made small talk with her until the game started, hoping Yelena would go back to sit with her family, but she never did. So they watched the game together—for Nikki it was an obligation, but for Yelena it was something else, screaming in excitement when things went well or, when she disagreed with the umpire, going into fierce attack mode, jumping up and yelling.

After the game, Nikki found Hannah and told her she'd

done great—what do you say when the kid's team has lost? But instead of slipping away like smoke as she had planned, she ran smack into Yelena, who insisted she come to the house for the post-game meal. Nikki politely declined, but Yelena kept insisting, and then Hannah joined in, saying, "Please, *please*, Ms. Nikki," and she found herself getting into an SUV with them and a couple of Hannah's uncles, all of whom were talking rapidly in an Eastern European language. Yelena turned around from the front passenger seat and said: "Ukrainian."

They arrived at the Brighton Beach apartment, and Yelena put out a huge spread: bowls of borscht, platters of pierogis, thick slices of rye bread spread with herring, and cookies with jam in the center. It was all delicious, and Nikki ate too much. Hannah's uncles, Marko and Petro, now talking with her in English, insisted she have a shot of vodka. She downed it. Okay, fine. And then another. And another. After a few, she started saying no, but they assured her she hadn't had enough. *"Ta, piy, piy, beelsheh, beelsheh!"* they yelled. She asked Yelena what that meant, and she said, "My brothers are saying, Drink more!" Nikki thought it was an awful lot of words for just "drink more."

Marko, the tall, blond one, put on Ukrainian music and urged her to join them dancing—she did her best and it was fun, more fun than she'd had in a long time. Petro, the short, dark-haired brother with the sexy smile, taught her some basic steps and she flubbed them, but it felt so good to be not thinking, just laughing and moving to music. At some point, she firmly refused more vodka shots, which would have forced her to stay the night. That would have been going way over the line—like into the stratosphere. She extricated herself from the rowdy brothers, leaving them to their dance party, and although Petro was really very appealing, she knew she had to leave before she did something stupid. She found Yelena and said her goodbyes. Hannah's mother walked her to the door. "If only my daughter Sasha could be with us today," she said, her voice breaking. Nikki nodded in sympathy, and Yelena threw her arms around her and sobbed.

"I understand," Nikki said, thinking: This is why it's not good to go to your client's soccer game. You end up with the child's mother sobbing on your shoulder.

Petro appeared and offered her a ride. "I give you ride home," he said.

"No, no, I'm fine taking the train. Besides, you really shouldn't drive."

"I drive fine. Where do you live?"

"South Slope, but really, I want to take the train."

"Is long train ride from Brighton Beach to Park Slope."

Yelena said something to him in Ukrainian, and he said, "Okay," and opened the door.

"I really don't want a ride," Nikki said.

"I understand. I walk you to station," Petro said.

Halfway to the station, she found herself walking arm-in-arm with him, like they were old friends. Petro, it turned out, was a furniture salesman, "But only until my business gets off ground." He and his friend Gustavo were going to open a restaurant. They already had a small storefront and they were fixing it up. "We will call it Pan-Brooklyn. You know, like Pan-Asian or Pan-African? The food will be part Ukrainian, part Mexican, and part Middle Eastern food." She said it sounded delicious. He asked her about her work and then took her hand in his.

The feel of his hand, which was both soft and calloused, loosened something inside her. She didn't usually like to talk about her work, but now she opened up, telling him the low points—like the time a young child had put her shoes in the toilet, and also the highs—the day a teen client wrote a song for her and sang it to her in perfect pitch.

Petro nodded, saying, "That is beautiful." He leaned over and kissed her softly, and then they were making out in the street, and it felt so *awesome*. Somewhere in the back of her mind she knew that Petro was her client's uncle and that there was a thing about boundaries. And that she wasn't supposed to be doing this.

The long train ride home gave her plenty of time to go over the events of the night. The meal with the family was bad enough, but the drinking and partying was going way out of bounds. She'd always thought the expression "one thing leads to another" was ridiculous. Surely she would never be swept away like a heroine in some bodice-ripper romance novel. But now she understood. Part of it was the vodka, but also it was seamless how the *one* thing, kissing, had led to *another*: a semi-secluded doorway, some serious dry-humping, groping, and laughter. Petro had seen her to the station and politely asked for her phone number. She'd given it to him. Which, she realized now, was *another* thing that was not a good idea.

It took her all of Sunday to recover from the vodka hangover. Petro called and left a voice mail saying he'd like to see her, "like for nice date." She didn't call him back. It was a bummer that the only guy she'd met in the last couple of years who she might want to go out on a date with was her client's uncle.

When Nikki got to work on Monday, Susan stopped her in the hall, asking to see her in her office after her next session. It was probably to talk about the agreement, and fortunately she had finally remembered to bring in the signed paperwork.

She prepared herself for the session with Hannah with a deep-breathing exercise. When she fetched her client from the waiting room, she was with the babysitter, who didn't even bother to look up from her magazine. Hannah smiled and took her hand—she'd never done that before. Nikki smiled back, squeezing her hand and letting it go right away, hoping no one saw.

Once in the office, Hannah went right to the sand tray. She selected a few miniatures and placed them in the sand: a table and chairs, with a woman and a baby perched precariously on the chairs. Then she searched through the tiny objects to find a green dragon, its jaws open in a roar. She used the dragon to knock over the woman. Nikki thought: The baby is Hannah, the woman is her mother. Is the dragon her sister's suicide? Or something else? Hannah picked up the dragon and woman figures and buried them in the sand. Finally, she put the baby on top of the table. "Done," she said.

"What happened to the dragon and the woman?"

Hannah pointed, saying, "Underneath."

"And the baby—she's on the table now."

"Yeah."

Why had Hannah buried the mother figure? Did she want more control over the situation and so she put herself on a higher level, on top of the table? Nikki almost reached out to dig up the miniature mother figure and move it to the table, but stopped herself. She had never, in six years of using sand tray therapy, had the impulse to invade a client's created world. She was clearly influenced by her sympathy for Hannah's mother, which would never have happened if she hadn't gone to their home for dinner, and if Yelena hadn't cried on her shoulder.

"Ms. Nikki?"

"Yes?"

"Aren't you going to ask me more questions?"

She turned her attention to Hannah and nodded. In this moment, her client was the most important person in the universe. Nikki smiled and Hannah visibly relaxed, her shoulders going down, her forehead uncreasing.

"Yes, I *do* have a question for you," Nikki said. "What would you like to do now?"

Hannah went to the padded armchair and settled in, stroking the arm. "You know what?"

"What?"

"I'm glad you came to my soccer game."

"Me too," Nikki lied.

"Now you're like family," Hannah said, smiling.

Nikki kept her placid therapist face on, thinking, Fuck, fuck, fuck. This is what came of having dinner with her client's mother and uncles. Not to mention the make-out scene with Petro in the street, but maybe that wasn't "like family" but just, like, stupid. Say something. "That's so sweet. Thank you. I'm not *exactly* family, though—more like a really good friend you can talk to, to help you understand your feelings and give you support. It works better that way, because then I can be dedicated to you and not the rest of your family." Was Hannah going to buy that?

Hannah's puzzled face crinkled. "My *mom* said you're like family. What's wrong with that?"

Nikki arranged her face in what she hoped was a reassuring smile. "Nothing's wrong with that." Jesus. Change the subject. Quick. "I really like the world you created in the sand tray. Tell me more about it."

After the session, she went down the hall to Susan's office. She handed her boss the agreement. "I'm sorry it took me so long to get it to you."

Susan didn't smile. "Would you close the door, please, and have a seat?"

This didn't bode well. Usually the door stayed open and they both sat in the guest chairs while they talked. With her desk between them, Susan sat down. She had her therapist look on, and the cords in her neck were tight. Wait a minute, Nikki thought: *Fuck*. Her stomach clenched and her armpits were instantly soaked. What if her boss had found out—somehow—about Nikki's weekend habit? Did someone see her, had *she* seen her? But that was absurd—what if they had —she was a free woman, it was none of Susan's business. Nikki could fuck whoever she wanted. But there was that one time she'd used the work computer, even though she'd sworn she'd *never* use the work computer to set up a meeting, she *always* used her dedicated laptop, which she kept at home. Her heart raced and she could barely breathe. Christ! Could she lose the job she loved and her livelihood over this fucking habit? It wasn't as if she was a sex addict or anything. It was like a hobby. And what about the kids? If she was fired, it would be like a betrayal of her clients' trust in her. And that would be so fucked up.

Susan cleared her throat. She picked up a rubber stress ball from the corner of her desk and pumped it a few times. "I'm sorry to have to do this, but it's come to my attention that —oh shit. I'll just cut to the chase. Someone reported they saw you at a soccer game with your client's family. She looked down at her notes. "Hannah Stevanovich. And her mother, Mrs. Stevanovich. They reported you getting into a car with the family after the game. I'm sure you realize that you were engaging in a dual relationship. This is precisely the issue we have discussed before."

Nikki's heart hammered. Please goddess, she entreated, let it be only that, not making out on the street with your client's uncle. "You're right—I know. Hannah asked me to come and I promised her I would. But you and I had discussed that attending a game or a school play would be all right. In terms of boundaries." Her voice was shaky.

"Yes, it would have been fine to just watch the game from the upper bleachers and then leave, except you didn't. Apparently you went somewhere with your client's family. Where did you go?"

Shit, shit, shit. She knew she shouldn't have done it. But it had seemed so natural at the time. Going with the flow. She swallowed, trying to get her voice back under control. "We went to their house."

"And what happened there?"

"We had a meal and then I went home."

"Also," Susan said, "The person who reported this incident said that you and Hannah's mother kissed."

"*Kissed?* When she greeted me, Mrs. Stevanovich gave me a peck on the cheek—it's a Ukrainian custom. People kiss on the cheek."

"This isn't personal, Nikki. We have to maintain ethics in the clinic. I'm concerned about this situation compromising your ability to work with your client. If you have a friendship with the parent, it's difficult to put the child client at the center of your concerns. We are a clinic for child therapy. We ask ourselves over and over again: what is the best thing for my client? The other family members are seen only in relation to that central focus."

Susan's voice changed now, to a gentler tone, and she had a look of compassion that Nikki had never before witnessed.

"But then you know all that. You're one of our most gifted therapists. I am wondering if you may be caught up in counter-transference issues, and if you're not already seeing a therapist or consulting with someone, I suggest that you do so."

Maybe, she thought, Susan really did care. But Nikki didn't entirely trust her. She took a deep breath, trying to calm herself down. "Look, I'm sorry for getting so defensive. It was uncalled for. And you know what? You're right. I have boundary issues. And I signed the agreement and all, so maybe we can give it some time as a kind of probationary period."

Susan grabbed the stress ball and squeezed it. "There's one other thing."

Nikki braced herself.

"There's no ethics rule about this, but I am concerned about the friendships you've had since I've been here."

"*Friendships?*" Nikki clenched her hands.

"With Vic, and before that with José, and before that with Tony."

Oh, for god's sake, Nikki thought. "Friendship" was a euphemism if she ever heard one. "What about those friendships?"

"It's another boundary. It's better to keep coworker relationships separate from personal relationships. Nikki, are you seeing a therapist or consulting with someone?"

"No. But maybe that would be a good thing." Things were spiraling downward. She told herself: Just say yes to whatever Susan says.

"I recommend that. And—as for the next step—I'm afraid I'm going to have to put you on leave. I'm also going to have to report your case to the Disciplinary Board. Once they make their decision—which usually takes up to six months, we'll take it from there. Depending on what the Board decides, we hope to give you your job back, but I can't promise anything."

A clenching sensation in Nikki's throat made it hard to get the words out. She sputtered, "But. Isn't that a bit harsh? Can't we give it some time, however long you want, and I'll work on the boundaries issue and consult with someone to work on my issues? People have been spared the review by the Board for a lot worse. Is it a crime to have issues with boundaries?"

With a sad smile, Susan shook her head. "Not a crime, Nikki. But it was not just a breach of personal boundaries. It was also a dual relationship, after you'd already been warned. I'm sorry. I'm putting you on leave from the clinic until further notice and submitting your case to the Disciplinary Board." She stood up, signaling that their conversation was over.

In a fog, Nikki made her way back to her office. Vic was more dressed up than usual today, wearing slacks and a button-up blue shirt. Seated at their shared desk, his shoulders sloping downward, he swiveled around to face her when she came in. She hoped he wasn't still pissed off. She closed the door behind her and sank down into the armchair. "You won't believe what just happened."

"I wanted to tell you *before* you talked to Susan," he said.

"Tell me what?"

Picking up a paper clip, he twisted it until it was straight and then attempted to bend it back to shape. "You didn't see my note?"

"What note?"

He held up a piece of paper that was sitting on their desk. *Please see me before you talk to Susan.*

"So she didn't tell you it was me?" he asked.

Nikki grasped the armrests. "*You?* You're the one who reported it? Jesus. I can't believe this."

"Look, I had to do it; it was a matter of ethics."

"You couldn't have talked to me first before gabbing to Susan? Okay, this is just fucking great."

Vic laughed angrily. "Oh, so this is *my* fault now? I can't believe you."

"Let's go outside. I don't want anyone hearing this," she said.

He set his jaw stubbornly, starting to refuse, but then shrugged his shoulders in agreement. Typical Vic, she thought, passive-aggressive.

They made their way out of the building in silence and walked down the street through the blustery morning to the corner, stopping just outside the bodega.

"How did you just happen to be at that game?" she said.

"My niece was playing."

"So you didn't follow me there?"

"You are such a narcissist. This isn't all about you, you know."

"Okay, what about *you*, then, Vic? You seem angry. Is this about us—our thing?"

"See, I knew you'd think that. It's about ethics, plain and simple."

"Because you've been giving me the cold shoulder, even though—"

"For god's sake," he said, "what a somatic expression—the 'cold shoulder.' I haven't been doing that. You're clearly dealing with your intimacy issues, and it's not about me."

Something inside her exploded and the words tumbled out. "Don't talk to me like I'm a client. 'What a relief that the sex doesn't *mean* anything'—those were *your* words, not mine." She realized she was yelling. She lowered her voice just in case someone from the clinic walked by. She tamped down the anger but still felt the back of her neck quivering. "And one day—boom—*you* wanted to stop. I said okay, fine, and then you acted like *I* had ended things, when you were the one who wanted to—not break up, because there was supposedly nothing to break—but you were the one who wanted to change our relationship from a sexual one to a nonsexual one. It's not like we even hung out. You acted like I'd abandoned you, when it was *you* who set the whole thing up, start to finish."

She thought he would yell back at her, but instead he just looked away. That was weird. But when he turned back, she realized, *Oh shit*, that there was a glimmer of tears in his eyes. Oh no. How could she have been so blind.

"I'm sorry," she said quietly. "It's not black and white. All the feelings got mixed in. I guess maybe I was insensitive to what you were feeling."

"You know, I didn't tell Susan about the dual relationship to be punitive," he said. "But when I saw you and her kissing—"

"What?" she said. "Me and who kissing?"

"Mrs. Stevanovich. Hannah's mother."

She exploded. "What the fuck are you talking about? She kissed me on the cheek, and I kissed her on the cheek. It was a friendly greeting. Jesus! For god's sake—"

"Fuck you," he snapped. And he was gone, striding away in the opposite direction from the clinic, his shoulders hunched. She watched as his figure grew smaller and smaller. Heading back to the clinic to pack up her things, she leaned into the swirling gusts of wind.

· · ·

Walking home, the more Nikki thought about Susan putting her on leave without giving her another chance, the more furious she got. As soon as she got back to her apartment, she pulled out her laptop, checked craigslist, and made a call. The guy wanted to meet downtown on Stone Street, which was all very cobblestoned and more upscale than her usual hangouts. And it was near the Financial District, also not her turf. But sometimes, she thought, it was good to get out of your comfort zone. They agreed to meet in a couple of hours.

They sat at the bar and talked. The guy, Tripp, was an investment banker, and Nikki had never met one before, so she asked him lots of questions about his work. Like most people, he enjoyed talking about himself, and he held forth. The bartender, her bronze skin covered in tattoos, came by and, smiling at Nikki, asked if they wanted more drinks.

"No smiles for me, Uma?" Tripp said.

"Nope."

One drink and as much talk about assets and securities as she could stand later, Nikki changed the subject. To her surprise, he was actually open to talking about other stuff—her community garden, cooking, and the latest Woody Allen movie, *Match Point*, which they had both seen. He was a bit of a frat bro, but she was warming up to him, and the sexual tension was building. When they got up to leave, he insisted on paying, much as she tried to split it with him. She gave Uma a giant tip—she was a good bartender, but more than that, there was something about her that was particularly sweet. Uma thanked Nikki and leaned in, about to whisper something to her, but Tripp put his hand on Nikki's elbow and steered her to the door. Looking back at Uma with a silent apology, she went out the door with him. She'd had only one glass of wine and then switched to mineral water, and she felt in control. Heading down the sidewalk, she said, "Do you live nearby?"

"Not too far. Want to go to my place?"

She wanted to, yes, the chemistry was good and she felt a sense of her sexual power in the moment.

Before she said anything, he said, "Not sure?" and leaned in and kissed her, and she kissed him back. Then he steered her around the corner of a building into an alley and leaned her against the wall, grinding into her, his dick hard, with so much force he was slamming her.

"Hey, easy, easy," she said.

He pulled back and something changed in his face. He jammed his body into hers even harder than before and rammed, grabbing for the zipper of her jeans.

"What the fuck?" she yelled.

"You know you like it rough," he snarled, one hand braced on either side of her shoulders, trapping her.

She slid down and wriggled out of the cage of his arms. "No, actually, I don't." She started to walk away, moving out of the alley and onto the sidewalk, but he grabbed her arm.

A man and woman stopped on the sidewalk and the man called out. "Are you all right?"

Tripp's back was to the couple and he ignored them. "Come on, bitch."

"Fuck you." Nikki yanked her arm away.

He punched her in the face. The shock of it sent her careening. On automatic, she jammed her knee into his crotch.

He bent over in pain. "Cunt!"

Dizzy, she managed to stumble down the sidewalk. The couple came up behind her and asked if she needed help. She looked behind them to see if Tripp was following, but he was nowhere in sight. Turning down their offer, she made her way back to the bar. Once inside, she sat on a barstool, looking for Uma.

Uma spotted her from the other end of the bar and headed over. Taking in Nikki's face, which was starting to swell, she exploded. "Fuck! Are you all right? I tried to warn you about him, but you were out the door." She ran out to the sidewalk and looked in both directions. When she came back, she said, "He's gone. That's it. I'm going to get that asshole 86'd. Here, let me get you some ice before we do anything."

Holding the ice on her face, she thanked Uma and turned down the offers to call the police or go to the emergency room. When she said she'd be fine to take the train, Uma crossed her arms and said no way, she was calling her a cab. Uma walked her out to the taxi and told the driver to charge it to the bar.

"Thank you. You are so kind."

Uma shook her head. "It's the least I can do."

A loud sound woke her. It was dark. Where was she? Home. She was lying on the couch, and she liked it there. She wasn't about to get up. What was that buzzing? Someone downstairs at the door to the building? She ignored it. Whoever it was must be leaning on the buzzer. She opened her eyes and squinted at the clock on her desk—it was just before midnight. Stereo was on—Billie Holiday. A CD. She didn't remember putting it in the player, but there it was. She got up and groped her way down the hall to the intercom and pressed the button. "Who is it?" Her voice sounded funny to her ears. Her face hurt. She touched it. It was puffy.

"It's me." Ira sounded pissed. "Are you okay? You left me that weird message. I've called you five times. I was worried about you. You couldn't pick up or at least call me back? Buzz me in."

"Ira," she said slowly.

"Oh Christ. Just buzz me the fuck in."

She pressed the button, opened the door, and made her way back to the couch.

He came in, locking the door behind him. He turned on the lamp. "Holy shit! What happened? Were you mugged? Oh my god, should we go to the emergency room?"

When she didn't answer, he said, "You want some ice for your face?"

"No, I did that already."

"I'm getting it anyway." He went to the kitchen.

"You should have some whiskey," she called out after him.

"No thanks. Oh, what the hell, yeah."

He came back with an ice pack and a glass. "Here, hold the ice pack here. Your voice mail—you were slurring your words and I couldn't understand what you were saying. Something about your job. Talk to me."

"I got fired."

"What?"

"Not fired, 'put on leave,' but what the fuck, it's like getting fired. She said I'm having a dual relationship."

"What does that mean?"

"It's like, a relationship outside the therapy room. Bad boundaries. Bad girl."

"Jesus." He poured himself some whiskey from the bottle on the coffee table. "So then what happened? She punched you? No, seriously, who did that to you? Did you call the police?"

"No, no. I did something stupid. Went for a hookup—shouldn't have used craigslist, should've used one of those dating sites, should've known better." She told him what happened.

He shook his head. "That fucking fuckhead. See, that's

why you should never have anything to do with an investment banker. They're scum. I wish I'd been there, I would've decked him."

She laughed. "You've never hit anyone in your life."

"True, but I'm taking kickboxing and I'm kind of into it now." He stroked her hand. "Maybe we should go to the emergency room. What if you have a concussion?"

"I'm okay. I didn't fall down or anything."

Ira went to the kitchen and came back with a big glass of water. "Drink this. Now."

She took the glass and gulped it down.

"I have to say," he said, "Maybe the universe is sending you a message, amiga. I mean it. Could be time to back off on the sex trolling."

"It's not *trolling*, for god's sake."

Ira shook his head, opened his mouth and then closed it. After a moment: "You know what? Let's talk about that later. For now, just tell me what happened with your boss."

She gave him a full account of her meeting with Susan. "I love that job. I can't fucking believe it. What am I going to do?" Her face was wet with tears. She put her arms around her friend and sobbed.

He shook his head. "Jesus. That seems harsh. She really should've given you a second chance. She could have put you on—like—probation or something."

"Already was. Kind of." Nikki laid back down on the couch and closed her eyes.

Ira picked up the bottle of whisky on the coffee table and swirled the liquid around. "When did you buy this?"

"Sometime tonight; I don't know."

"Christ, you made quite a dent in it."

When she didn't answer, he said, "When was the last time you ate?"

76

"Oy vey, Mama Ira. I had lunch. A while back. Whenever that was. Not hungry."

He went to the kitchen and she heard him pulling out stuff from the cabinet and refrigerator.

"Where's the bread?" he said.

"Top of the fridge."

She must have dozed off, because when she woke up, Ira had a sandwich for her on a tray, along with another glass of water. She drank the water and devoured the sandwich. She closed her eyes as she savored it. It tasted fantastic. "This sandwich is *mind-blowing*. What did you put in it?"

"It's salami and cheese. *Trayf*."

"What's *trayf*? I forgot."

"Not kosher to eat meat and cheese together."

"That's all it is—salami and cheese? There's something else, right?"

"Mustard. And pickles," he said.

"Pickles! I'll have to remember that." She chewed carefully, her jaw sore. "Ya know what?" she said, peering at him. "You . . . you're far out."

He laughed. "Thank you. You're pretty groovy yourself, mademoiselle."

The next morning, Nikki woke up with a pounding headache. She found herself on the couch with all her clothes on and a Mexican blanket draped over her. She blinked her eyes to clear away the sleep. The room looked oddly clean. Then it came back to her: Ira was here last night. Not only did he make her a sandwich, but he also must've straightened up the place and then found, in the closet, the most aesthetically pleasing blanket to drape over her. Just behind these thoughts came a wallop of memory. Her job at the clinic: gone.

Chapter 8

Friendly Fire

Deb eased herself into the swimming pool. In the balmy night, the water sparkled aquamarine. Thank goodness it was quiet. The whooping prepubescent boys of earlier in the day were gone. She stayed underwater as long as she could hold her breath, then came up for air. The Palms Motel was her little secret. She'd never told any of the rangers about it—she always said she was going to visit a friend in Palm Springs, when really she came to this tacky Ridgecrest motel. It had a wireless connection, so she had 24-hour access to the internet. The motel had become her go-to place to work on her website whenever she could manage to get a couple of days off. But it wasn't only that. There was something about the motel that was so utterly California, so the opposite of Michigan, her home state. But it had been a long time since she'd considered Grand Rapids "home."

She floated on her back and looked up at the sky, gray-black, tinged with purple. The three palm trees ringing the parking lot were like a gathering of souls. She pushed out of the pool, wrapped herself in a towel, and headed back to her room.

Perched on the lumpy queen bed, her laptop propped on a pillow, she opened up the website. It was still exciting to see it fully realized. They'd gone live a few days ago, and she and Ming had celebrated with a long-distance launch party. Ming had shown her this new way of talking by video, and even though it was a little fuzzy, there was Ming drinking champagne, while Deb nibbled on cannabis cookies. She'd hoped Ron would show up like he had before, as a voice in her head or even a dream, and that he'd thank her for the website, but nothing like that had happened. She'd imagined, too, that as soon as she put up the site she'd hear from throngs of bereaved family or friends of vets who'd lost someone to suicide. So far, only two people had signed up to post their loved one's names on the Suicide Veterans Memorial Wall. But then, maybe it was scary to go public with it. The first email was from a woman named Cindy.

Dear Deborah,

Listing my son Steve on the Suicide Veterans Memorial Wall has finally got me to acknowledge what happened to him. My years of writing to his commanding officer, to my congressperson, to the VA, have come to nothing. Here is a place where I can say: My son died as a result of war wounds. It was an injustice that after his service and all, the VA and his community couldn't help him out when he needed them the most.

Cindy

Duluth, Minnesota

Deb read it over again, still with a rush of excitement.

This was why she had conceived and built the website—for people like Cindy and her son, Steve. And for Ron.

But the other email she'd received had surprised her.

Dear Deborah,

Your Suicide Veterans Memorial Wall is for veterans. But what about soldiers who commit suicide when they are on active duty? My husband, Luis, took his life while he was stationed in Fallujah. We will never forgive the army for allowing this to happen. Please post his name on the Wall. I put all the information below. Thank you.

Rosa

La Puente, California

She got up from the motel bed and went outside, past the parking lot, to a rickety picnic table in the middle of a scrubby patch of dirt. There was no one around, so she lit up a joint and sat on top of the table, smoking and looking out at the chaparral. Rosa was right. The website should be for anyone in the service who'd died by suicide, not just veterans. Maybe the soldiers who killed themselves during this war were caught in a kind of friendly fire. Shoot the enemy within. Ron always said friendly fire was a bullshit term invented by the military to cover up their mistakes. For Rosa's husband, maybe he couldn't live with the massacre of civilians in Fallujah. What if he shot the enemy inside him because he could not bear another day of shame.

She got her guitar and notebook from the motel room and returned to the picnic bench. Strumming and singing, *I shot the enemy/the enemy inside/easier that way/could not bear/another day*. She found her way through the rest of the melody and lyrics. Setting down her guitar, she jotted down the words by moonlight. In the sky, the medallion of a moon was higher now and crispy white. After a while the coyotes started up. She yipped back but they didn't answer—they never did. They could tell she wasn't one of them. Just once, she wished they would respond.

Back in the motel room, she checked her inbox and found an email from Matt.

Hi Sis,

I looked at your website. I know you put your heart and soul into it, and I admire you for that, but I have to say I haven't changed my mind. We've talked about this before. There's no evidence that he did it because of the war. Mom and Dad always agreed with me about that.

But I will say that if you feel the website is an important memorial, then I'm proud of you for doing it.

Love,

Matt

Deb shook her head. Typical Matt. Good cop/bad cop. His theory was that their brother had died by suicide because of "mental health issues." He thought Ron was bipolar but undiagnosed, so he never got treatment. Matt "knew" he was right because of the "evidence"—that Ron was seeing a counselor at the VA, that he would always withdraw into stony silence at family gatherings. Of course Matt was fond of evidence. He was a cop.

In her family, everyone had their own unique theory about why Ron did it, and because there was no suicide note, each of them considered theirs to be the only correct version. Mom's view was that Ron did it because he was so lonely, out there in San Francisco, and that he always had his *moods*, the last word spoken in a whisper. And a few years ago, at Christmas, not long before her dad died, he'd pulled her aside, taking her into his study and shutting the door. His new theory was that the real reason Ron moved to San Francisco was that he was *gay*. In the 1970s, he said, he hadn't known any homosexuals. He'd made fun of them when they visited Ron in San Francisco. Even worse, he'd called them *homos* and *sinners* and said they would burn in hell. But now things had changed, and he'd found out his nephew Brad is gay, and Joan at church, too, and it turned out that all these years there have been gays everywhere, and they were decent people. And he'd learned that being homosexual isn't a sin. All those terrible things he'd said about homosexuals the last time he saw Ron. Maybe Ron was a homosexual, her dad said. And that was why he did it. Ended his life. Maybe, he said, his voice breaking, the whole thing was his fault for making Ron feel ashamed. Deb told her father no, it wasn't his fault. No, Ron wasn't gay. And if he *had* been gay, San Francisco would have been the perfect place for him to explore that and to come out, but he never did. Her dad, his eyes full of regret, just shook his head, because he believed his theory was the right one.

Eleven years after Ron died, Deb went to a Veteran's Day poetry reading. It was 1986. A Vietnam Vet, one of the authors, dedicated his poem to all the vets who had committed suicide from "hidden war wounds." Listening to him read, the tears rolled down Deb's face. Afterward, she waited in line to talk to him. When it was her turn, she told the poet about Ron. "Do you think—that might be why he did it? Because of the war?" The bespectacled man nodded quietly. "Yes, of course." A wave of relief washed over Deb at his matter-of-fact affirmation. It was a strange sensation—the feeling in her body that she was hearing the truth. The poet added, "Did you know that more Vietnam-era military personnel died from suicide *after* the war than from injuries *during* the war?" The next day, on her lunch hour, she dug through newspaper and magazine articles at the library for everything on the subject. The data backed up the poet's statement—there were more suicides of Vietnam War veterans than there were US casualties during the war, though the US military refuted those findings. Apparently, numbers—those seemingly stalwart markers of proof—even they proved ambiguous when it came to military suicide.

In the Ridgecrest motel room, Deb reread the text from Rosa about her husband. A quick internet search confirmed that suicide among US soldiers while deployed in Iraq was on the rise. She hadn't known the scope of it, but now that she did, it was more important than ever that she call attention to it. She spent a couple of hours on her website, changing all the references to veterans to include all military service members.

She opened the curtains the next morning, casting a harsh light on the bleak motel room, with its mustard shag carpeting and maroon-flowered bedspread. How could she spread the word about the website? What about people who had cared about Ron? Maybe they would want to post their memories of him.

She made a list of the people close to her brother. First she wrote down: *Travis Family*. Her mother wouldn't want to be a part of it; she was such a private person. Matt had already said he didn't agree with her about why Ron died. Their Michigan cousins? She and Ron had lost touch with them once they moved to San Francisco.

She crossed out the heading and started over with a new one: *Ashbury House Family*. Mama Linda was kind of the power figure in the family—a cushiony woman with a perfect

Afro and a laugh like creek water over rocks. She had worked odd hours—was she a nurse? Right, she'd worked at the hospital a few blocks away from the house. You definitely didn't want to get on her bad side; but on the other hand, she was generous and forgiving. Linda used to write her a holiday card every year, and at some point Deb had stopped writing back. She wished she had kept in touch.

And what about Nik-Knock? She'd be in her midthirties by now. And her mother—Willow. Nik-Knock's real name was Phoenix. The sweetest child, with an uncanny way of examining you with big dark eyes, then homing in on your feelings and reading you like a book. It had been so great to have a little sister, really that was how it was, for the five or so years that Deb had hung out at the house.

Then there was Che. They'd had a thing the summer before she started college. Ron had *not* been happy about that, but she was eighteen by then, and she told Ron she could do whatever she wanted. She remembered the hot make-out sessions and Che's expert fingers, so unlike anything her old boyfriend in Grand Rapids had known how to do. He'd tried to convince her to have "real sex," but she'd hung on steadfastly to her virginity.

And the other woman housemate—a dancer, kind of self-absorbed. She led the rituals. She was the first woman Deb had ever met who was open and proud of being sexually active and turned it into a feminist thing. Deb paced the room, trying to recall her name. Stretch! Of course. That was it. That reminded her to do her exercise routine. Training to be a ranger had kicked her butt, and she'd had to do a daily regimen to keep up with the younger recruits. She got down on the carpet and did her sit-ups and push-ups. She made it to the last push-up and, panting, pulled herself to her feet. She wiped her face with a towel and sat back down at her laptop.

She thought of doing a search for "Haight-Ashbury" along with each collective member's name, but she only knew their house names. She closed her eyes and called up a picture of the Ashbury Street family sitting at the big table, but she couldn't seem to summon up a real name for any of them except Mama Linda—her real name was Linda, but what was her last name?

After Ron died, she'd packed up a few of his personal things and shipped the box to her parents' house. There might be something in the box with his housemates' names. She looked at the clock—it would be almost noon in Grand Rapids. She called her mother.

"Hello, this is Fran." Her mother's upper midwestern accent came through the phone loud and clear.

"Hi, Mom."

Deb heard her mother's faint inhale of surprise and pictured her picking up the yellow phone, with its lengthy cord, and carrying it from the kitchen to the couch in the living room, where she would settle in.

"Deb! I was just thinking about you."

"What were you thinking?"

"Just that I hadn't talked to you for so long. And with the time difference, I'm never sure when I can reach you. Are you still in the desert?"

Deb sighed at the implied criticism in her mother's question. She tried to keep the irritation from her voice. "Yes, still in the desert."

"Oh, for Pete's sake. I hope you go back to your job after your sabbatical."

"I probably will, Mom." She really did not want to argue.

"How's Andy?"

"Fine. She likes her new job. Loves Philadelphia. She calls it 'Philly.'"

"What's she doing again? Is she a stockbroker?"

"She's a junior trader."

"She was always good at math."

Deb paced the length of the motel room and kicked the carpet. "How are you, Mom?"

"I'm fine, just fine."

"There's something I want to ask you." She listened to the silence—a skill she'd picked up in her childhood, when she'd learned to interpret her mother's disapproval, anger, or sadness through the texture of her particular stillness. This one sounded like resignation or disapproval. "Mom?"

"Yes." Fran's voice was tight.

"You know that box of Ron's stuff in the basement?"

"Yes, of course."

"Would you open it and look for something for me? I'm pretty sure there's something there from Linda—Ron's house-mate and friend. I need to find out her last name so I can get in touch. She was really nice, and I was just thinking about her, and how I'd like to see her again." Deb looked out the window at the parking lot while she waited for a reply. This time the silence had softer edges. "I wouldn't ask unless it was really important."

Her mother sighed. "Linda," she said sadly.

Deb felt a prickle of excitement. "You remember her?"

In a soft voice: "The Black lady. I always liked her the best of his housemates. The other ones were strange. She was a Christian, you know."

"Would you look in that box and see if there's a letter from her? I need to know her last name."

More silence on the other end of the line. What Deb wanted right now was to smoke a joint. Waiting for her mother to answer, she rummaged through her backpack, found a cannabis cookie, and took a bite. Just one. It would take some time before she felt anything but it was enough to know the sensation was coming.

Fran sighed, a drawn-out, quiet sound like the desert wind on a spring night. "Okay, dear. I'll look and call you back."

The phone rang a half hour later. "I didn't look in the box."

"Okay," Deb said, trying to keep the anger from her voice.

"Didn't need to. I looked in my Christmas cards file. Linda used to send me one every year; it was very nice. Her last name is Joiner. The cards are from that same address on Ashbury Street. Do you want that address?"

Of course Deb knew the address, it was imprinted on her memory. "I remember it. Is there a date on the last card she sent you?"

"Let's see. Postmark is—1994. Eleven years ago."

"Thanks, Mom."

"And now," her mother said, her voice sounding small now. "Let's talk about something else."

They talked for a few more minutes about the something-else topics Fran preferred and then said their goodbyes. Deb immediately started searching online for Linda Joiner. There were a zillion Linda Joiners, but no reference to a "Mama" Linda. Of course there wouldn't be, but it was worth a try. She tried the name along with "nurse," "Haight-Ashbury," and a few other things, but she didn't get any hits.

She got up and made another cup of crappy motel coffee and drank it standing up, swilling it like medicine. In moments, the caffeine starting doing its job: her neurons firing, passing their signals along their pathways, perking up her cannabis-laced senses, and—bingo—producing a memory flash: rent checks were always made out to Linda. The house on Ashbury Street had belonged to Mama Linda's aunt, who gave her a deal on the rent; that was why it was so cheap. Deb climbed back on the motel bed and tapped at the keyboard, searching the real estate websites. Amazing that she still remembered the address thirty years later: 232 Ashbury. There it was. It showed that the owner, Linda Joiner, had sold the house in 1999 for just over a million dollars. Deb whistled. That was quite a chunk of change. So Linda *was* the owner. Or maybe she inherited the house from her aunt. Where had Mama Linda, a retired nurse with the financial means to go wherever she wanted, moved? Deb picked out the Linda Joiners who sounded like a possible incarnation of the woman Deb remembered: a textile artist in Santa Fe, New Mexico; a community activist in Santa Cruz; and a women's health advocate in San Diego. She sent an email to each of them and then went out to the pool for a few laps. She did the rest of her exercises and went to the local diner for a grilled cheese sandwich. That night, she checked her email obsessively, but no response from Mama Linda. She curled up with a Sue Grafton novel that kept her up half the night, turning the pages and rooting for her favorite private investigator, Kinsey Millhone.

When she checked her inbox the next morning there were still no replies from potential Mama Lindas. Packing her bag, she said a silent goodbye to the motel room. As tacky as it was, with stains on the carpet, a lumpy bed, and paint-by-the-numbers art on the wall, it still felt connected to her journey. If she could connect with Mama Linda, then maybe she could find other members of the house family, too, who cared about Ron and might want to post on the website. She felt a tingle of anticipation. Just thinking about the house gave her a buzz. Those few years there, even encompassing the horror of Ron's suicide and all that came after—it was still the time in her life when she felt the most expansive.

She was zipping up her duffel bag when she thought she'd

take one last peek at the website for comments. Pulling out her laptop, she opened up the site and right away saw there was a post in the comments section. The first line knocked the breath out of her:

ARE YOU SURE RJ KILLED HIMSELF?

Chapter 9

Mama Linda

1975

"R-E-S-P-E-C-T," Linda sang along with Aretha on the hi-fi. Spraying Pledge on the coffee table, rubbing it in with a cotton cloth, she got a whiff of lemon that brought with it a memory of her mother, intently polishing the dining room table every Saturday.

She still missed her.

Cleaning the parlor wasn't Linda's chore this week, but she wanted the house to be extra beautiful for the May Day ritual and party. Consuelo said she'd be on call Saturday but would try to come. Yeah, right. Whenever Consuelo said she'd "try" to be anywhere, she never made it.

Sitting back on her heels, Linda surveyed the front parlor. The sagging couch had a burgundy slipcover, courtesy of Stretch, a reject from her parents' house. It was damask—that girl came from money, even though she wouldn't admit it. RJ had just cleaned the bay windows, and they sparkled. She glanced through the archway to the expanse of the two connecting rooms. The middle room looked good, with its shelves full of books and a couple of easy chairs. It led to the dining room, and, at the far end, the view through the windows, showing the deck and garden. That reminded her to check out the deck later, make sure it was in good shape for the party. The burnished redwood floors surrounding her stretched through all three rooms, glowing in the afternoon light. It was amazing—even after five and a half years, she couldn't quite believe the house was hers.

All property is theft, Che liked to say, quoting some anarchist. He wouldn't understand wanting to buy your own damn house—he didn't grow up in the projects. He goes on about how he's "working class" and all, and okay, he grew up in a rented house in South Central, and okay, his parents worked in a factory, but still—he got a scholarship to UC Berkeley and since then he'd skated by, living in squats or supported by girlfriends. And what did working class mean, really—he didn't seem to have *worked* until after college. Linda had always worked—after school and summers, ever since she was twelve. So of course she worked her way through nursing school. And then once she started working as an RN at St. Mary's, it was no big deal to pull extra shifts to save money for the down payment. She'd bought the Victorian in the Haight-Ashbury at a time when no one else would, with the drug house on the corner and the neighboring houses all falling apart. The realtor said the property had "deferred maintenance." But when she laid her eyes on it, it was with the starry eyes of a girl who thinks she can change her man. And change it she did, stripping and refinishing the floors, fixing the windows, putting in new linoleum in the kitchen.

The house was too big to live in all by herself, and she'd needed to rent out rooms to pay the mortgage, but she hadn't wanted plain old roommates. She'd lived in a Good Earth commune for a year when she was younger. That was a wild time. Fun for a while, but then it got too crazy. When she got the house, she wanted something more stable: a housing collective, not a hippie commune. She'd started looking for members and put up notices at the Food Conspiracy, the Western Addition Cultural Center, and Marcus Books, the Black bookstore, hoping to find folks looking to share meals, chores, and political interests. She'd assumed she'd put together a multiracial household and had asked her Black friends if they were interested (no one was) or knew anyone who wanted to join (no one did). It turned out the only people who responded to her notices or who she found on her own were white; but that was all right, she figured that would change over time.

After the housemates moved in, they had worked together to paint the inside of the house, all three stories. Whenever it needed repairs or fixing up, she'd say her auntie, the make-believe landlady, was paying for it. Linda couldn't tell them she owned the house because they'd look at her like she was on some kind of power trip. The whole dynamic of the collective would change, and she couldn't have that. Consuelo kept telling her she should be honest, she shouldn't keep a big secret like that from the collective. Well then, she thought, why do I have to keep *your* big secret? Dammit, she was going to bring it up the next time she saw her. How long did she have to wait for Consuelo to get a divorce? Linda knew, of course she did, that she was a fool to be having an affair with a married doctor. And an even bigger fool for risking her whole career. Consuelo, too, was at risk—a *woman* physician and a *Mexican American*. Even though she was a doctor, she would still be seen as a woman cheating on her husband with a dyke nurse. They were both crazy. Linda shook her head. The hospital administrator wouldn't hesitate to fire both of them. All right, now, stop it, she told herself. She took a deep breath and said a silent prayer. They were fine. They were good at their little charade; she always called her Dr. Hernandez, and Consuelo called her Ms. Joiner, and they made a show of being frosty to one another. It was such a good act that when the staff had a birthday party for Consuelo, they didn't even invite Linda—everyone thought the two women did *not* get along. But, she thought, it was possible to be in a long-term, committed relationship and keep a low profile—she knew gay couples who did it and kept their jobs and everything. They could do it too; they would just have to keep their personal and professional lives separate. But every time she got up her nerve to give Consuelo an ultimatum—divorce your husband or we're through—something would happen to make her put it off. She'd see her girlfriend's kindness to her patients; or the graceful sway of her wide hips; or the way she respected everyone, from the hospital administrators to the nurses to the janitors; or Consuelo would whisper *"Mi cara"* in her ear. When her beloved was near, it was like there was a golden butterfly in Linda's heart. Consuelo always said "be patient," reminding her of the road ahead. Once divorce proceedings began, they would have to be even more discreet. Consuelo's husband would go to battle for custody, and his attorney would have a field day: Your Honor, this is a woman who spends nights with her Black lesbian lover in a hippie commune in the Haight-Ashbury, where drugs are rampant and group sex is commonly practiced. How could she possibly be a good mother? How could she provide a stable home?

Linda shook away the voice of the phantom attorney and pushed herself up to standing. Her knees creaked. My word, Linda Jean, you're only thirty-two; that's not old. She did a last check of the room. It looked good. Maybe she'd take a smoke break before doing the upstairs. She patted her pockets but found nothing; she was about to get a pack from the kitchen when she heard the slamming of car doors. Through the window she saw RJ and his sister getting out of the Rambler. Meadow looked all grown-up, in her overalls and hiking boots and with a new air of confidence. When they came in the front door, Meadow threw her arms around her. "Mama Linda!"

"Hi, sugar." Linda smiled to herself. Meadow was as enthusiastic as ever.

Che, coming downstairs, saw the cleaning supplies and said, "A woman's work is never done."

"For god's sake, Che. Don't be a sexist pig," a voice came from above, and Willow followed him down.

"It was a *joke*," Che said. And then, with a nod to the women: "I'm with you in the struggle. I'm going through the women's movement too."

Willow rolled her eyes. "Right, you're going through the women's movement . . . one woman at a time."

RJ burst out laughing, slapping his thigh.

"My work is done, but yours has just begun," Linda said.

"You're a poet and you don't know it," Meadow said. "I take it back. You probably do know it. Anyway, I'm here to help. What can I do?"

Linda gave Meadow the vacuum cleaner and supplies and sent her upstairs to clean the common areas. She went to the kitchen and searched the drawers for the packet of cigarettes she'd stashed. Shoot. It had disappeared. Well, okay, she hadn't written her name on it, so it was up for grabs. She went out the back door and surveyed the deck. It looked fine; whoever had it as a chore this week had done their job. Leaning against the railing, she felt it wobble. Damn! Why hadn't she noticed that before? Why hadn't *anyone* noticed? She went back inside and asked Che to reinforce it before the party on Saturday.

"Sure. I'm off Friday. I'll do it."

"That's a commitment, right? Because it's a real safety hazard. We're going to have a big crowd."

"Absolutely. Right on, sister."

"Screw you."

"No, I mean it. I'll definitely do it."

"All right. But I'm not your sister," she said, her lips pursing, holding back a smile. He grinned; it was their inside joke. She went upstairs and, passing by RJ's room, saw him staring out the window, lost in thought. Even from the hallway she could see it, in his face and shoulders. Despair. Should she reach out? No, when he was like this, it was better to leave him alone. Lord knows she'd tried to get him to open up. It was like he wanted to talk, but he didn't want to talk. Heading down the hall to her room, she thought of the first time they met.

Two years ago, RJ—or Ron, as he introduced himself—had arrived at the house on time to meet with her about possibly joining the collective. Her first take on him was that he was uncommonly beautiful for a man—and a gentle soul. As they talked, he reacted in such a positive way. They talked about growing vegetables (which he said he would love to do in the backyard of the house), living alone (he wanted to live with housemates), his volunteer work (at the Haight-Ashbury Food Conspiracy), his part-time job (at a printing company), and movies. She had just seen *Watermelon Man* on TV. He'd never heard of it, and she had to explain that it was a satire about a white man who wakes up one morning to find out he's Black. He nodded and said solemnly that every white person should have that experience. She snickered and then he did, too, and then they both cracked up. She would start to try to get serious, but his chuckling was so infectious, she couldn't stop laughing and neither could he. Finally, their laughter dying down, she wiped her eyes and tried to steer them back to their conversation about movies. He said he'd seen *The Exorcist* and it scared the heck out of him. She brought up *M*A*S*H*, which was playing at the Red Vic, the revival movie theater on Haight Street.

His sunny expression faded. "I don't want to see it."

In that moment, he reminded her of her cousin James, who was such a sweet guy, and came back from the war such a different person. He was still a good person, but with a ragged edge. "By any chance," she asked, "were you in Vietnam?"

He went still. "How could you tell?"

She shrugged. "Just a feeling."

He nodded. "People say that even though *M*A*S*H* takes place during the Korean War, it's really about Vietnam."

"I've heard that too. It's supposed to be very funny, though. Sometimes laughter is the best medicine."

"True. But I don't need to see it."

She nodded slowly. "You don't need to see it, because you were there?"

His taut expression slowly relaxed, turning into a half-smile. "You understand. Most people don't get it."

Not long after he moved in, it turned out that even though their backgrounds were different—their color, their class, where they grew up—they had something big in common. It was Sunday morning, and she was on her way out the door, in her polka dot dress and her white hat.

RJ had never seen her in a dress, and he looked surprised. "You look nice."

"Why, thank you," she said in a mocking femme voice, batting her eyelashes.

"Where are you going?"

"Church." She waited for the inevitable: a shocked look and thinly veiled disapproval.

But instead, he said, "Cool."

That was not at all what she expected, but even more surprising was his expression. He looked wistful, and maybe even a bit envious.

When she got home that afternoon, he asked if he could go with her to church sometime.

"Of course," she said. She thought she'd better tell him. "Just so you know, it's a Black church. But everyone is welcome."

The following Sunday, when they walked into the sanctuary, the whole congregation turned their heads to look. But there were only a couple of raised eyebrows. It wasn't unheard of to see an occasional white face in the pews, and besides, she'd grown up in the Fillmore and had been coming to Third Baptist since she was a child. So if he was with her, he was all right. After the service, he'd seemed so happy, and he'd thanked her over and over. He joined her for a few more Sundays, but then one day he stopped. She'd asked him a couple of times if he wanted to come back, or if he might want to try a different church in the city, but he just shook his head. Eventually, she stopped asking. She didn't want to push it. Religion was such a personal thing.

In her bedroom, she changed out of her housecleaning clothes. It was her day off, and she was going to put her feet up. She lit a cigarette and stretched out on the couch. Damn, she was tired. She took a drag and felt the comforting rush. Exhaling, she closed her eyes for a second. When she opened them, her cigarette had burned down to almost nothing. Brushing the ashes off her jeans, she put the stub in the ashtray. Something on the coffee table caught her eye—the edge of a book, buried under yesterday's papers. She leaned over and picked it up. It was the paperback Sherice had handed her at work a few days ago. "Linda, I am here to tell you, you gotta read this. It's so good." Linda smoothed the creased cover with her palm. *Sula* by Toni Morrison. She opened to the first page and started reading.

That night, after dinner, she was back in her room, watching the news about the fall of Saigon. There was a knock on her door.

"It's me. Can I come in?"

"Sure."

RJ closed the door behind him and stood beside her, his eyes glued to the images on the screen. The reporter's voice in the background summarized the events: "With American fighter planes flying cover and marines standing guard on the ground, Americans left Saigon yesterday by helicopter after fighting off throngs of Vietnamese civilians who tried to go along."

The footage showed hundreds of figures trying to climb over the embassy wall, and a whole bunch of Marines pushing them back down. She glanced over at RJ. He stood, his feet in a wide stance, his fists clenched. Pulling his eyes away from the screen, he turned his gaze to her. "You know what they call it, when an innocent person is harmed or killed? Collateral damage. Military-speak for murder."

The voice from the TV: "After the last Marines left, hundreds of civilians swarmed into the compound and onto the roof. On the roof of a nearby building that had also served as an emergency helipad, several hundred civilians huddled together, hoping there would be more helicopters to carry them away."

He was riveted to the television set.

"RJ?" she said.

Turning his gaze to her, blinking his eyes, he said, "I've

been listening to the radio all day. I knew this was coming, but it's so much worse than I—fuck. I don't know. We thought we were fighting for justice, but we found out we were fighting for nothing. And now the people left behind, supposedly our allies, will be slaughtered. Only the rich and well-connected will get out. It's all our fault. It's my fault. I don't want to see it, I can already see it in my head."

She got up and turned off the TV. "You're right. It's criminal. But I don't think you should blame yourself for an entire war."

He stood, his eyes fixed on something she couldn't see.

"Do you want to talk about it?" She gestured for him to sit down beside her on the couch.

"No. I mean—" He cleared his throat and sat down. "I wanted to, actually, ask you about something else."

She wondered if he was pissed off at a housemate—maybe even her. She lit a cigarette. "What's happening?"

He swallowed. "Did Meadow mention anything about her new boyfriend?"

Here we go again, she thought. She hoped they wouldn't have a repeat of what happened last summer. "She said she might bring him to the ritual and party."

"But did she say who he is, or what he's like? How she met him? Anything like that?"

"She said he was nice. Why?"

"I just wondered."

"Are you worried?"

"No, just—she doesn't always make the best choices. With the guys she goes out with."

She nodded slowly. "Let's see what happens with this new fellow. Maybe give him a chance."

"Yeah, sure. Of course." With a resigned look, he smiled sadly.

Oh my, she definitely hadn't gotten through to him. Maybe she should meet him halfway. She touched his shoulder. "If you want, I could do some detective work."

He laughed. "That would be far out. Thanks." He stood up and started moving to the door. In a choked voice, he said, "She won't listen to me," and darted out.

She prayed for him every day.

Chapter 10

Wack Job

2005

D eb stared at the first line of the comment, her heart racing. ARE YOU SURE RJ KILLED HIMSELF? She continued reading.

I never thought RJ committed suicide. Meadow, someone killed him. The cops claimed they had forensic evidence that it was suicide. That was bullshit! Never trust the fascist pigs. RJ was a police informant. It was a coverup.

The name of the commenter was "a friend." She jumped up and paced the motel room, her stomach clenching. A police informant? What the fuck? Who was this so-called friend? Ming had warned her against a comments section because "there are so many wack jobs out there, you'd be opening yourself up to some crazy shit. Just stick to email contact." Deb had insisted on including it anyway, in the spirit of openness. Ha. The anonymous commenter knew their house names, so obviously he was either one of the housemates or someone who had been a regular. A conspiracy fanatic. But was it a conspiracy or could it be partially true? Deb and the other housemates *had* wondered at first if Ron had been murdered, and she'd pressed the police detective about it. At first he'd said they were investigating and he couldn't talk about it. But eventually he'd contacted her when they closed the case because the fingerprints and other forensics all pointed to suicide. When the investigation was complete, he arranged to meet with her to give her Ron's journal. It was, he said, one of the main pieces of evidence in ruling the death a suicide.

She remembered Detective Murphy meeting her at school, between classes, in the San Francisco State cafeteria. He'd seemed old to her, back then, but he was only in his midforties, with a ruddy face and intelligent blue eyes. She never forgot his words: "I've seen a lot of strange things, believe me . . . we don't know why people do the things they do." After he left, she'd stayed at the cafeteria table, looking through the journal, which was not a notebook at all, but a stack of typewritten pages on onionskin paper. Her hands trembling, she had glanced through the first few pages—it was a jumbled diatribe about a bloody, suffering Christ and sinful, powerful women bent on destruction. Ron had also detailed a conspiracy featuring Johnson, Nixon, Watergate, the fall of Saigon, the CIA, Charles Manson, and the military-industrial complex. She hadn't read the rest.

Deb sank down on the motel bed. Where was Ron's journal? The detective had given her an accordion folder filled with clipped-together pages. Had she thrown them out in the angry period just after Ron died? Or had she saved them, which would mean they would be in that box in her mother's basement?

The comments section on her website was public, so she opted for a professional tone in her reply to "a friend":

Thanks for contacting me. I'm interested in talking about this. Please email me at info@soldierswiw.net.

On the road back to the national park, she tried to keep her mind on driving while mulling over the weird comment. It had an "I know what you did last summer" sort of horror-movie feel. She had a feeling who it was from but wanted to think about it rationally. It couldn't be Mama Linda; it just didn't sound like her voice. The tone of the comment was that this person didn't particularly like Ron, especially if he or she was calling him a police informant. So that ruled out Willow, who'd always had kind of a thing for Ron. Stretch was kind of a strange person and maybe could spin out a conspiracy theory, but she'd always been friendly with Ron and maybe even, like Willow, had a crush on him. The child, Nik-Knock, would be in her thirties now and probably more internet-savvy than the rest of them, but she had always idolized Ron, and besides, hadn't they all colluded in telling the child that Ron had "moved on to a better place" until eventually one day Nik-Knock announced that Ron had moved to Oregon? No one had set the child straight; it seemed cruel to remind her that he'd killed himself. So, yeah. By process of elimination, the comment must have come from Che. It sounded like him anyway; he always called the police fascist pigs.

She shook her head—why had she gotten involved with him? The thought of it now embarrassed her. When she started college, at the end of the summer, they'd agreed to part as friends. It could be he now wanted clarity about what was really the cause of Ron's death. Maybe he had struggled over it, too, for all these years. Or maybe he was just one of those guys who trawls the internet looking for former flings.

In a weird way, the comment gave her hope. All the times she'd imagined his death wasn't a suicide after all—maybe she hadn't been crazy for thinking that. She would search for and locate Detective Murphy and every one of the housemates from the Ashbury House. She was a research librarian—she could find anything and anyone.

The next morning, she got an email from Linda Joiner from Santa Fe, who said yes, she was Mama Linda from the house on Ashbury Street. Deb called her right away, and they stayed on the phone for an hour, as if it was still thirty years ago and they were drinking coffee at the breakfast table by the window.

The only real names of housemates Linda recalled were for Willow and her daughter—Sarah and Phoenix Gold. It turned out Willow had died a year ago, which gave Deb a shock—in her mind, Willow was still in her twenties. The only housemate Linda was still in touch with was Phoenix, and she gave Deb her contact info. When Deb told her about the weird comment on her website, Linda's response was: "Sounds like Che."

Deb had one more day off. There were still some things that couldn't be found online. It was time to go to the library. She got in her truck and made the four-hour drive to Bakersfield in good time.

At the library, she headed to the information desk, where a sleepy young woman looked up from her computer.

"Can you tell me where to find the Polk directories?"

The librarian smiled and stood up. "I'll show you."

"That's okay, I can find them."

"No, really. I need an excuse to get up."

"Got it. I'm a librarian, too," Deb said, and then thought: Am I?

The woman tilted her head and examined Deb. "I wouldn't have pegged you for a librarian. It's usually the private investigators who want to look at the reverse phonebooks."

"Really. You thought I might be a PI." Deb smiled to herself. She was investigating something, after all.

The librarian led her to a section with shelf after shelf of reverse phonebooks. Deb had woken up that morning with a flash: when she lived with roommates in college, each person had an individual listing in the phonebook. Everyone used to do that before cell phones came along, she remembered, especially if you wanted friends to be able to find you. So maybe she would find each housemate from Ashbury House listed separately. She pulled out the reverse directories for San Francisco for 1972–1975. In 1972, at the Ashbury House address, only Linda Joiner was listed. But the next three years showed two other names at that phone number: Sarah Gold and Katherine Stewart-Ross. Deb sat back in the chair and grinned. Sarah was Willow, so the hyphenated Katherine had to be Stretch. It made sense that Che wasn't listed; he was always so secretive and probably too cheap to pay for a phone. But it was a surprise that her brother wasn't. He'd always been part of a group of friends growing up, and she thought of him as a social person. But, she thought, that was before Vietnam.

She found a public computer and searched for Katherine Stewart-Ross. She got two hits, and one she ruled out right away—the organizer of a church supper for an evangelical Christian community. The other, in Marin County, looked promising. This Katherine Stewart-Ross was the leader of an organization called Ritual Design. For a fee, Priestess

Katherine offered to create, plan, and lead a ritual for you or your organization. The photo showed a fifty-something woman with expertly applied makeup on a face that miraculously had no wrinkles. Deb squinted at the image. It was Stretch—older and plumper—with a surprised look on her face. She had clearly had some work done. Deb clicked on one of the tabs: *Opening the Flower* was a three-day workshop for Spiritual Sexual Opening for Women. Deb sat back in the chair. Wow. This was definitely Stretch. Or rather, "Aphrodite," as she called herself on the site. Her photo showed her wearing a form-fitting black bustier with lots of cleavage. The site proclaimed, "We guide women in opening to their sacred sexuality. Among our offerings are: *Yoni Opening, Living Your Orgasmic Life,* and *Vibrational Juices.*" On the "About Us" page of the site, the bio read, "Aphrodite has a PhD in Sexology and years of experience leading pagan rituals."

Deb wrote Stretch an email, saying she wanted to reconnect after all these years, which was mostly true, and asking if she knew how to get in touch with Che, which was totally true. She included the link to her Soldiers with Invisible Wounds website.

When she got to the ranger station that evening, everyone had gone home for the day. That suited her fine; she didn't want anyone to know she was working on personal stuff, especially Gretchen, who always seemed to take the opportunity to look over her shoulder. She was okay, but Deb just wasn't interested in engaging in Gretchen's favorite activities— gossiping about coworkers; analyzing which guys were hot or not, available or not, or both; and drinking copious amounts of beer at the bar. Deb logged on and checked her inbox, and there it was, already, a response from Stretch. With a jolt of excitement, she opened the email.

Hi Meadow,

How awesome that you found me on the internet. Wow, i checked out your website and it made me so sad. It's a beautiful tribute to RJ. You know, it brought that whole time back to me, how devastating it was when RJ died. i've done a lot of work on my divine path, and even though it's been part of my practice to let go and let be, i have to say i've never been able to really let go—on a spiritual level—of RJ. i'm happy with my husband, Forest (he's so awesome!), but i've never been able to forget RJ. There is a place in my heart where i still love him.

That comment on your website—wow, that's pretty heavy. Because that person is implying it was murder because what else could it be, and i can't imagine anyone in our house could've done it. The police did a really thorough investigation. Plus they fingerprinted all of us and questioned us and it was really scary. And Che was their prime suspect because he was home at the time—god, I know he was kind of paranoid and all, but he was a good person; he couldn't possibly have killed RJ.

Che and I kept in touch for quite a while, but that was before the internet, so i don't have an email address, but i do have an old phone number. Last time we talked was about twelve years ago. He was working as a carpenter and he had a kid—not sure if he was living with the mom or what. He wouldn't give me his address—he was always so cagey about his whereabouts, but the last time he called he gave me his home number, and it was a Montana area code, so that's where he was at the time. His real name is Joshua Brown.

If you're ever in the Bay Area, i'd love to see you. Keep me posted about what happens with the weird-comment person.

May the Light Be Within You,
Aphrodite (Stretch)

Deb read the email and shook her head with wonder. Stretch's note read like an older version of the young dancer who was always moving and stretching—the woman who taught her the word *yoni* and showed Deb how to undo some of the sexual shame she was raised with. Stretch had clearly reinvented herself—and she had the means to do it. The housemates all thought Stretch must've had a trust fund or something back then, because she always had money for her dance productions or trips to Europe or Asia. Must be nice, Deb thought, to have money to do whatever the fuck you want, change careers or lifestyle, to not have to be a single mom and stay at the job you started out with so you can provide a stable life and support your kid. Not that being a librarian had been awful, but still . . . if she'd had money, she could've played and sung music and traveled and . . . maybe become a park ranger earlier.

Getting up from the desk, she went to the break room and made a cup of tea. Stretch said Che couldn't have killed Ron, but Deb had only asked if she knew where he was, not if he'd murdered her brother. Maybe Stretch was watching too many *CSI* shows. Or maybe Deb was reading too many detective novels.

Back at the computer, she checked once more for an email from the creepy comment person. Nothing. She'd deleted the comment a few days ago. There was a follow-up email from Stretch with Che's old phone number from twelve years ago. Should she try it? It was just before six pm, and mountain time was only an hour ahead. He probably wasn't even at that number anymore. If he was, though, what would she say? Are you the psycho who put a comment on my website? Part of her wanted to believe the message because it would have meant Ron hadn't killed himself and hadn't willingly abandoned her. But another part of her still thought he had died by suicide.

If he was like the other vets and soldiers who'd killed themselves because of inner wounds, was there something that triggered him around the time of his death? She searched the newspaper databases for what was happening in the world around that time, the end of April 1975. The Fall of Saigon. The Symbionese Liberation Army robbed a bank and murdered a customer. Ron hadn't been interested in the SLA, but he'd always followed the news about Vietnam and had been furious about the events leading up to the fall of Saigon, all through April.

Then she found an article that spurred a memory. April 4, 1975: Operation Babylift. The crash of an Air Force rescue flight that killed 138 people, including 78 Vietnamese orphans.

She flashed back to one night when she was at the house and the collective was gathered around Mama Linda's TV, sitting on the bed or the couch, all except Ron, who leaned on the wall by the door. On the television, the newscaster reported the crash of Operation Babylift and the death of 78 orphans.

"Fuck!" Ron exploded. He punched the wall and left the room.

Deb followed her brother down the hall and stood in the doorway to his room. "What's wrong?"

"I don't want to talk about it." His voice was rough with anger. He sat down at his desk with his back to her and opened a book. She could tell he was only pretending to read.

"That was awful. The orphans. Unbelievable," she said.

"Believable," he said. He kept turning the pages.

She folded her arms. "What's happening, Ron?"

"Okay," he said. "If you really want to know. Come in and shut the door behind you."

He took out a big manila envelope from the bottom drawer of his desk and took out some photos. He spread them out on the bed and she looked through them. They were from when he was in Vietnam, in Da Nang: black-and-white snap-shots of him and his Marine buddies with a bunch of Viet-namese children. In the photos, Ron and his friends were playing games with the kids, or reading to them, or they were all eating ice cream cones.

"We used to visit the kids at the orphanage a few times a week. I learned to speak enough basic Vietnamese to commu-nicate, and we taught them some English. It was the only thing we did in Da Nang that was positive. It would never make up for all the civilians we slaughtered, but—" He stopped, took a deep breath, and blew it out.

She pointed to one photo—Ron with an arm around a skinny boy, about seven years old. There was a way the child held his body that made it look like he was poised for flight. Like a scared bird. Yet he was looking up at Ron with such joy. "Who's that?"

He looked down at his hands. "Tuan. I was going to adopt him after—after I was done." His eyes were glassy and it looked like he was going to cry, but then he kept blinking and his eyes cleared. "One day, I was at the base, fixing a genera-tor. Howard—we used to go to the orphanage together—stormed into the shop. He was yelling and crying, saying we had bombed a Viet Cong outpost near the orphanage. It was gone. The orphanage. No buildings, no survivors. We went to our commanding officer for permission to go there, but he said there was no point. It was collateral damage. He ordered us to talk to the chaplain. The chaplain gave us more of the same

110

bullshit, that it was friendly fire, that it happens during war, and even though it was wrong, we had to accept it." His hands formed into fists and then, in a flash, he was on his feet. He planted them in a wide stance and pulled himself up straight, his chin into his chest. He was no longer there in the room with her, wasn't looking at her, was gazing someplace far away. She'd never seen him do that before. He looked like he was ready for a fight. He wasn't her brother, he was a Marine.

"Ron?" she whispered.

He looked at her and then he *saw* her. Something shifted inside him, and his shoulders softened and his fists uncurled. He was back to being her brother. He sank down on the bed.

"It wasn't your fault," she said.

"Yes, it was. The next time I got permission to leave the base, I went back to where the orphanage used to be. To the rubble. I buried my soul there. In Da Nang."

It was dark in the ranger station now, the glow of the computer the only light. Deb put her head down on the desk and cried.

Chapter 11

Painting Houses

T his was the part Nikki liked best. Laying down the
paint with the roller. The sticky wet sound. When
she first started working for Charles, he was such a
stickler, she thought she'd go nuts. The scraping, the sanding,
the repairing, the taping, the masking; each step of the way,
everything had to be just so. But now, three weeks in, Nikki
realized it was his perfectionism that made Charles so good at
what he did. When they'd finished the first job, Nikki had
looked around the sunny apartment and thought, Wow, the
results are so tangible. When it's finished, it's finished. In her
job—guiding a child through the hallways of his or her psyche,
without a road map—the progress was subtle; it was never
exactly clear when the work was done. But watching a child
grow and heal was the thing she loved to do.

She moved the ladder and climbed back up again to start
on the next section. When Charles had first offered her work,
"just until you get your job back," Nikki had turned it down,
assuming it would be easy to get a bartending job—she'd
tended bar all through college and grad school. Besides, she
worried about her dad being her boss—would that mess up

their new-found relationship? She'd helped paint several rooms in the House as a kid, and she and Christopher had painted their apartment. But would she be able to do a professional enough job of house painting, up to Charles's standards? When she discovered that Brooklyn bartending jobs were not so easy to come by any longer, she accepted her father's offer. It turned out to be a good thing; working together was making her and Charles closer, not driving them apart. She carefully layered on the lemon-yellow paint, watching for drips. It was the exact shade of the lemon pudding she used to make for Christopher. He loved it so much. The memory of its sweet tartness was overshadowed by the pleasure she used to have in making it for him. She braced herself for the sorrow to sweep through her, but—something was different. It was as if when she felt around in there, it didn't hurt like she expected. Was this what "moving on" meant? She felt lighter.

The main thing she kept obsessing about now, though, was whether she'd ever get her real job back. The initial shock had worn off, and now she was just plain pissed off. At Susan. At fucking Vic. She laughed bitterly to herself. Wasn't it the fucking of Vic that had gotten her into this mess? No, it was more than that. When she'd called Susan yesterday to check in, her boss had said she hoped to bring Nikki back "if possible." But, Nikki thought, what if she lost her license? Every therapist colleague she'd talked to said that was unlikely. If anything, her license might be suspended for a short while, and she'd have to take an ethics course or something like that.

The worst part of it, though, was knowing how hard it must be for her kids. She'd asked Susan if she could send letters to her clients for a sort of temporary goodbye and closure, and her boss had agreed, as long as she could see the drafts before she sent them. Nikki was especially worried about Hannah. The child had asked her, just a few weeks ago, "Are you going to go away?" And Nikki had said no. But now she had abandoned her after all, confirming Hannah's worst fears. It was one more loss, one more betrayal for the child after the trauma of her sister's suicide. The guilt seeped through Nikki, catching in her throat. She swallowed. *Her* actions had led to this debacle. She'd mailed her letter to Hannah yesterday, explaining that she had to go away for a while to help her father, that she hoped to be back, and in the meantime, her friend Imani would be a really good person for Hannah to spend time with. It was mostly bullshit except for the last part—her coworker was an excellent therapist, and she'd be a good fit with Hannah.

Petro had called her again, said he didn't want to stalk her but he really liked her and hoped he could see her again. She felt like a jerk about not calling him back the first time. He was actually a nice guy, sexy as hell, and funny, too, and it was too fucking bad that she wouldn't be able to see him. Fortunately, she got his voice mail when she called, and she left him a message explaining that she couldn't possibly go out with him because he was Hannah's uncle, and Hannah was her client.

Trudging up the stairs from the train after work, coming up into the soft spring evening, a display in a bookstore window caught her eye. It was chock-full of children's books, from *Goodnight Moon* to *Cricket in Times Square* to *Harry Potter*. She stood on the sidewalk, peering in, and a wave of regret washed over her: she missed her clients. Their eager minds, agile sensibilities, and the light that came into their eyes when they recognized something. She missed their intense concentration as they arranged the objects during sand tray therapy. She even missed their personal questions: "Why are you so tall?" or "Are you married?" or "Why don't you have any candy?" And then there were the children who were shut down; whose listlessness, or dissociated gaze, or hyperactive rampages were their only expression. She never thought she'd miss them, yet she did. She missed all her kids. Would she ever get them back? Maybe not those clients, but other children? With whom she could go into that magical world, no matter how painful? The world that was more real to her than this one?

Her mother used to ask her: If you like children so much, why don't you have children of your own? Nikki hated that phrase "of your own": children as real estate, the whole fucking American-dream thrust of owning property—the spouse, the kids, the house, the car, the dog. Her friends who had children had all moved away, some upstate, others to a Brooklyn-esque suburbia: pile the kids in the car to go to soccer games, ballet, and parent-teacher conferences. Christopher had pressured her to start a family, but she'd kept putting him off. She didn't trust that he'd do his share. And there was always a part of her that wondered if the marriage was going to last. She never wanted to end up a single mom, like her mother. He always asked if she was afraid of having mixed-race kids, which of course she wasn't. And now, she thought, in a weird twist of fate, it turned out she was mixed herself, but they were no longer together. Okay, so she was single and thirty-seven. Instead of *having* kids, she got to be with them in their world, work with them, witness their growth and—at best—their healing. It was the perfect job. At least it had been until she'd fucked it up.

When she got home, she found some left-over chicken soup in the fridge and put it on the stove to heat. While it warmed, she checked her inbox. An email with the subject line "Meadow Reconnecting."

Dear Phoenix,

I got your email address from Mama Linda. I don't know if you remember me—I'm Meadow, RJ's sister. I knew you back in the seventies, when you were a child and lived in the house on Ashbury Street.

I am so sorry to hear that your mother passed away. I send my condolences.

I would like to connect with you, if you're willing, and also to talk about my brother Ron. I hope you are up for reconnecting, but if not, I understand.

Best,

Meadow (aka Deb)

P.S. I've been working on a website. I think you might find it interesting. Here is the link.

Nikki read the email twice. *Of course* she remembered Meadow. How could she ever forget her? She was like a figure in a fairy tale, a braided rope of blond hair, long skirts and gauzy peasant blouses, and the scent of sandalwood oil. She'd stayed with them a couple of summers, and then she was in and out of the House for a few years, visiting. She'd forgotten that Meadow was RJ's sister. How amazing that Meadow would look for her now, thirty years later, just when Nikki was trying to unpack her past. Or maybe it wasn't a coincidence at all. Maybe Mama Linda had contacted Meadow and instigated this whole thing.

She went to the kitchen, ladled the soup into a bowl, and took it back to her desk. She took a few bites and read the email one more time. Meadow was a teenager back when they knew each other at the House, so she'd be in her late forties now. Funny how when they were kids, the age difference of a decade was huge, but now it was nothing. Meadow said she wanted to reconnect "if you're willing."

Of course I am, Nikki thought; I always had a little-girl crush on you.

> Dear Meadow,
>
> Thank you for contacting me. Yes, I would love to reconnect. You said you'd like to talk about RJ, and I would also like that. I was fond of him, though I was so young when I knew him that my memories of that time are somewhat occluded and—

She stopped. *Occluded?* Just say—fuzzy or blocked or something. But she left it alone, there was no reason to dumb it down. She continued:

> I would welcome a chance to talk with you about that time, as I am wanting to learn more about my past at Ashbury House and all the stuff that went down—

Her fingers froze on the keys. "Went down"? Too much hippie lingo. She started to delete it, then told herself, Stop censoring yourself. She continued typing.

> at the collective.
>
> How is RJ? I think about him sometimes.
>
> It would be great to talk with you or even to get together sometime. I live in Brooklyn now. Where do you live?
>
> Sincerely,
>
> Phoenix (I go by Nikki now, but you can call me Phoenix. I like it.)

She checked over what she'd written, added her phone number, and hit Send.

There was something in Meadow's email she wanted to look at again. She went back to check it and saw the postscript about her website, *Soldiers with Invisible Wounds*. Why was Meadow sending her this? Maybe she worked with veterans at a nonprofit. Nikki clicked on the link. It was about veterans and soldiers who had died by suicide. She clicked on the "About Us" section.

"This website is dedicated to my brother Ron—soldier, brother, friend, and humanitarian. 1948–1975."

Nikki bolted out of her chair. Ron. That was RJ's real name. She didn't know he'd died, or even that he was a Vietnam vet. She had a brief flash of him in the garden, carrying her on his shoulders, the light coming through the leaves of the trembling birch trees. She tried to take a few deep breaths. Her whole body was shaking. The photo of RJ was just like she remembered him—in his twenties, long hair, intense brown eyes. Out-of-this-world beautiful. The date of his death—1975—how could that be right? She was seven years old then, and RJ still lived at the House. But it was right around the time he moved. To Oregon or somewhere in the Northwest. So he must've died by suicide right after he moved.

She went to the window and looked out at her tree. She was no longer trembling, but she still felt a swirling sensation in her chest. She had always thought RJ must have been a sort of father figure to her, even though her memories were hazy. But when she'd tentatively brought this up with her mother several years ago, her mom had dismissed it, saying, "Everybody loved RJ." But Nikki was sure of it—she and RJ had been close. So surely it must have been traumatic when he suddenly moved away. Maybe she'd lost a sort of father she never really got to have. That made her think of Charles, and something he'd said when they were sitting up on her roof a few weeks ago. He'd said RJ had died, and Nikki had told him, no, he was wrong about that, and he hadn't pressed his point. So Charles knew too. Did everyone but her know? She pounded the wall. Why the fuck didn't they tell her that RJ died, or that she had a father in New York who wanted to be in her life, and that her dad was Black, by the way, and she was mixed race, which would've have been nice to fucking know who she fucking was and that it was part of her fucking *identity* and *history*?

"How is RJ?" she'd asked Meadow in her email, and Meadow must have thought that was a weird question to ask about her dead brother. Nikki quickly wrote a PS to Meadow with her condolences, explaining she hadn't known RJ had died.

The next day, at the house in Greenpoint, she applied eggshell paint to the kitchen walls. Her correspondence with Meadow had left her with a wash of sadness. There was a reservoir of grief from her childhood; she knew that even before these feelings started coming up. Maybe when she and Meadow talked on the phone or in person, she could find out if all of this stuff coming up was related to RJ.

She stayed inside for her lunch break, the windows cracked open to dilute the fumes. The patter of rain on the roof was comforting. She ate her bag lunch and then pulled her cell phone out of her backpack. There was a voice mail. "Hi, this is Deb Travis. I mean, this is Meadow. I'm calling you. (Nervous laugh.) Obviously, I'm calling you. I work in a remote area—I'm a ranger at Death Valley National Park—so cell service is spotty. But you can try me at the ranger station landline or my cell. I really want to talk. Um, okay. Thanks." Meadow left both numbers.

Her voice sounded younger than Nikki would have thought for a woman in her forties. It had a vulnerable undertone to it, not like a park ranger. Or not like the edge of toughness she'd seen in the women rangers she'd met back when she and Christopher used to go backpacking. With that thought, an image of Christopher came into focus. He was naked under a waterfall, surrounded by boulders and the electric green of ferns, his sepia skin gleaming in the sunlight. If she were her own client, what would she say? Let Christopher go? That whole let-go thing had never made sense to her. How about just being with what is. The image of Christopher flowed into the pool and down the river, away and away, becoming smaller and smaller, with the soundtrack of the crashing water and his laughter getting softer and softer until it was gone. Audio silent, screen blank.

She called Meadow's work number at the ranger station first, but she wasn't in, so she left a message. When she tried her cell, it rang and rang, but didn't go to voice mail. It must be ringing in desert cyberspace, she thought, where there were no cell towers, just cacti and sagebrush.

She called the number for the Board about her ethics case, and, after waiting on hold for several minutes, talked to a snippy man who told her once again that it could take anywhere from three to six months, and no, he didn't have any more information, but she would receive a letter after a decision was made. After she hung up, she stared out at the bare windows across the street, just as she had as a child from her room upstairs, where she would sometimes catch a glimpse of a naked man doing yoga. But in the opposite building today, a fully dressed Brooklynite paced back and forth, yelling into his phone.

An hour later, Nikki was done with the front room. Painting was a series of steps, one after the other; you finished this room, then you did the next and the next, and finally, you'd completed the job. It seemed like all she did now was wait—to finish painting each house, to get a decision from the Board, to get her job back, to retrieve her childhood memories, to open the door to love. What? She set the roller down in the tray. *Door to love?* How corny can you get? She pictured an old-fashioned oak door with a brass knob, burnished by age. Maybe she was permanently fucked-up and would never be able to open the door to love, or be loved. She saturated the roller and went back to the laying on of paint. Not too much, not too little.

The jingle of keys, the front door opening. "Hey man, what's happenin'?" Charles called out.

"Good. Almost done with this room."

Her father walked around, inspecting, nodding his head. He pointed at one corner. "You got a holiday here, missed a spot. Otherwise, looks fine."

"I'll fix it."

He stood there for a moment and it seemed like he was going to say something, but then he didn't. She waited.

Then he said, "Bernice reminded me to ask you again to come for Sunday lunch, she keeps on me. I told her I asked you to come before, but you're always busy. Like I said, we want you to meet the family."

She set the roller down in the tray. She was nervous about meeting his family, which was, or could be, *her* family. But she'd put it off for too long. "Okay. When?"

His face lit up. "Really? Cool." He grinned. "Family lunch every other week. How about this Sunday?"

"*This* Sunday?"

"Yeah."

"Uh. Okay."

"You look real happy," he said sarcastically.

"No—I want to come. I really do," she lied.

"Great. Here's our address. I know you have it, but here it is again." He scribbled it on a slip of paper. "Everyone wants to meet you—your aunties, uncles, your cousins. Your grandma."

She nodded and pasted an upbeat expression on her face. "I'll be there. Sunday." She took a deep breath and told herself, Ask him if he knew about RJ. That he'd died by suicide. Ask him. Ask him why no one had ever told her.

"Okay, then. Gotta go, get to another job site. See you Sunday," Charles said, and he was gone.

She exhaled in frustration. She could've asked him, and he would've hung around and talked with her. She looked down at the slip of paper in her hands. He was right—it was time she met the family. But she was dreading it. She smiled at the irony. Family was supposed to be a good thing, right? Yeah, tell that to her clients' parents, who not only paid for their kids to go to therapy, but who had been in therapy themselves (and maybe still were) to work out their family issues.

At the end of her workday, she was packing her bag to go home, when her phone went off. She didn't recognize the number but picked up anyway.

A woman's voice. "Hello, is this Phoenix?"

Only her mother, Charles, and Mama Linda called her that. And now there was one more person.

"Hello?" the voice said again.

A shiver of excitement ran up her spine. "Yes, this is Phoenix. You must be Meadow. I'm so glad you called." She sat down cross-legged on the tarp and got a flash of how Meadow might look now: freckled, her long hair pulled back in a knot, or maybe it was cut short? And instead of a long skirt she'd be in a ranger uniform. Nikki got up from the floor and paced the room. Say something, she told herself. "I apologize for asking you how RJ was. I had no idea. I didn't know he'd passed away. No one told me. Suicide—I'm so sorry—"

"No need to be sorry. I guess I thought someone would have told you by now."

She felt a twinge of anger—why hadn't Mama Linda told her? Maybe she didn't know either.

Meadow went on talking: "I got in touch because . . ."

She heard, or maybe she felt, the faint sound of Meadow's breath. Silence. When Meadow started talking again, there was a tremor in her voice. "Reconnecting with Linda, it was the first time in ages I could communicate with someone who was willing to go there—to really talk about RJ and what happened to him. For years, people have told me to move on. How do you move on when there's no 'on' to move to?"

The carved-out sensation in Nikki's chest was back and she was finding it hard to breathe. "I know what you mean. That 'moving on' thing is such bullshit."

"You think so?"

"Yeah." Nikki took a deep breath and blew the air out like it was too much to hold.

"Crap," Meadow said, responding to her noisy exhalation. "Is this too much? I was worried about getting in touch. Maybe you don't want to revisit all that."

"No, it's fine. I do actually want to." Okay, Nikki told herself. Ask her. "The date he died—1975. I was surprised. He must've done it right after he moved away from the House, right?" There was a silence on the other end of the line, and she thought they'd been cut off. "Hello?"

"Yeah, I'm here," Meadow said, and her voice sounded different, almost hollow.

"Suicide is such a hard death to come to terms with." Nikki heard herself using her therapist voice, but she couldn't help it.

Meadow cleared her throat. "It is."

Her tone had changed—it was almost maternal. Were they both reverting to their kid selves, when Meadow was like her older sister?

"I really want to talk with you more about this," Meadow said. "Sometime when we can have a longer phone conversation. Or maybe we could see each other in person. I visit my daughter in Philadelphia sometimes and I could come up to New York and meet you. Or you can visit me here—Death Valley is beautiful. But you'd have to come in late May or in June because the heat is intolerable in July or August. I wouldn't wish that on anyone." She laughed.

Nikki took a deep breath. "I would love to see you again. And just so you know: about your brother's death. I can only imagine how tough it must have been. Must be still, after all these years."

The phone went quiet again. This time she knew they weren't cut off. She felt Meadow's presence and pictured her silently parsing out her thoughts before she spoke.

"The thing is," Meadow said, "everyone says not to feel guilty, that I couldn't have saved him. But what if I could have? You know? I was eighteen years old when he died—I wasn't a child anymore. After he came back from Vietnam, I knew he had changed, but I didn't realize—the interior damage."

"How could you possibly have known?"

Meadow went on as if she hadn't spoken. "When I was little, he used to carry me on his shoulders and then throw me up in the air and catch me. And I'd beg him to do it again. And he would, over and over. But when it was my turn to catch *him* before he fell, I blew it. I let him fall. There I was, living in the same city, coming over to the House regularly, and I didn't *see* it. I was too caught up in college and my new friends and—all that bullshit. If I'd noticed, I could've told my parents, "There's something happening with Ron. He's in trouble." They could've come out to San Francisco and—I don't know. Convinced him to come home. To get some kind of professional help. Except for there was kind of a stigma to therapy back then—it was like, if you went to therapy you were crazy. Or I could've told the House family. But how could I tell them about something I didn't even know existed?"

Nikki shook her head. "You couldn't have. There's no way anyone could have caught him before he fell. It sounds like he was really good at hiding his pain. I sort of remember him as being good at taking care of people. He was like a—." She stopped. Silence, while each waited for the other to speak. The room was slowly darkening, the sky through the windows a deepening blue.

"Like a—?" Meadow said.

"I was going to say he was like a father to me. My mom always told me not to call him Papa, I wasn't supposed to." Nikki felt a whisper of a sensation in the center of her chest. The memories, instead of coming in sequence, seemed to fall out of their cubbyholes, one by one, covered with dust. In the garden with RJ, just the two of them, working the compost into the soil. Or in the kitchen, RJ teaching her how to scramble eggs.

They talked for a few more minutes, and before they hung up, Meadow said, "I really want to see you and tell you—tell you more."

When Nikki disconnected the phone, she realized Meadow had never answered her question: Did RJ commit suicide after he moved away? What she hadn't asked outright was—or did he do it at the House?

Chapter 12

Stretch

1975

She laid out her ritual tools on the table in her room: the chalice, the athame—a dagger, really, but athame sounded better—and the bell. The May Day festival was only three days away. This was her first time leading a Beltane ritual, and she was nervous. The Celtic ceremony was all about fertility, but how could she make that work for a community of friends more interested in birth control than procreation? She jotted down in her notebook: *Frame in symbolic context: Fertility = creativity.* What about renewal, she thought? Beltane was also a celebration of renewal. She nodded to herself and wrote: *Renewal is super-important in this time, to heal from the aftermath of the Watergate shit and the fucked-up ending to a fucked-up war.* Except she'd have to find a way to say it more elegantly.

Stretch circled her shoulders, thinking, What else? The spiral dance, of course. Setting down her pen, she got up from the table and began to wind her way around and around the room, imagining her and RJ hand-in-hand, with all the other

Ashbury House collective members and friends following in a snaking line, forming a spiral. In her fantasy, RJ gazed at her with quiet adoration.

Back at her table, she started a list. She still had to make the Beltane cake, a luscious treat with cardamom and choco-late—she'd planned to use hash butter—she'd just scored some really nice Lebanese hash, but Mama Linda had vetoed it. That was okay, though, because the bigger question on the table had been the bonfire, an essential for Beltane, and Mama Linda agreed to it, but only if they built a firepit in the back-yard and someone would keep an eye on the fire and douse it if there were even a hint of it getting out of control. Jesus, she thought, Ashbury House had so many fucking rules. The collective she'd lived in back in Cambridge had them, but she'd thought that was all about uptight New England stuff and that the Haight-Ashbury would be more loose, like anything goes. Mama Linda said she'd lived in a Good Earth commune in the sixties and there were no rules at first, but eventually all the members agreed by consensus that they needed them because the place was "dirty, riddled with used needles, and there were frequent altercations among the members." Stretch shook her head, thinking about the way Mama Linda talked—sort of formal, almost literary. Stretch could deal with some of the Ashbury House rules, like no hard drugs—she only smoked pot and sometimes tripped. One chore a week—that was cool. But the no-food-in-your-room rule was ridiculous.

Just thinking about it, she felt the anxiety rising up from her stomach to her throat. She got down on her hands and knees and pulled out the cosmetic case from under her bed. The small powder-blue valise had originally been her Aunt Beth's, who'd used it in her vaudeville days, and had handed it on to her niece with her blessings when Stretch was touring with the ballet company. The tour from hell—the ballet master missed no opportunity to make "adjustments" to her hips, or brush against her boobs, or corner her after class to say, "When are you going to admit you want me?" All the other dancers said, Yeah, he's handsy, and just shrugged it off. She tried to ignore it, too, but one evening on tour, after everyone else had left the studio, he shoved her against the wall, yanked her leotard and tights down, and unzipped his jeans. She managed to break free by biting his hand and running out. But when she reported him to the company director and staff the next day, they told her she was imagining things. In tears, she'd quit and moved to San Francisco, hoping to start over. It turned out that was the best thing she could've done, because now here she was, the artistic director of her very own political dance theater collective.

Opening the cosmetic case, she surveyed her stash. She dug around for some Oreos, but there was only an empty packet. She opened a package of Nutter Butter cookies. Anticipating her first bite, she felt a mixture of excitement and guilt. If she ate too many she'd get fat, but she could always throw up and it would be okay. She took a bite, and the sweet, peanut buttery taste brought a memory of when she was eleven, in the kitchen of the house on Beacon Hill, and how her mother used to be, back when she would actually listen. "Do you want a cookie, Kathy honey?" her mom would say. Stretch ate a few more and then finished the package. All that was left in her stash was a box of Red Hots, some peanut brittle, and a few jelly beans. She wanted something seriously chocolate. Nik-Knock was the only other housemate who craved sweets as much as she did. But Willow and Mama Linda had rules for that, too. Willow believed white sugar was the root of all evil, so desserts had to be made with honey, brown sugar, or molasses. Nik-Knock was only allowed sweets on Wednesdays and Sundays. Which was crazy. For goddess's sake, the kid was only seven. In solidarity, Stretch would sometimes sneak her a candy bar. The child never ratted her out. She locked the case and slid it back under the bed. Maybe there was something sweet downstairs. Sometimes Willow or RJ (*goddess*, he was the best cook; his banana cream pies were *amazing*) would bake and hide the treats so Nik-Knock wouldn't get to them on her own.

When Stretch came out of her room, Meadow was there in the attic studio, sitting cross-legged on a futon, writing in a notebook, her sleeping bag beside her. "Hi, Meadow." No response. "Orchid is crashing in the studio tonight, too. Just so you know."

"Uh-huh. Writing a paper for school," Meadow mumbled, without looking up. "Can't talk." With her long hair hanging loose, her filmy peasant blouse—no bra—and long Guatemalan skirt, she was a hippie goddess, transformed from the midwestern girl who'd arrived at the house for a summer visit a few years ago. Back then her hair was in a neat plait, and she wore khaki pants, a white buttoned blouse, and a gold cross necklace. Stretch smiled to herself as she headed down the stairs. Over the last few summers she'd taught Meadow to say yoni instead of vagina, given her the classic feminist article about how to take charge of your own orgasm, and taken her to Planned Parenthood for birth control pills.

On the second-floor landing, she paused outside RJ's room. Was he in there? She put her ear against the closed door. Silence. She balanced her butt on the newel post, pushed off, and slid down the bannister to the first floor. Something smelled faintly of—was she imagining it?—chocolate! She searched the kitchen cupboards and pantry, finally sniffing out the goods in a cookie tin on the highest shelf.

In the empty dining room, she ate two brownies in the

semi-darkness. They tasted of whole wheat and honey—a sure sign that Willow had made them. They tasted too healthy, but still, chocolate was chocolate. Moonlight fell on the cherry-wood hutch and glinted off the glass panels, reminding her of how, when she'd first moved into the house, she'd taken a snapshot of it—slightly blurred so you couldn't see the mismatched thrift shop dishes—and sent it to her mother to prove (theoretically) that she lived in a nice house. Her mother was worried that Stretch was "losing her way" while she was "finding herself" in that "hippie commune out in San Francis-co." Mom, it's a collective, not a commune, she'd told her. We even have a chore wheel. Of course she'd had to explain what that was: a paper wheel you turned every week to get assigned a different household task. Her mother had stopped doing housework years ago, when she'd climbed out of her working-class family to marry into a blue blood Boston clan and inher-ited a full-time housekeeper, but she still had respect for work of any kind.

At first the housemates used to ask Stretch what she did for work and how she made a living. She'd say she made enough money at the Lusty Lady a couple times a week. Which wasn't true; the meager pay and tips she made at the club weren't enough for rent, food, and rehearsal space. Mama Linda asked her why she was objectifying herself by stripping, saying it was oppressive to her and all women. With the glass booth, Stretch argued, she was in control; no one could touch her. For once, Willow backed her up, agreeing that Stretch was empowering herself by owning her sexuality. Che was skep-tical that dancing at the club was her sole source of income. He had a thing about going through the mail before anyone else, and when the letter with the check from the trust account came every month, he'd hand her the envelope with a raised eyebrow. Maybe because the return address was an attorney's office in Boston, he'd figured it out. He probably saw her as a spoiled little rich girl, living off her capitalist pig parents. But, she often argued with him in her head, she was using the money for radical change—her company, Working Women's Dance Collective, gave free performances for the community and did fundraisers for social justice organizations.

Stretch finished the brownies and, curious about the light on in the front parlor, moved quietly into the hallway to check it out. She peeked in, staying out of sight. There was RJ, lying on the couch reading, the lamplight creating a golden glow around him.

"Who's that?" he said, his eyes glued to his book.

"It's me." She stepped into the room.

"Hi," he said, not taking his eyes off the page.

He looked good enough to eat—but she wouldn't say that out aloud, it would freak him out. With his long hair, big brown eyes, and curly eyelashes, he was so pretty, and so unaware of it, which made it even better. His soft looks were offset by his moustache and muscular arms. He was an androgynous pastry. She wanted RJ. Ronald James Travis. They had originally dubbed him Papa Ron, but for some reason it infuriated him, so they'd eventually made a house name from his initials. "You're beautiful," she said, trying that on for size.

He flushed and looked up from his book. "Not really," he said awkwardly.

"What are you reading?"

"Carlos Castaneda. *The Teachings of Don Juan: A Yaqui Way of Knowledge*." He showed her the cover: two profiles, a white man and a brown man, and between their brains, psychedelic flowers bloomed.

"I've heard of it." She plopped down in the armchair. "Magic mushrooms in the Mexican desert with a shaman."

He shook his head. "Peyote buttons, not mushrooms. And datura, or devil's weed. But it's more than the substances. It's about altered states and expanded consciousness. His exploration of the nature of reality—it's mind-blowing."

"Wow. Outta sight. Peyote is mescaline, right? You can get that on Haight Street. Hey, maybe we should do an Ashbury House mescaline trip. Oh goddess, we can drop mescaline for Beltane! For the party after the ritual."

"Not a good idea," he said. "It's important to have a guide for the trip. Someone who stays straight. I wouldn't want you or anyone else I care about to be tripping without a guide."

"Okay, Papa Ron."

He smiled. "But don't just say okay and then go ahead and wing it. Promise me you won't trip without a guide." Turning down the edge of a page, he closed his book and set it down.

She smiled slowly. This was amazing. It was always so hard to get him alone, and now it looked like he actually wanted to *talk*. "I promise. I grok that. We can get a guide, no problem." She pulled out a joint from her pocket. "Want some?"

"Sure."

His eyes in the soft light were hazel, almost golden. She'd always thought they were dark brown. She lit the reefer and passed it to him. Knowing he liked silence, she pressed her lips together, willing herself not to chatter.

"How are Crystal and Fritz?" he asked, blowing out a plume of smoke.

Okay, that was weird. He'd never asked her about her lovers before. Crystal and Fritz had been to the house for dinner once or twice and had spent the night a few times, and all the housemates were cool with her being part of a threesome. Ashbury House was a place where you could be accepted no matter what your bag was. "They're good." Then she added, just in case: "We have an open relationship."

"Really?" His eyebrows shot up. "So you have—a ménage à trois—but you see other people? All of you?"

"Yeah."

"Isn't that complicated? If each of you is seeing someone else, that's six people." He smiled. "What if each one of those other people had a lover, it would be, like, nine people. It's *exponential*, right?" He handed her the joint. "Do you ever get jealous?"

Was he teasing her about it because he wanted to be one of those exponential lovers? Probably not. She'd tested the waters before, and he was never interested, and besides, she wasn't getting any kind of vibe from him now. "Sometimes. But if people get jealous, we process it."

"That's great, that you're all so—free and open."

"Yeah, well. Mostly. So how about you, are you seeing anyone?"

"No, not really."

She took a toke and handed the joint back to him. She wanted to kiss him. Maybe she would. She moved over to the end of the couch, her thigh grazing his feet. He looked a bit freaked; it was like his whole body was shrinking, pulling away, and he sat up, leaving a vast expanse of couch cushion between them. Okay, so maybe she scared him. A minor setback. "What about your cute friend from the food co-op?" she asked. "Deirdre? I thought maybe you . . ."

"We're just friends. It's pretty funny, though, everyone at the co-op assumes we're a couple, and we used to deny it, but no one believed us, so now we just play along with it and pretend we're together." He laughed. He took a hit, held it for a moment, and then exhaled. "Your relationship—it sounds so

—utopian. I don't think I could do it. I couldn't handle an open relationship."

"Why not?"

"The jealousy, for one thing. But mainly—the way I was brought up—it was a sin to have sex outside of marriage. Period. And sex was for procreation. So already you're talking about an immoral act, and then sex with multiple partners, it would be like a triple, quadruple sin." He laughed. "I'm not saying I believe that anymore. And I don't judge you or anyone. I'm just saying conditioning dies hard."

"But lots of people were conditioned that way and they broke free of it."

"Right, and I have. Mostly. See, you're a few years younger—but when I was a teenager, the sexual revolution hadn't really started yet—at least not in Michigan. I had a girl-friend in high school and we messed around, but neither of us wanted to go past second base—remember that? The bases?" Shaking his head, he snickered. "Then, when I was in the service, there was this guy in my unit who was a big reader. He lent me some books that blew my mind, like *Tropic of Cancer*—here was this book that was banned for a long time and now you could read it, and it was explicit but it wasn't pornography, it was full of ideas and insights. It opened my eyes to this whole other world where sex didn't have to be shameful. And then on leave, I saw this French film, *A Man and a Woman*—I'd never seen people making love, in a movie, and it was beautiful. But even so, when I had my first time, I still had the voices in my head from the pastor and Sunday school and the Bible about sin. It's hard to unlearn that. When I came to San Francisco, I tried to join the free-love thing, you know, have sex just for the pleasure of it, and everyone else was doing it and it was supposed to be easy and fun, but I just couldn't. I like to have feelings for someone." He smiled his radiant smile and flushed. "You probably think I'm really square."

She didn't think he was square, she thought he was fucking far out. So honest and self-effacing, so willing to be vulnerable, not like so many of the guys who pretended to be into their feelings but then wanted to control and dominate you. She shook her head. "I don't judge you at all. I think I see where you're coming from. So then, do you believe in God—I mean a Judeo-Christian god?"

He didn't answer at first. "I argued with my father about it for years. He would say unless I took Jesus as my Lord and savior, I wouldn't go to heaven. Meadow went through the same thing, starting when she was around fourteen, but by that time I was gone, so I couldn't back her up. They'd tell her that Christianity was the one true way—no other religion or belief system was legitimate. Our brother Matt never strayed, though, he was a good little sheep. Still is. So Matt and our parents are still waiting for me and Meadow to come back to the fold." He took a deep breath and blew it out. "I used to have long talks with the chaplain on the base about my doubts; he was more understanding than my parents, but he still pushed me to keep the faith."

"Wow, that's the second time tonight you've mentioned something about Vietnam—I've hardly ever heard you talk about it before."

"Yeah. I usually don't tell people I was there—the only reason the housemates know is because when I interviewed to live here, Mama Linda somehow picked up on it and asked me straight out if I was a vet. I wasn't going to lie to her. Mostly I don't talk about it because no one understands what happened over there. The doves hate us because they're anti-war, and the hawks hate us because we lost the war. People don't get it that for so many of us, once we were there, in Vietnam, we found out what the war was really all about and how the military was lying to us. And we turned anti-war too." He stopped talking and stared into the distance, his eyes unfocused.

"But it wasn't your fault—you were drafted," she said softly, not wanting to break the spell.

He shook his head and took a deep breath. "Actually, I enlisted in the Marine Corps. That's even worse, right? I graduated from high school and I wanted to prove something to myself, I guess."

"What did you have to prove?"

He looked at her, and a flash of fear passed over his features and then disappeared. "Never mind. I can't explain it. Anyway, as soon as I finished my service, I moved out here. I'd heard about the Haight-Ashbury, the Summer of Love, all that, and I thought maybe I could still get in on all the peace and love things I missed out on because I was fighting a meaningless fucking war clear across the ocean. So I got the GI bill and started taking classes at San Francisco State. 'Literature and Spirituality'—that class changed me. The teacher was a Jewish woman from New York. I'd never met anyone like her —first of all, I'd never really known any Jewish people, and secondly, she believed in spirituality as separate from religion. Like you do, Stretch, but to me it was a radical idea. We'd have these discussions, and it turned out everyone else in the class was an atheist. I felt like a freak—so I'd just listen quietly and not contribute. We read a bunch of books, but Hesse's *Siddhartha* really tripped me out. I started to realize you could be a spiritual person—a good person, even—and you wouldn't have to believe in the whole pile of bullshit I learned in church."

"So—you think it's bullshit, then?"

He shook his head. "No, I don't mean that. It's not black

136

and white. I *do* still believe in God and Jesus, but just in my own way. How about you, did you go to church when you were growing up?"

"No—I was raised without religion at all, and we never talked about it. But I still got a big dose of the puritanical sex shame stuff you're talking about. I was always a sexual person, ever since I was like—twelve—and I liked playing around with boys and girls. The girls kept it secret but the boys didn't. I got a 'reputation,' and by the time I got to high school, they all looked at me like I was the local slut. It didn't matter that I was an "A" student and a ballet dancer. And in college, it was better, but there was still this Madonna/whore dichotomy. That's why I volunteer at San Francisco Sex Information, to help people to be free of shame and proud of their sexuality."

"People call in to the hotline, and you talk to them?"

"Yeah, I work the switchboard. You wouldn't believe how many people call in—sometimes they want to talk about herpes, something like that. Other times it's a question about technique. But really, most of the time, they want to talk about their shame. It's so beautiful to reassure people that *all* sexual desires are fine and healthy."

He nodded slowly and looked down. When he brought his gaze back up, he said softly, "What are they ashamed of?"

"Look, anyone who lusts for something outside the mainstream thinks they're a freak. So that's—all of us, right? We all wonder if the special thing that turns us on makes us a pervert. Let's say the caller is a woman attracted to women, or a guy who's into S&M, or anyone who needs a particular object, like a fetish, to get off." She shrugged and opened her arms in a gesture of acceptance. "I tell them it's all okay, it's all wholesome, there's nothing bad about any of it."

He went still, his eyes faraway in thought.

What, she wondered, was his secret? She didn't say a word, just waited.

After a bit, he looked down at the joint in his hand. It had gone out. Setting it in the ashtray, he came back from wherever he'd gone in his head. His expression shifted, and with a smirk, he said, "Sounds groovy. Are you hinting around to find out what kind of kinky sex I'm into?"

She laughed and grabbed a strand of her hair, twisting it around her fingers. "Sure, why not?"

He laughed too. "No-no-no, I was just kidding. I'm basically a heterosexual meat-and-potatoes kind of guy when it comes to sex. Boring."

Bullshit, she thought. Aloud, she said, "So the guilt you were talking about—from your Christian upbringing—is that the only thing? I mean . . ." Should she ask, or just leave it? "I was wondering if maybe there was something else you felt shame about. Believe me, whatever you're struggling with, there is *nothing* you could say that would shock me or make me judge you." She smiled, hoping he would trust her with this. It was true, she would accept him just as he was, no matter what.

He jumped off the couch and moved to the armchair. "No, nothing like that," he said, his voice shaky. He laughed nervously.

"Oh—fuck. Sorry, did I hit a nerve, or . . . ? I didn't mean to imply—"

He shook his head and shrugged. "No, it's fine. Fine. I just —I was in that same position on the couch all this time, and my back got stiff—needed to move around a bit, you know."

She sighed. What was he so afraid of? Whatever headway she'd made with him tonight, it was gone now.

"The May Day ritual will be cool, huh?" he said.

His open smile didn't fool her. He was shaken. But she

knew better than to press it and didn't bother trying to steer him back to their conversation. They chatted about the ceremony for a couple of minutes until he said goodnight, giving her a platonic hug before he bolted upstairs.

Stretching out on the couch, she lay back and stared at the ceiling. She took a deep breath, held it, and exhaled, trying to release all her disappointment. What was it about RJ that made her want him so much? There was something deep inside him that was so sad and untouchable. Why couldn't she get through to him? If only he would let her in, she knew she could help him heal.

Chapter 13

Sunday Lunch

2005

The train to Queens was late. Nikki paced back and forth along the platform, a band of tension already threatening to blossom into a headache. She'd allowed extra time for the Sunday train schedule, but obviously not fucking enough. She could *not* be late, though. If it meant running from the station to Charles's house, fine, she'd do it; she wanted to make a good impression on the family.

She exited the station and jogged the half mile to Charles's house. The St. Albans neighborhood had a well-kept, working-middle-class feel in stark contrast to her jumpy internal state. When she got to the Tudor-style house, she checked her phone. It was 12:02. Okay, Nikki. Calm down. She took a few deep breaths and rang the doorbell. The door opened and a large woman with bronze skin and a broad smile said, "You must be Phoenix."

Nikki liked her right away. "And you must be Bernice."

Bernice threw her arms around her, and Nikki,

surrounded by bosomy padding and the smell of coconut oil, felt herself relax for the first time all day.

"Baby, we had to wait for you a long time. From now on, you'll come to every Sunday lunch," Bernice said. "Come in, come in, come in."

Nikki stepped into the entryway, and Charles appeared, smiling and taking her arm. As they moved toward the living room Nikki heard Bernice say under her breath, "She looks just like Auntie Judy."

In the crowded living room, she was introduced to four or five aunts and uncles, and so many cousins she lost count, until her head was spinning with names and faces. But no one named Judy.

A series of long tables, placed end to end, stretched from the dining room to the living room. As soon as she sat down, an elderly lady across the table eyed her sharply.

"I'm Grandma Faye."

Nikki stood. "Pleased to meet you."

"You're Phoenix. Charles's daughter." Grandma Faye examined her sternly, nodding her head. "It's true, you look just like Judy." Faye's piercing stare was intimidating.

Okay, yet another Judy reference. Where was Auntie Judy?

"Now you come on over here and give me a hug," Faye demanded.

Nikki circled around the stretch of tables to reach her and leaned in for a hug.

"I'm your grandma now," Faye said, with a genuine smile.

Nikki was surprised by the tears springing to her eyes. A whole new family.

Once all the food was on the table, a hush came over the group and everyone lowered their eyes. Bernice started saying grace, and Nikki quickly looked down, something she'd learned to do from grace with Christopher's family. Bernice was giving thanks in a way she'd never heard before, in a kind of poetic riff. "For the love. For the bounty. For the grandchildren. For the beauty on this earth." She continued a recitation of things to be grateful for, and then she said: "We give thanks for Charles's daughter. We welcome Phoenix to the family."

Nikki felt a tingle of excitement that turned into a rush of joy. She started to look up and smile but everyone else was still looking down at their plates with a grave expression, so she did the same. Bernice said a few closing words and *Amen*, and Nikki joined in the chorus. Instantly, the family perked up and started passing the food around and talking loudly and laughing, as if the solemn prayer had never happened. The woman on her right, Sherry, one of her many cousins, engaged her in a conversation that ranged from the skyrocketing rents in Brooklyn (where she also lived) to Sherry's job (post office), to a who's who of family relationships (cousin once-removed, third cousin, auntie, great-uncle). She whispered that the two sisters, Grandma Faye and Auntie Judy, weren't speaking to each other, so Bernice always seated them at opposite ends of the table.

"The famous Auntie Judy," Nikki said. "Is she here?"

Sherry grinned. "Yeah, she's *infamous*. She's late, as usual, but she'll be here soon."

The lunch was a cross between traditional Southern cooking (fried chicken, macaroni and cheese, candied sweet potatoes) and gourmet vegetarian (arugula salad, quinoa pilaf, hummus). Nikki devoured the food, which was both comforting and delicious, so much so that by the end of the meal, she was beyond full. When Bernice brought out a strawberry shortcake, Nikki tried to turn it down, but Bernice wouldn't hear of it. Bernice gave her a big piece and waited for her to take a bite, watching her face. It was so good, Nikki actually groaned in pleasure, which got a big grin from Bernice.

"This is amazing," Nikki said. "How on earth do you make this?"

"Trade secret." Bernice moved down the table to the next guest.

"Bisquick," Sherry whispered.

"You're kidding, right?"

"Serious as a heart attack. Fresh strawberries, real cream. Hand-whipped."

Nikki savored every bite: the sweetness of the strawberries, the crustiness of the shortcake, and the rich, round taste of the cream.

After lunch, she went out to the backyard. Sherry and the other cousins, who were all roughly Nikki's age, were standing around smoking and talking, while the older family members sat in lawn chairs gossiping. Nikki joined the cousins, and Sherry was about to introduce her when something—fear?—flickered across her face as she looked at something or someone behind Nikki. With a tense smile, she said, "Hi, Auntie Judy."

Nikki turned around and almost gasped. Aunt Judy looked like someone had done a computer-generated simulation of what Nikki would look like when she reached her late 70s. Or, rather, she hoped she'd look as good as Aunt Judy when she got to be that age. Judy's straightened hair fell to her shoulders, but aside from that one difference, their tan skin, brown eyes, heart-shaped faces, and big-framed, curvy bodies were so similar it was eerie. Like her, Aunt Judy could pass as white.

Sherry introduced them, and Nikki said it was nice to meet her, but beyond that she wasn't sure if she was supposed to hug or what. She waited for a cue. Judy gave her

143

a cool hug and kiss, and Nikki responded in kind, as if it was no big deal to meet a zillion new family members all in one day.

Aunt Judy examined her from head to toe. "Finally, we get to meet Phoenix. So. Where do you live?"

"Brooklyn. South Slope."

"Are you married? Kids?"

"No. Neither."

"Divorced?"

"Yes." Nikki thought—I've got to turn this around—ask her a question, quick!

But before she could, Aunt Judy asked: "What do you do? For a living?"

"I'm a therapist at the Brooklyn Child Therapy Clinic. How about you, Judy? What was your job or profession? Do you have kids? Maybe I've met them or your grandchildren already today."

Her great-aunt glared at her out of eyes so dark brown they looked black—just like Nikki's. "Mind your manners, young lady. Asking me all those questions." She looked at Sherry. "Tell your cousin what's what."

After she walked away, Sherry whispered, "You'll get used to her." She then filled her in—retired schoolteacher; married and divorced twice; three kids, five grandkids.

Nikki looked around for Charles. She felt like bolting. As much as she was happy to meet her new family, she was equally overwhelmed. She told herself to hang in there a little longer. Besides, she wanted to ask her dad about the House— if something had happened to her there, as a kid. If he even knew about it. She spotted him in a corner of the backyard, smoking a cigarette. When she reached him, the tobacco smell reminded her of her mother, who always said she would quit, but never did.

144

Charles gestured to his cigarette. "The one habit I haven't been able to give up." He smiled.

"You should give it up. Smoking. It's what killed my mother," she snapped.

His smile faded. He shook his head and dropped his cigarette, grounding it out with his heel and picking up the butt. "You're right."

Her voice softened. "I just don't want to lose you, too."

He didn't say anything, just shook his head sadly.

She took a deep breath. Say it, she told herself. "My new family is amazing. I mean it. I like it. Everyone."

He laughed. "You can tell the truth. It's a bit much, right? I can dig it."

She breathed a sigh of relief. "Yes, exactly. I'm loving it, but it's kind of freaking me out. It's so different from the House family I had when I was a kid, and my mom was so cut off from her family of origin that I've never really had this. Now I have *you*, and I'm meeting everyone, which is really nice, but it's a bit confusing." She thought, Okay, now. Before you lose your nerve. "Um—I want to ask you something."

He tensed slightly but nodded. Nikki pushed on ahead, her heart slamming. "I reconnected with Meadow. Remember her—from the house on Ashbury Street? Ron's sister."

"Meadow, yeah. I never met her, but I heard about her."

"There's something I want to find out. About my past. I think something might have happened to me at the Ashbury House. Something maybe—traumatic. But I can't remember it."

"You know," Charles said, "I only stayed with Willow at the house a couple of times before she cut me off. So I don't know much about what went down there." She felt a weird vibe coming off him. It was like a door was slamming shut. His words were friendly, but his body language was remote. He looked around the patio like he was searching for an escape route.

Nikki felt a surge of anger. Why was he being so evasive? True, men of his generation didn't talk about their feelings. But still, he was in AA; he must've gotten used to opening up with people at meetings. So, what the fuck? "Did you know Ron died by suicide? After he moved away? His sister Meadow told me about it. I'm about to fly out and see her where she lives out west. I'm hoping to get more information from her, but I thought I would try you as well," she said.

A series of emotions flashed across her father's face—confusion, sadness, maybe even fear, before his expression went back to neutral.

"I heard he died," Charles said. "So that was—*after* he moved?"

"Yeah."

"Right. It was such a shame. A terrible thing. I don't know what to say." He wiped the sweat from his upper lip.

"Charles!" Bernice was standing at the door to the patio, hands on her hips. "There you are."

"Gotta go," Charles said.

Nikki watched her father retreat. Why did he look so relieved, like Bernice's summons was the best thing that ever happened to him?

Chapter 14

Push-ups

On a break from work, Deb found a bench close enough to the ranger station to get cell service, but far enough away from nosy coworkers. She braced herself to make the call. Stretch had said it was an old home number, and he might not live there anymore. He lived in Montana—maybe he was a survivalist or some kind of hermit and wouldn't want to talk to her. Or what if he was the one who posted the comment and he was mentally ill or . . . what if he was right, and Ron was murdered or . . . stop it, she told herself. Just call. You have nothing to lose.

A woman answered the phone.

"Hello, my name is Deb Travis, and I'd like to speak with Joshua Brown."

There was silence. Then: "What is it you want?"

Deb swallowed. "I knew him a long time ago, in a house in San Francisco where we both were housemates. I'm organizing a reunion with everyone from the collective." Okay, that wasn't entirely true, she thought, but close enough.

"Where was this house?"

"In the Haight-Ashbury."

The woman sniffed. "I've heard him talk about that place." She didn't say anything for a few moments. "He doesn't live here, but I know him; I can give him your phone number, and if he wants to, he'll call you back."

Deb asked the woman to tell him that Meadow called, and she left her phone numbers. After she got off the phone, she thought it was funny that the woman seemed secretive, just like Che had always been.

For her next call, she got a recorded message: "You have reached the San Francisco Police Department. If this is an emergency, please hang up and dial 911. If it is not an emergency, please hold."

She waited on the line, examining the cacti and sagebrush surrounding the bench. She didn't see any creatures, but she knew they were there. You just had to keep looking.

When the woman came back on the phone, Deb told her she needed to get in touch with a Detective Murphy who'd worked on a case in the 1970s and who was probably retired. The woman at the police precinct laughed. "Do you know how common that name was for a police officer in the 1970s?"

Deb gave her the exact dates and the Ashbury House address, and the housemates' names, and the woman said she'd look it up, but it would take a while before she'd be able to get back to her. Deb disconnected and, looking over the boulder next to the bench, caught a slight movement. It was a chuckwalla lizard, doing push-ups. "You're just showing off," she said to him. Or her.

That night, at home in her trailer, she warmed up a can of tomato soup and ate it in the breakfast nook, reading *R is for Ricochet*. She wanted to stay up all night reading to find out if Kinsey was going to get into terrible danger like she always did, and then find her way out, like she always did. But Deb put the book down. She had to straighten up the trailer—

Phoenix was coming for a visit that weekend, and even though Deb would put her up in a tent, they'd still be spending time in her little home. She cleaned the table and the banquette bench and dusted off all the surfaces, then swept the floor. "Good enough for government work," she said to herself. She hoped she and Phoenix would still have something in common after all these years. She couldn't stop the anxious feeling in her stomach. Phoenix said she had a feeling something traumatic had happened when she was a child at the house. Deb knew it was time; she had to tell her that Ron had died by suicide there in the house and that the young Phoenix had made up a story about Ron moving away, and they'd all gone along with it. But now Phoenix was an adult, and Deb had to tell her the whole truth. It would be nice, Deb thought, if she knew what exactly that truth was.

Chapter 15

Reunion

Nikki got in the rental car at the Las Vegas airport and began the three-hour drive to Death Valley National Park. She opened all the windows with the push of a button, and the hot wind blew in. Fuck, it was like a furnace. Meadow had said she was lucky, the weather was nice, "only 80 degrees." She was about to close the windows and put on the air conditioning but something stopped her. The dry heat was so unlike New York. Get out of your comfort zone, she told herself. She left the windows open.

Driving through the desert scrub, the mountains looming in the distance, she was both wired and tired. She passed the ENTERING DEATH VALLEY NATIONAL PARK sign and, an hour later, parked at the Furnace Creek Visitor Center. Inside, she scanned the open space for someone who might resemble the Meadow of her childhood. Of course, Meadow wouldn't look like the girl she knew thirty years ago.

A woman in a ranger uniform approached. "Phoenix?" A slow smile started at the corners of her mouth.

Nikki's memory of the shy teenager with long blond hair

merged with the present image of this confident woman standing before her, with short brown hair, a sprinkling of freckles, and laughing hazel eyes. "Meadow!" She threw her arms around her and instantly smelled sandalwood—the same scent as the incense they used to burn at the House. It was at once familiar and jarring.

Moving out of their hug, Meadow said, "How tall are you? Jeez, I can't believe it."

"5 foot 10."

Meadow examined her, shaking her head. "Awesome. Now *I'm* the one looking up to *you*." She laughed. "Come on, let's split this crazy scene."

Nikki trailed her out to the parking lot and then, in the rental car, followed Meadow's truck for several miles. Just beyond a campground, they turned off onto a dirt road and arrived at a vintage trailer with a silver, bubble-like shell.

Meadow showed her around her Airstream and then grabbed a couple of lunches and water bottles, and they took off in her jeep. Nikki had been too anxious on the drive there to really take in the landscape; now with Meadow at the wheel, she took in the sight of the blue-hued mountains, the desert scrub, and the splashes of wildflowers. She let out her breath in a huge sigh.

Meadow grinned. "Yeah, the desert has a way of forcing you to relax." She turned off the road and pulled into a parking lot, where the sign said MESQUITE FLAT SAND DUNES.

Hiking the sandy slopes, they saw a few tourists at first, but after a mile or so, they were completely alone in a vast expense of sand. Finally, they sat down at the top of a dune, staring out at the mountains, and Meadow unpacked their lunch. Nikki took a bite of the sandwich. She could tell Meadow wasn't into food. It was cheese slices on bread; no mayo, no lettuce, no nothing. Plus some carrot sticks. But it was sweet of her to make a picnic for them. "Thank you for the lunch."

"My pleasure." Meadow munched on a carrot stick. "I'm curious about your job. What's it like, being a therapist? Do your clients tell you about their dysfunctional families, their affairs, their fantasies about killing their bosses?" She grinned.

"Not really. I work with children, so it's more like parental neglect or abuse, sibling conflict, learning disabilities, bullying. Or the aftereffects of trauma." She smoothed out the warm sand with her palm, and it reminded her of the sand tray, which in turn reminded her of Hannah. Once she started telling Meadow about Hannah, it all came pouring out: how something about her client had triggered her; the fiasco with the soccer game and the party at Hannah's house; the boundaries issue with her boss; and how she might've lost her job, or worse, her license. She even told her about the messy affair with Vic and the making out with Hannah's uncle in the alley.

Meadow listened and—this was so nice—she didn't give her some bullshit advice. She just nodded, a look of understanding on her face. "Jeez, it seems kind of harsh to lose your license for doing something that isn't entirely a *bad* thing," she said.

"In the therapy world, it's considered a really bad thing."

Resting her eyes on the sandy expanse, Nikki saw a sheer stretch of land in every direction, unfettered by buildings or people. The dunes were silky and curvy and the mountains bosomy, in contrast to the outcroppings of brush.

Meadow grabbed her binoculars and peered through them. "Hello, Buddy."

"Who's Buddy?"

Meadow handed her the binoculars. "A coyote. I sometimes see him when I'm here. I call him Buddy, but he doesn't know it."

Nikki looked through the lenses. "I don't see him."

"Gone. He's like that."

After a silence, Nikki realized Meadow was looking at her with piercing eyes. She turned to her.

Meadow spoke softly: "You said working with Hannah brought up feelings in you. Like about the House, when you were a kid. Do you know why?"

"No." She sifted the sand through her fingers. "She's had a terrible loss—her sister died by suicide while she was stationed in Iraq. I don't know what it is about her that triggers me." She scooped up the sand and, patting and shaping it, made a rounded hill. "It made me wonder if something happened to me when I was a kid."

Meadow's face, which had been flushed from the hike, paled.

She knows, Nikki thought. "What is it?" Her heart was racing and she realized her voice had gone up a few notches. She tried to tone it down. "I work with a lot of kids who were sexually abused and I wonder if—"

"No, no," Meadow interrupted her. "It wasn't abuse. I wanted to tell you in person; I was waiting for the right time."

Nikki had a sense of the landscape tipping underneath her, and her breath turned shallow. "You sound like you *know*. Tell me."

Meadow nodded and gathered herself. "Ron died by suicide at the house."

"What?" Nikki stood up. She started to move away, the sand squeaking beneath her boots, but then she stayed put. "Were you there?"

Meadow's voice was shaky. "No. Mama Linda came to get me at school. I was a freshman at San Francisco State at the time. It took her a while, but she finally found me in the library. She drove us back to the House and when we got there, it was so chaotic, with the police and everything. I can't remember if you were there or not—I'm sorry, I don't remember that part. But anyway, it must have been devastating for you; you were only seven." She reached up and took Nikki's hand. "It was so hard for everyone, but now I'm thinking of how especially hard it must have been for you. For little Nik-Knock. I'm so sorry."

Nikki pulled her hand away. A rolling series of shivers ran through her body, a sensation like she had the night she'd looked at Meadow's website and discovered Ron had died. "When I saw it on your website, that he died by suicide, I assumed he did it after he moved. Did he come back to the House after he moved? I don't understand."

Meadow shook her head. "He never moved anywhere."

"Yes, he did. I remember." A wave of dizziness came over her. She sank down onto the sand. "Are you sure? Christ. Of course you are. How—how did he do it?"

Meadow took in a deep breath and blew it out. "We think he shot himself."

She swallowed and shook her head. "What do you mean you *think* he did?"

Meadow handed her a water bottle. "You look shaky. Drink."

She gulped down some water. "Tell me," she said, choking on the words.

"By the time I got to the house the cops had taken his body away, and they were still doing their investigation in his room—they wouldn't let me in. There was a lot of blood," Meadow said.

Nikki's thoughts tumbled, one on top of the other. She had worked with clients who had lost the memory of a trauma. And now—Hannah's anguish about her sister's suicide had triggered her. "A lot of blood. . . . What did the police come up with—after they investigated?"

"They ruled it a suicide."

Nikki blurted, "Why didn't Willow or Mama Linda ever tell me about this, once I was older and I could process it?" She punched the sand in frustration. "Just like they didn't tell me that I was Black. 'Hello! You're Black but we're not telling you!'"

"What? You are?"

"Oh yeah, another family secret. After Willow died, my father contacted me. She kept him away from me, my whole life. And it would've been nice to know—this is who you are. Where you came from. All these years, I was passing and I didn't even know it. It turns out my dad had wanted to be in touch and to see me and have a relationship with me, but my mom refused."

"Wow," Meadow said. "I had no idea. Why didn't Willow want you to see him?"

"I don't know. I'd like to think it was some sort of protectiveness, but I also wonder if it wasn't also racism. Or maybe she just thought it would be an easier life, for me to be white. But I need to talk more with Mama Linda about it to find out. The good part is, now I have a really nice relationship with Charles—that's my father—and I just met my whole new family, and they're amazing. I'm still kind of catching up to it."

They were quiet for a while, looking out at the dunes.

"So," Nikki said, "Willow kept that from me, and now I find out about RJ. Maybe I was even there when it happened. Jesus. If they knew I blocked out the memory, okay, but then why didn't they tell me, once I was older? Do you know?"

Meadow looked down at her hands, and when she looked

back up, there was a look of resolve in her eyes. "After he died, you kept asking where Ron went, over and over, and Mama Linda always said he'd moved on to a better place. It was a figure of speech, right? But then one day, your child mind or—heart—latched on to that, and you decided RJ had literally moved. You kept asking us where he moved to, what state, was it New York? And after a while the family just decided to go with the flow and say he moved up north. Not long after that you came up with the idea that he had moved to Oregon. And the collective went with that, too. RJ moved to Oregon. At first, I fought with the family on it—I really did. I thought it was best to tell you the truth, but I wasn't a collective member, so I didn't get to be part of the consensus. They had a house meeting and decided to go along with your Oregon fantasy. When I contacted you recently, I figured you'd know the truth by now. I guess I shouldn't have assumed—should've asked Mama Linda."

"All I remember is that he moved, and I missed him terribly."

"You're trembling." Meadow put her arms around Nikki. "Back then, it wasn't the usual thing to take your kid to a therapist. They didn't have grief groups and support groups like we have now. Plus it was expensive, and Willow didn't have much money. Maybe that's how the memory got buried—you had no way to process it. But Phoenix—you don't have to remember a trauma to heal from it."

Nikki pulled out of the hug and examined her friend. "That's true; that's what I tell my clients' parents when they keep trying to get their kids to remember. How did you know that?"

"Years of therapy?" Meadow smiled sadly.

"Why did you say you *think* RJ shot himself?"

Meadow looked away, chewed on her lower lip, and

heaved a big sigh. "Here's the thing. Sometimes I had my doubts, like maybe he didn't do it—I just couldn't believe he would do something like that. But the police investigated and they ruled it a suicide, so I accepted it." Then she told Nikki about a message on the comments section of her site from someone who implied RJ had been murdered.

"What? That's bizarre. Who could've sent it?"

"I don't know. But it's someone who knew my House name. And Ron's."

On the hike back, Meadow told her about reconnecting with Stretch and about her Ritual Design business.

"That's perfect! She's still creating rituals, but now she's an entrepreneur. A ritual capitalist. A capital ritualist," Nikki said.

"Wait, it gets better. She has *Yoni Opening* and *Living the Orgasmic Life* workshops."

Nikki guffawed. "All right! Right on, sister! Open that yoni!"

"Oh my god, you're the only person who would understand that." She grabbed Nikki's arm and they held onto each other, chanting, "Yoni, yoni, yoni," which then turned into "Yoni pony, yoni pony, yoni pony."

"Maybe I'll get my yoni opened," Nikki said.

"I haven't had mine opened for quite a while," Meadow said.

"Why not?"

"I've kind of given up on relationships; it's just too much work. I feel like I *should* get out there and date, you know, especially now that my daughter's off on her own. But I rarely meet anyone, and if I do, they're too old or too young, or they have a girlfriend or an addiction, or they're boring."

"Huh. You've covered the six top reasons why a woman stays single. So have you ever been married or lived with someone?" Nikki followed Meadow's lead, stepping into her footprints.

"I was living with someone and got pregnant by accident. In retrospect it would've been better not to get married, but for some reason—actually I know what the reason was—it was my Christian upbringing; I just couldn't face my parents' freaking out if I had a child 'out of wedlock.' So we married, and a few months after our daughter was born my so-called husband went off to India to join an Ashram. Never came back, went completely off the grid. It took a number of years, but I finally located him and got a divorce. I didn't even try to get child support, didn't want to have anything to do with him."

Hiking through the dunes, their footsteps leaving imprints in the sand, Nikki thought about Meadow raising her daughter completely on her own, just like Nikki's mom.

"What about you?" Meadow continued. "You're divorced, right? Are you seeing anyone?"

"No. I really only want to get together with someone occasionally for sex. Maybe that's a double standard, like if a man does that, we think he's a jerk. A 'male chauvinist pig,' like my mom used to say. But ever since my divorce, I haven't been into emotional intimacy. I love my friends. But that romantic partner/marriage thing? I just don't know if I want that anymore. If I could trust someone again. So then when I get this drive to get naked with someone and fuck, or not always fuck, but—whatever—cunnilingus, once we do that, I'm like— yeah, that was what I wanted. And then some time goes by, and I don't think about it, and then I want it again. You'd think I'd miss the romance and the lovey-dovey thing, but I just don't."

"So you, just, I guess you 'hook up'?"

"Yeah." She wondered if Meadow would judge her.

"I've never known how to do that. I had a relationship once that I knew wasn't going anywhere, and in a way we were both just in it for the sex, and after a while it didn't work out, but I've never actually had a one-night stand. It just doesn't—I mean, I have to feel something for someone, I guess."

They started walking again. "Yeah, I know. My best friend says the same thing," Nikki said.

"How do you meet these guys?"

"Online."

Meadow laughed. "Oh, right. Of course. My daughter wants me to do online dating. She says it's the best way. I don't know why she keeps pushing me to do it."

After a dinner of stir-fried veggies with tofu, they sat in camp chairs under a half moon. Nikki had offered to cook, but Meadow refused. Meadow brought out a cigar box, opened it and rolled a joint. She offered it to Nikki and started to flick her lighter.

"No thanks." She shook her head. "Not my thing."

Later on, in the tent, as Nikki was dropping off to sleep, she heard the coyotes. Yip, yip, then an extended, arcing howl. At times it sounded almost plaintive, but she was probably projecting. The coyotes were communicating with each other, she was sure of that. Maybe one of them was Buddy.

The next day, they went to Saline Hot Springs for skinny-dipping and a campout, which was fun, in spite of the heat and some strange people—Meadow called them desert rats.

But Meadow was good at keeping the peace, and the time passed peacefully. They came back to the trailer and spent another night before Nikki had to leave.

On the morning of her last day, Nikki insisted on making breakfast. Her friend kept trying to help her. "Just go sit outside and relax," Nikki said. "I want to do this for you." What she didn't say was that, after a few days of Meadow's cooking, she was determined to make something tasty. With ingredients she scrounged from the meager kitchen in the trailer, she threw together oat-raisin-pancakes. There was no maple syrup, so she made a caramel syrup from brown sugar and butter.

The two friends sat outside in camp chairs, eating the sticky pancakes and drinking coffee. "These pancakes are blowing my mind. Wow! How did you do that? I would never be able to put those ingredients together." Meadow said. She squinted at Nikki. "You're a cook, aren't you?"

"I enjoy it."

Meadow cleared her throat and, Nikki thought, looked kind of nervous. "You know how I was telling you about that comment on the website? And how I'm looking for the other housemates?"

"Yes."

"I know it's weird," Meadow said, "But all these years, I always wondered if he really did it. Ended his life. I've always felt like something was off, but I've never been able to put my finger on it. And then I got that comment. What if it's true, what if someone killed him? I just can't be at peace until I know for sure. And I wanted to ask if you would—I don't know—be a sounding board for me as I find stuff out?"

"Okay. I could do that," Nikki said, "But I don't understand. You said the police investigated, and they ruled it a suicide. Right?"

"Yes, but what if they got it wrong?"

They said their farewells in the soft morning air. Meadow tucked a green sprig into Nikki's shirt pocket. "No one is supposed to take anything out of the park—no magical rocks, no plant life, nothing," Meadow said. "So, technically, this is breaking the law, but I want you to take a piece of the Mojave with you. Don't tell anyone."

"I won't tell on you, Ranger Deb. You go by Deb now, right?"

"Yeah. Everyone but you. But keep calling me Meadow. I love that."

"And I love that you call me Phoenix, too." Nikki picked the sprig out of her pocket. "This is from a plant?"

"Mesquite. Technically a tree, but most of them look like bushes. It's a very smart plant—it survives in the desert because it has a long root that goes down deep to draw from the water table. But it's also flexible—it can use water from the upper part of the ground, and it can switch back and forth."

"Digging deep for sustenance but accepting whatever is on the surface as well. Isn't that cool. You and me, we both like digging deep. You should come to Brooklyn for a visit. I have a very nice foldout couch. You're visiting your daughter this summer, right? Come up to New York."

"I might just take you up on that." Meadow opened her arms.

Stepping into her friend's hug, Nikki felt a wave of comfort and love around her. What was that feeling? Of being nurtured. It was something she hadn't experienced for so long. Grounded and light, at the same time. Her roots were getting sustenance, just like the mesquite. She pulled back from the embrace and looked into Meadow's eyes. "I feel like I've found a long-lost sister. Thank you."

"You have," Meadow said. "But I'm the lucky one." The angle of light caught her amber eyes, glinting gold in the morning light.

Nikki didn't want to leave. She got in the car and turned the key. Rolling down the window, she yelled out, "Yoni power!" with a show of mock solemnity, and drove off. In the rearview mirror, Meadow was bent over laughing. Slowly, she stood upright and raised her fist in a power-to-the-people salute. Meadow stayed like that, eyes on the car, gradually turning her salute into a slow-motion wave. Nikki watched her gesturing figure grow smaller and smaller until the road turned, and Meadow was gone.

Chapter 16

Cover-up

D eb did the slo-mo royal wave as the car got smaller and smaller. She wished Phoenix didn't have to leave. She considered smoking a joint but decided against it; she had to be at work in a couple of hours. It was amazing—except for the first night of Phoenix's visit, she hadn't even felt like getting high.

She got in her truck and drove a few miles, then parked on the side of the road by the salt flats. The minute she stepped off the paved road and her boots hit the playa, she had a familiar sense of homecoming. This was the Mojave in its own skin. Heading across the cracked earth, she felt the satisfying crunch of its salty crust beneath her boots, and it bolstered her. Unlike other national parks, in Death Valley it was acceptable to go off-trail. The first time she'd tried it, almost a year ago, she'd anxiously checked her compass every few minutes to make sure she didn't get lost. But now, after countless forays, she knew that even if she lost her way, she'd find it again. Now she *liked* getting lost. She smiled. Being lost was considered a bad thing in Western culture. We're conditioned to set and achieve goals, stay focused, map and plan and organize and do, do, do. The past few days with Phoenix had brought back the same sense of pleasure in being lost to time that she used to feel at Ashbury House. The sense that anything could happen, that the world was a dreamy place, full of magic and surprise.

She hadn't had much chance to practice being lost for all of the years of raising Andy, working every day except for vacations, providing stability for her daughter. When Andy went off to college, she thought maybe it would give her a sense of freedom, but she was surprised at how untethered she felt. She and her daughter had been close through the childhood years, up until Andy became a teen and started inching away. Deb read everything she could find on the stages of child development, adolescence, and young adulthood, and realized it was the healthy thing for her daughter to separate from her. Still, after Andy went off to college, Deb felt she was no longer *of use*. She'd tried to talk to Ming about it, but Ming didn't have kids and didn't understand. So she'd brought it up with Matt, thinking that because he was so involved with his two children—really, he was a helicopter parent—that he'd relate. But he'd dismissed her feelings, saying of course she was *of use*, they weren't living in the 1950s, and she didn't have to be defined by motherhood like their mom had been. Her brother was always so literal about everything. It's more a feeling, she told him, not an actual belief. Matt's kids were preteens, so his nest was far from empty, and maybe even when they left, he still wouldn't get it. A burst of orange caught her eye and she knelt down beside the brilliant blooms: *Castilleja chromosa*. Desert paintbrush.

She got to her feet. Maybe her visit with Phoenix was about being lost and found, too. It surprised her that with

Phoenix she'd felt a sense of home. The Ashbury House had been a family to her in a way that her own family never was. Spending time with Phoenix was exciting—like a romance, but without the sex.

When she got to the ranger station, Gretchen handed her a pink slip of paper with a phone number and the message: *Call Che.*

"Who's Che?" Gretchen whispered. "A love interest?"

"Uh, no," she said, "Gotta go." She hurried to a free desk and examined the message. The area code looked familiar, and she dug in her bag for her notebook. She looked up the number Stretch had given her—yes, same area code, but different number.

She checked in with her supervisor and he gave her an assignment of multiple trash pickups. It was better than being stuck behind a counter talking to tourists all day. She made her way out to the truck and started to climb into it, but the seat was too hot, so she spread a towel over it. Settling into the seat, she took out her phone, inhaled a deep breath, and called the Montana number. A man answered.

"Hello, this is Meadow."

A pause on the other end. "It really is you."

"Yes. Che?"

"Sure is. Where did you get the number you called me at before?"

"I tracked down Stretch, and she gave it to me."

He chuckled. She exhaled in relief—he was laughing; that was a good sign.

"Is she still doing that cockamamie ritual stuff? And the yoni thing?" he asked.

His voice, and the way he said *yoni* brought back a memory of being in bed with him, the afternoon light coming in through the upstairs window, the lazy look in his green eyes, and the pure adolescent lust that had flowed through her.

"Meadow? You there?"

"Yeah, I'm here." Now that she had him on the phone, she wasn't sure if this was such a good idea, after all. "What made you move to Montana?"

"I like that it's near the border. I like that it's quiet, and people respect your privacy." He paused, and she heard him breathing on the other end of the line. "I saw your website, Soldiers with Invisible Wounds."

"How did you happen to find it?"

"I was searching for something related to Ashbury House and I stumbled on it."

"What were you looking for?" He didn't respond. "Che? Or should I call you Joshua now?"

He made a sound like a snort. "Whatever. Neither one is—"

"Neither one is what?"

"Never mind. I guess you want to know if I was the one who left the comment on your site. Right? Yeah, it was me."

"What the fuck? Why did you post that?"

"You don't have to yell," he said quietly. "I sent it because —I thought you should know. He was working at the Food Conspiracy, and there were a lot of drugs going in and out of there. I think he was dealing as a front, to work with the cops in an undercover operation."

Deb pounded her free hand on the steering wheel. "This is crazy. He would never have—"

"Meadow. I bought a lid of grass off him. Okay? You think you knew him, but you didn't really."

That stopped her. Could it be true? "Did you ask the police about this after Ron died—did you tell them what you thought?"

"Jesus. I couldn't do that—if they were in on the cover-up, they would never have revealed that he was their confidential informant. There was no way I was going to trust the fascist insect."

"Fascist insect?" Deb asked.

"I mean—I meant the fascist pigs."

Her stomach was churning. Was Che right or had he gone off the deep end? "So what if he was dealing some weed," she said. "That's not such a big deal." Actually, it was a pretty big deal in the 1970s; she knew that, but she didn't want to fuel his conspiracy theory.

"No," Che said, "The weed wasn't the point—I'm saying there were hard drugs around the communes and they were all connected to the food co-op where he worked. It was like a hub. We're talkin' heroin and cocaine. Pills. So he was an informant about pushers in the Haight. He was either killed by the dealers, and the cops ruled it a suicide so they wouldn't look bad, or the cops killed him because he found out about the pigs dealing drugs from inside the police force, and then they covered it up by staging it as a suicide. Listen, Meadow, have you talked to the other housemates from Ashbury House? Did you talk to Willow?"

"Oh." Deb felt a clenching in her stomach. She would have to tell him, of course.

"What does *oh* mean—have you talked to her?"

"I'm sorry but—" She started over again. "I have to tell you that Willow died about a year ago."

"What? No, that can't be."

"It is. I found out recently from Mama Linda."

Silence. Then he said, softly, "What about Nik-Knock? Is she okay?"

"She's fine," she said gently.

"I have to go," he said, his voice breaking, and the line was disconnected.

Chapter 17

Willow

1975

"Thanks." She put the baggie in her pocket. "Don't tell anyone, okay?"

"Of course not." Wrinkling his brow, RJ examined her face. "But it's just to help you sleep, right? Don't take them otherwise."

He's such a dad, Willow thought. "I never take them during the day," she said. "And I promise I won't tell anyone where I got them."

"I only give them to people I know and trust. So it's not breaking—you know."

"House rules?" She smiled. "Valium isn't a hard drug."

"Right. But you start with pills and one thing leads to another, and before you know it, you're a junkie," he deadpanned.

She laughed. "How about you? Do they help you sleep?"

He shook his head. "They don't work for me. Sometimes I smoke some grass before bed."

"Do you still have the nightmares?"

"Don't worry about me. I'm fine."

"I was reading a book about soldiers returning from the First World War—they used to call it shell shock, and, I mean, maybe it's something like that, and you shouldn't feel alone—"

"Not like that. I never saw combat. I'm okay. I mean it." He smiled. "I'm at peace with all that; I really am."

She nodded. She didn't quite believe him.

"Hey," he said. "Want to work on the firepit some more before dinner? We're almost done."

"Sure. Meet you in the backyard in a bit?" She gave him a quick hug and started to leave, but he held on for a moment longer. That was weird.

"Yeah, see you in the backyard in a while," he said quietly, stepping away.

When she closed the door of RJ's room behind her, Che was coming down the hall. He cut his eyes at RJ's door but didn't ask what she'd been doing in there. "My bed still smells like you," he said, his voice husky. "So fine."

She started to shake her head at him, but the memory of their combined scents and heat stopped her. A twist of delicious tension coiled inside her, and with the hint of a smile, she started up the stairs. "Stay tuned," she said, tossing the words back to him, over her shoulder. In the last few months, the sex, instead of fading out, had become more intense. They might go for a few weeks or even a month without fucking and then something would happen and the door would blow open again. They were both surprised by their feverish connection, how reliable the chemistry was, how it would start up with a touch or a word, but she didn't have real feelings for him, and as far as she knew, neither did he for her. She never spent the night. Always came back to her own bed afterward, checking first on Nik-Knock before going to sleep.

At first, she'd gone along with the crazy sexual healing idea partly to call Stretch's bluff and partly because it had been so long since she'd touched or been touched. She hadn't slept with anyone since Charles—six years. She'd finally given up on RJ, settling for friendship, even though a part of her harbored a fantasy of him as Nik-Knock's adoptive father. So the weird experiment with Che—seeing if a few nights between the sheets might stop them from constantly bickering —had been appealing in a through-the-looking-glass kind of way. What was supposed to last for a week or two had been going on for almost a year. It had turned into the weirdest relationship she'd ever had. But then they'd agreed it wasn't a *relationship*. They were both free to see other people. Except they hadn't, for the most part. Che's little fling with Meadow last summer didn't really count. She hadn't minded their romance, because it had given her a break from Che and time to think. But then Meadow had broken it off with Che once she started college and moved across town, and somehow Willow and Che had fallen back into their old pattern.

These days, when Meadow would come to the house to visit, she and Che were friendly enough, but it was clear there was nothing between them. Meadow had apparently taken to heart Stretch's speech about the art of the zipless fuck, a feminist take on sex without consequences or feelings. Stretch had lectured the house women about it as a model of sexual freedom after reading Erica Jong's *Fear of Flying*. Ridiculous, Willow thought, but then caught herself—she shouldn't be so judgmental—maybe she'd been doing the zipless fuck with Che, after all. But she'd read the book after Stretch had pressed it on her, and the act was a one-time sexual encounter between two strangers, not what she'd been doing at all. She shook her head—was this what the so-called sexual revolution was? Women were liberated to have sex without feelings? She *did* want feelings, just not marriage and all its baggage. The whole nuclear family thing was unpaid slave labor for women. Historically, most tribal cultures didn't even do monogamy, and they certainly didn't look on family as a biological-mother-and-father unit, but more as a community collectively responsible for the children. The mother was still the mother, though, and often the mother's brother assumed the role of what we think of as father. In a way, she'd been hoping for that ideal at Ashbury House, trying to create a tribal family for her and her daughter. But the only house members she could really depend on for childcare were Mama Linda and RJ.

When she reached the top of the stairs to the attic studio, the area between Stretch's room and hers that they'd turned into a creative space, Nik-Knock was at her little desk, drawing on a sketch pad. Willow pushed the bag of pills deeper into her pocket. She'd planned to stash them in her work table drawer, but if she did, her daughter would pick up on her furtive vibe and have a million questions. Her seven-year-old had become so perceptive—nothing got past her.

"Mumma!"

"Yes, honey."

"I'm going to help you and RJ make a pit fire."

"Firepit. Did you ask him if it was okay?"

"Yes, Mumma." She stuck out her bottom lip, like she did when she was spoiling for a fight.

Willow sighed. She'd rather have the time alone with RJ, but she didn't feel like arguing. "Okay, pumpkin."

She went into her bedroom, out of Nik-Knock's view, and hid the pills in her underwear drawer. Taking off her work clothes, she breathed a sigh of relief: knee-length skirt, flow-ered cotton blouse, tights, and flats. She'd managed to put together a few work outfits from the thrift store on Haight. Some of the clothes had to be ironed, which she hated. It reminded her of her mother, endlessly at the ironing board. She took off her bra and pulled on a Jefferson Airplane tee shirt and red drawstring pants.

On her way downstairs, she stood in front of her daughter. "Nik-Knock." Her daughter didn't look up. "Phoenix." Her child's gaze was glued to her drawing. When Nik-Knock was like this, nothing would tear her away. Willow was annoyed, but another part of her thought: Thank goodness she loves to draw and has the ability to focus. She would make damn sure Nik-Knock would be able to make a living doing something she loved, whatever it was. She didn't want her daughter to grow up to be like her, a wage-slave secretary in a fucking office. When she first got the job at the university, she'd thought it would be a hip environment. But it wasn't. It was still the straight world, and she hated it. Her fascist supervisor made sure she clocked in every minute of her eight-hour shift and watched her breaks like a hawk. She hadn't realized her degree in anthropology wouldn't lead to a job in the field. She really thought that after volunteering at the dig in Mexico and becoming fluent in Spanish, she might have a chance to become an archeologist or get some sort of cultural anthropology job. But it turned out those jobs weren't out there. At least not for her. Maybe if you had connections, like some of the rich kids she'd met on the dig, who seemed to know all the right people and could keep working for free until they landed an actual job.

After college, when she'd moved from Santa Cruz up to the city, she'd thought there'd be more opportunities, but instead she ended up waiting tables. She'd been saving her money from working at the restaurant, planning to go off on another dig if she could find one. But then she got into the relationship with Charles, with all its alcohol-fueled craziness.

A couple of months after Willow first met Mama Linda, she found out she was pregnant. Mama Linda asked around and found out about a safe place to get an abortion. But Willow wasn't sure—how safe could it be? She'd heard so many gruesome stories about back-alley procedures. But her options were limited, so she went ahead and made an appointment. She canceled it and made another and canceled that one too.

Her grandparents had emigrated from Poland around the time of the First World War, but none of their relatives joined them, so their whole family back in Europe was wiped out during the second war. There were some things from her upbringing she knew she would never shake, like the obligation to repopulate the earth with little Jews. Replacements. For the sake of the six million. She'd rejected so much of what she'd learned from her parents, her grandma, and Hebrew school, but that particular injunction stayed with her. Along with a couple of other fucked-up teachings from her mother, like "Sarah, don't confide in anyone except your family, because you can't trust the goyim or the State, or anyone who isn't your flesh and blood." In addition, her mother would whisper to her that you couldn't trust Mrs. So-and-So from the synagogue, or don't tell the rabbi, or don't talk to any number of other congregants her mother didn't trust.

Willow wasn't even aware that she had inherited the secrecy trait from her mother until Linda called her on it one day, asking her why she wouldn't tell Nik-Knock that she was mixed race, that her daughter was Black and it was an important part of her identity. She told Linda she was afraid if she did that Nik-Knock would push and push to meet Charles, and she just couldn't have her daughter growing up with an alcoholic father like she had had. Maybe if she were completely honest, she'd have to admit she was okay with her daughter passing. She'd promised Linda she'd tell her later, when Nik-Knock was older.

So much for keeping trust inside the family—all of them, except her bubbe, had disowned her for having a child 1) with a *goy*, and 2) with a *Black goy*, and 3) *out of wedlock*. Her parents, and even her sister, pronounced her dead and sat shiva for her. Bubbe said what her parents did was wrong. After all, they were Conservative, not Orthodox. So they didn't have to disown her. But Willow knew what was at the root of it. Her parents were always trying to fit in, to out-pious the Jews in their San Fernando Valley synagogue. Her grandmother had stayed in touch, faithfully writing letters, calling, and sneaking in the occasional visit. Bubbe had been there for Willow when no one else in the family had.

Willow waved her hand in front of Nik-Knock's face, and her daughter finally looked up, blinking. "Phoenix. If you want to work on the firepit, come with me now."

"Just go, Mumma! I'll come."

Willow smiled to herself. That probably meant Nik-Knock wouldn't make it in time to work with them, or, more accurately, to get in the way. That was fine with her. She headed downstairs and checked the backyard, but RJ wasn't there yet.

In the kitchen, Mama Linda was chopping onions, her eyes tearing.

"You just go ahead and cry. Let it all out," Willow joked.

"No, I'd rather hold it in," Mama Linda said. "In the traditional way of strong women."

"Right on, sister." Willow grabbed a cutting board and a knife. "What can I do? Put me to work."

Mama Linda shook her head. "It's my night to cook. You just sit down and put your big fat feet up."

"I want to do something. But just until RJ gets down here. We're going to finish making the firepit."

"Oh, so you're going to dump me for a man?" Her friend smiled.

"Never."

"Okay, chop those up, then." Mama Linda motioned to a bunch of carrots on the counter. "Did you go to the 5:30 meeting?"

"Went this morning before work."

"The usual suspects?"

"Yeah. You?"

"Last night. Community Center."

Willow started chopping, and they worked in silence. She'd first met Linda at an Al-Anon meeting eight years ago, when she was pregnant and still dealing with the fallout from her breakup with Charles. Linda was also getting over a bad breakup with an addict, and over time the two became friends. When Linda fixed up the house she'd recently bought and was looking for housemates, she'd invited Willow and her new baby to move in.

Willow brushed her eyes with her sleeve. The onions were making her cry too. "Who's going to be here for dinner?"

"Everyone but Stretch; she's at rehearsal. Plus Meadow and her new boyfriend are coming."

"Ooh, a new beau. What's his name?"

"Gary."

RJ came into the kitchen just then. "Who's Gary?"

"Meadow's new boyfriend. Guess who's coming to dinner? Sidney Poitier," Willow said.

"She has a Black boyfriend?" Mama Linda said.

"No, I was just kidding. Or maybe he is Black, I don't know."

RJ's jaw tensed. "She's bringing him for *dinner?* Tonight?"

"Yeah. What's wrong with that?" Mama Linda said.

"Nothing. I just wish she'd told me." He turned to Willow. "Are you still up for working on the firepit?"

"Yeah, I'll be out there in a minute."

RJ went outside, slamming the back door. Willow raised her eyebrows at her friend.

Mama Linda shook her head. "I guess he's having a hard time letting go of his baby sister. He's going to have to let his precious little bird spread her wings and fly away."

"Yeah, well. I just hope he handles it better than he did when she was with Che," Willow said.

Mama Linda snorted. "He better. But it might be completely different with this Gary guy."

"It was pretty awful. You weren't here," Willow said.

"I know."

Willow really didn't want to think about it, but there it was, playing like a movie, in her mind.

She'd been in the parlor, reading aloud to Nik-Knock, when they'd heard RJ and Che's raised voices in the kitchen, their voices getting louder by the minute.

"Leave her alone, motherfucker," RJ shouted.

"You son of a bitch, you don't own her," Che yelled.

"You just fucking keep your hands off her, you dick."

"What are you, her boyfriend? You're acting like a jealous asshole."

There was a crashing sound and then silence. Willow's stomach seized up. She was paralyzed, stuck in a flash of the sound of her parents screaming at each other while she froze, alone in her bedroom. Nik-Knock started to get up and move toward the kitchen. Willow grabbed her and held her down.

"Let me go!" Nik-Knock said.

"No, sweetie," she said, choking on the words.

From the kitchen, Che shouted, "You want to take this outside, we can take this shit outside." The back door banged open and slammed shut.

Meadow came clattering down the stairs. "What the *fuck* is going on?" She started toward the kitchen.

"Mumma, Mumma, I want to see," Nik-Knock said, yanking herself free of Willow's hold and running to catch up with Meadow. Willow followed behind, and the three of them burst out the back door, onto the deck.

RJ and Che were in a face-off, the anger between them palpable. Willow held on firmly to Nik-Knock.

"Don't do this!" Meadow shouted.

RJ swung wildly, his face contorted. Che drew back, but not in time to miss RJ's fist, which landed with a resounding smack. Che roared and swung back, but RJ was too close, and the punch stopped short. Che grabbed at RJ's T-shirt and clawed at the bared flesh. He jammed his other hand into RJ's face, mashing his mouth and nose.

For a second, RJ flailed, but then he closed his arms around Che's neck, trying to choke him. Tied together, they swung side to side, each trying to gain an advantage, but they only succeeded in falling to the ground.

Willow, coming out of the deep freeze she'd slipped into when they first started fighting, yelled, "Stop it!"

The two men, pushing away from each other on the ground, scrambled to their feet. They faced off again, seething and breathing heavily. RJ's T-shirt was ripped, and red welts were rising on his stomach. His lips were swollen. Blood dripped from Che's nose.

Willow tried again. "Stop, you're scaring Nik-Knock."

"I'm not scared," her daughter said, pulling away from her grasp, but Willow held on tight.

"Mumma, you're hurting me!"

At that, RJ and Che turned to look.

Now Meadow spoke up. "You're behaving like little boys," she said, her voice steely. "Grow up. Ron, I'm an adult now, and I can do whatever I want. Che, stop acting like a macho pig." She turned on her heel and went back inside.

The two men moved away from each other. Che put his hand to his face and then looked down at his bloody hand. "Man."

RJ touched his swollen lip.

Nik-Knock tried once more to yank away, and this time Willow let her go. The child went over to the two men and put her hands on her hips. "This is not good conflict revolution. You two should learn how to talk. To. Each. Other." She pivoted and exited, slamming the kitchen door behind her. Willow glared at Che and RJ and, shaking her head, followed her daughter back inside.

Under any other circumstances, "conflict revolution" would have been something they all laughed about. But nothing about that whole scene was humorous, even now. Before the fist fight, Willow had always thought of RJ as a gentle guy. And Che— she'd assumed his macho edge was just an act. But she was wrong about both of them. What had she expected, really? RJ had been in the Marine Corps, and Che had grown up in South Central LA. And men are bred for violence.

She handed the diced carrots to Mama Linda and went out to the backyard. RJ was setting a brick in the center of the shallow crater they'd dug and surrounded with a ring of stones a few days before. "Are we just covering the bottom of the pit with bricks? Do we need mortar or something?"

"No, it's cool—after we set them all down we pour sand over them, and it gets caught in the cracks and locks them in place."

She set a brick next to his. "Is there something about Meadow's new boyfriend you don't like?"

He shook his head. "I haven't even met him."

He looked up at her and tried for a smile, but it was forced. It wasn't his usual playful grin. What was going on with him?

"I just don't want her to get too serious with someone when she's so young, you know. She's only eighteen," he said.

That sounded like bullshit to her. Maybe it wasn't just protectiveness. Maybe he was actually jealous. But, then, she'd never had a brother. It could be she just didn't understand the whole brother-sister dynamic.

Nik-Knock came out on the deck and down the stairs to the yard. RJ's face transformed from cloudy to clear in a heartbeat.

Her daughter threw her arms around him from behind and climbed on his back. "Show me how, RJ!"

He gently peeled her off and demonstrated how to lay the brick down, and then he explained about pouring the sand. When he gave her a brick she put it in sideways, so he showed her again. The second time she put it in the right direction but then started scooping up sand and piling it on top in a heap. "No, it's not time for that yet," he said gently, reminding her that they'd sweep the whole thing with sand at the end and encouraging her to lay another brick down. Willow wished she could be as patient as he was, and that her daughter would listen to her like that.

She gazed at the two of them working together. Nik-Knock would put in a brick correctly, and RJ, with a clown face, would pretend to do it wrong, and her daughter would laugh hysterically. Then they would repeat the whole pantomime. As much as she dreamed of taking her little girl and moving to the country, to some woodsy town in Sonoma County where they could have a more peaceful life, she would never leave this house as long as RJ lived here.

Chapter 18

Threshold of Revelation

2005

Nikki waited for Ira at their usual spot in the park for their Saturday morning run. Where the fuck was he? He was never late. Nikki called him again and his phone went straight to voice mail. She felt the first shard of anxiety—what if something had happened to him? The fear had never really gone away, ever since those wrenching hours on 9/11 when she didn't know where he was, if he'd made it out of the office in the tower, if he was hurt or trapped or dead. Nikki had gone to their apartment where she and Javier had waited, silently. When Ira walked in the door a few hours later, dazed and ash-covered, his boyfriend fell on him, crying and laughing. Nikki, overwhelmed with relief and joy, watched the couple until they beckoned, and she joined in their sooty hug.

Now, waiting in the park for Ira, she checked her watch for the umpteenth time. Finally, she saw her friend hobbling to meet her. "Why didn't you answer your phone?" she snapped.

"The battery went out and I couldn't find the charger. My knee is fucked. I can't run. You go on ahead without me."

She shook her head. "No, no. Sorry for barking at you. I don't have to run; it's more important to hang out with you. Come on, let's go get coffee."

Balancing two mugs, Nikki approached the café table. There was a part of her that didn't want to talk about the visit with Meadow and the details about RJ's suicide; it would be easier to keep all of that stored away.

"So, how was your trip? Did you find anything out from Meadow? Anything you didn't already know?"

She set down the mugs, sat down, and took a sip of coffee.

"Well, what already?" Ira said.

"The housemate I told you about, RJ, who died? It turns out he died by suicide in our house. While I was there, maybe. When I was seven. Except I can't remember it."

"That's intense," Ira said. They sat in silence for a while. "Do you think you have PTSD?"

She shook her head. "People with PTSD usually have flashbacks—it's like they have *too much* memory. What I have is not enough memory. Dissociative amnesia."

Ira shook his head in confusion. "What is that? Please translate."

"Basically, it means you can't remember a traumatic event." She had a sensation of something opening in her chest. And then her eyes were filling with tears.

Ira reached across the table, placing his hand on hers.

"Maybe I should go back into therapy," she said, "after this revelation."

Ira smiled sadly. "Threshold of revelation."

"What's that?"

"In *Angels in America*, remember? Harper tells Prior they're on the threshold of revelation, where you can understand things you wouldn't ordinarily perceive, and so she asks him to tell her a revelation about herself. He says, "Your husband's a homo." See, Harper wasn't exactly aware her Mormon marriage was about to explode, but somewhere in the back of her mind, she knew there was this secret ticking away. When you get the big reveal, you're on the threshold of something that's going to change your life. Even if you're not entirely conscious of it."

Nikki nodded slowly. "But that was a play, right? In theater, everything is bigger than life. But in real life, like for me, it's something from my childhood that happened that I can't access with my conscious mind. Or are you saying I'm on the threshold of some other kind of revelation? God, I hope so, because I could use something like that." She laughed.

Ira nodded slowly. "Okay, maybe not a big giant revelation. Maybe a flash of understanding? A missing piece of a puzzle. I don't know. So was it hard—being with Meadow, talking about all that stuff?"

"Yes and no. The trip, and my time with her, was magical. I felt so connected to her from sharing that time of our lives. I mean—I was a small child and she was a teenager, so it doesn't seem like we would've been in the same world, but we were. And there's this kind of shorthand where we don't have to explain things because we were there together, and even though there was some crazy-ass hippie stuff, still, there was so much wonder and mystery in those times. Not like now."

Ira opened his mouth and closed it.

"I know what you're thinking," she said. "Tra-la-la."

He laughed and choked on his coffee. "I am *not* thinking *tra-la-la*! I get that it was like the best of times and the worst of times, right? At the house? No, I was just thinking about

184

when we met, and how your life in Petaluma was so different from what you're talking about."

"It was kind of a culture shock, to go from that big house in the Haight with all those people to just me and Willow in that apartment in Petaluma." Something clicked into place then. When she thought about the House, in her memory, RJ was always there. "Okay, threshold of revelation: RJ was kind of a surrogate father. Maybe I can make peace with the missing piece of the puzzle. Too much alliteration?"

Ira touched her hand. "It's good timing to make peace with the piece. You have Charles now. Your lost-and-found father. There's a symmetry there."

"True." She thought about Meadow's conflicting theories about RJ's death.

"What is it?" Ira said. "You have a weird look on your face."

"Now Meadow is saying she isn't sure RJ died by suicide, that he may have been murdered."

Ira sat back in his chair. "Okay, that's weird. Do you think it's a possibility? Or is she—how to say this—is she nuts?"

"I have no fucking idea."

After they parted ways, Nikki walked to the community garden. Her plot was looking good, but it needed cleaning up. First she did the weeding—her least favorite part, but it was always satisfying once she finished. She chopped up the weeds and put them in the compost. The smell of compost always brought back pleasant memories. An image of RJ rose up in her mind. He was showing her how to turn the compost, add the rice hulls, and rotate it again. He watched as she tried it herself and then nodded and smiled, his teeth white against his dark beard, his eyes delighted. Then he did the whole thing again himself, but he didn't say that she'd done it wrong, nothing like that. He just showed her again, and nodded encouragingly when she did it one more time.

One of her fellow community gardeners threw some weeds into the compost, snapping her out of her reverie. Okay, she thought. The visit with Deb had stirred up some memories. It was sort of like being triggered, except in a good way. She surveyed her vegetables and knelt down to take a whiff of her tomato plants. They smelled and looked good; maybe the tomatoes would be ready in a month or two. There were a couple of early zucchinis, and she picked one for dinner. Then she watered her plot and, because her garden neighbor was out of town, watered his too. After she was done, she sat on a bench and turned her face up to the sun. It was hot, but nothing like Death Valley. She tried to empty her mind, like she used to do when they had meditation sessions at the House. When she cleared away as much as she could, a voice in her head said, "Mama Linda." She opened her eyes and sat up straight. Ever since she got back from Death Valley she'd been putting it off, but now the time had come. She would call Mama Linda. Threshold of revelation.

"Why didn't you ever tell me that RJ died?" Nikki, back at her apartment, looked out the window at the bright green leaves of her tree, her voice shaky.

With an audible sigh, Mama Linda said, "Willow made me promise. The last time I saw her, just about a year before she died. When I said I was going to reconnect with you, she made me swear not to tell you. She said it was better to keep the story that RJ had moved away; she thought it would freak you out too much if you found out about his suicide. I felt I had to honor her wishes. She was your mother."

"You were my mother too," Nikki said, her voice tight with anger.

"I know, sugar." She sniffed. "And that's why I feel so terrible about it. It was the same with the big secret about Charles, how she kept me from telling you. She'd burdened me with these damn lies."

Nikki heard the anger in her voice and had a glimmer of understanding.

"So when Meadow contacted me," Mama Linda continued, "and said she was going to get in touch with you, I thought she might tell you. I didn't tell her *not* to talk about it. I figured what would be, would be." Her voice broke. "But I do believe: the truth will out."

Nikki's jaw, clenched tight, slowly relaxed. Mama Linda had always been there for her, and of course she'd done what she thought was right, thirty years ago, and even in the recent past. She pictured her—by now her hair was probably gray, her deep brown eyes as empathetic as ever—sitting by a window with a view of the desert sky. "Meadow said she doesn't know if I was home when he killed himself," Nikki said. "Was I?"

There was silence. When Mama Linda started talking, her voice sounded different. "I don't know. I was at work and didn't get back until late. I went to pick up Meadow right away, and it's all kind of a blur. Sugar, when are you coming to visit? We can talk so much better in person. I'll tell you everything."

Chapter 19

East Coast

Deb sat at Andy's patio table on the terrace of her daughter's new apartment in Philadelphia, contemplating the bloody hamburger on the white-flour bun, with iceberg lettuce and a slice of tomato on the side. Andy had insisted on cooking the burgers on her brand-new gas grill, which she was eager to show off, and which looked to Deb like it cost a zillion dollars, but she wasn't going to bring *that* up.

Andy took a big bite of her burger. "Mmm, it's so good."

Her red hair, inherited from her father, glinted in the sun. It was pulled back in a ponytail, and her blue eyes, also a reminder of her absent father, crinkled at the edges. Her daughter always had a knack for looking perfectly fresh and natural, in spite of the time and money she spent on mascara and blush and lip gloss.

"Mom. Go on, taste it. It's not going to kill you. God, you're still such a hippie."

"I'm trying it. See?" Deb took a bite, chewing slowly. "This is actually tasty. I don't usually eat red meat. How does that make me a hippie?"

"You know, the whole crunchy granola thing."

Deb sighed. "I *was* a hippie in the seventies, and back then it meant something brave and principled, like protesting the war, marching for civil rights, the women's movement. Not an oat-based cold cereal."

"It wasn't only politics, though, right? Sex, drugs, and rock 'n' roll. Right? Flowers in your hair. But you know what? I accept you as you are." Andy guffawed.

"And I accept you, too, honey, that you're a trader, doing—whatever it is you do with stocks. I'm okay with it. As long as you don't become a Republican."

Andy rolled her eyes. "Not *stocks*. Remember? We talked about it. *Hedge funds*. And I'm not a Republican, I'm a Libertarian. You realize I'm one of the few women in my field? A pathfinder. Blazer. Trailblazer." She chomped on her burger.

"I'm proud of you, sweetie." Deb didn't really want the bloody burger but she ate it anyway. It would make her daughter happy.

"You are? Seriously? Wouldn't you rather I was working at some nonprofit on environmental issues? Ecofeminism? Habitat for Humanity? Or all of the above?"

Deb coughed, the bun and meat sticking in her throat. "I am truly proud of you. Let's not fight on my last night."

"We're not fighting."

"You know what I mean—let's not—accentuate our differences." An uneasy silence.

Deb took a bite of potato salad and gasped. "Mmm. So good. Wait a minute." She took another bite. "Oh! This is your grandmother's recipe, isn't it? This is such comfort food; I haven't had it in so long."

Andy smiled proudly. "Yup. Got the recipe from Grandma. Isn't it delish?"

"Yes. It reminds me of church picnics and backyard

barbecues. It was Mom's summer go-to dish." She closed her eyes, relishing the taste. "So good. It's probably really bad for you, all that mayo. I want the recipe."

"It's easy, you just cook the potatoes and you hard-boil some eggs, and you dice everything, add mayo, mustard, vinegar, salt and pepper."

"Very Michigan." Deb took another bite. "Celery, too, right? And onion?"

"Yeah. Forgot to say."

"Really good, honey." Taking another helping, Deb said, "Want some?" the spoon poised above the bowl.

"I'm good," Andy said.

"Do you want some more?"

"I *said*, I'm good."

"What does 'I'm good' mean?"

"Seriously, Mom, you don't know?"

"I think I've heard it from the students who come in the library, but I have to say it always confuses me."

"It means I've had enough, no thanks, I'm okay like this. God, I can't believe it. You're still the language police." Andy took a swig of beer and burped.

Deb laughed and her daughter joined in. A truce, of sorts. She should say something nice to counterbalance. "Andy, I'm glad you found a nice guy. I really like Ed. I'm happy for you." She held back from saying what she really wanted to: And don't rush into marriage, you have plenty of time.

"Thanks, Mom. He's amazing, right? I've been meaning to tell you—I want you to know, we're really *serious*."

Uh-oh, Deb thought. She hoped that didn't mean Andy was about to get engaged. She was only twenty-three years old, for god's sake. Andy was peering at her, waiting for a reply.

"That's great, sweetie."

After dinner, they worked together clearing the dishes and stacking them in the dishwasher.

"Oh, I checked out your website," Andy said. "Your updates are really cool. It looks like you took my advice and added some images. You know, I feel like I *knew* Uncle Ron, even though I never met him. I guess it's all the family stories and the photos of him. So when I look at your site, and the tribute you wrote for him, with the pictures and all, I'm like, *yeah*, that's my uncle."

Deb felt herself tearing up. "Oh, honey. That means the world to me."

The next afternoon, she arrived at Phoenix's building after a train ride from Philadelphia, plus a subway ride and a bus ride. Phoenix met her at the door to her building and took her pack from her. They trudged up two flights to Phoenix's apartment.

"Jesus, it's fucking hot," Deb said.

"This is from the woman who lives in Death Valley?"

"But that's a dry heat. The humidity—how can you stand it?"

"It's not the humidity, it's the stupidity," Phoenix said.

"I don't know what that means, but it's funny."

"Yeah, my eighty-nine-year-old neighbor says that—born and bred in Brooklyn, so she must know what she's talking about."

Phoenix had made lunch—salad with smoked trout, a crusty Italian bread she got at a local bakery, and iced hibiscus tea. Deb took a bite of the salad. It tasted divine. "You are such a good cook. And this is healthy, too. Will you marry me?"

"Yes," Phoenix said, grinning. "It would have made Willow so happy."

"Mama Linda would be thrilled too."

They discussed Mama Linda's relationship, which she had told them was a "friendship" with her ex-partner Gena, and even though they didn't want to be in a relationship anymore, by mutual agreement, they still went on vacations, celebrated major holidays, and were there for each other if either one of them got sick.

"That sounds like a relationship to me," Phoenix said.

"Yeah-huh," Deb said.

They finished their salads, and Phoenix said, "Let's leave the dishes. There's something I want to show you in my neighborhood."

"A hipster artisanal brew pub?"

"Hey, smartass, I moved here *before* it gentrified. No, actually. What I want to show you is a cemetery. Green-Wood, it's a historic place. Have you heard of it?"

Deb laughed.

"Why are you laughing?"

"I'm laughing because you think it's a cool outing to go to a cemetery. But I'm with you on that. I love cemeteries."

Trudging up the hill to the gates of Green-Wood, she had second thoughts. There were hardly any people on the street. That's because they were all inside, with fans blowing, or sitting in air-conditioned cafés or bars, drinking tall, cool beverages.

"Here we are," Phoenix said.

Above the sign that read GREEN-WOOD CEMETERY were Gothic arches, the spires reminiscent of a European cathedral, complete with flying buttresses and a faded elegance.

"Wow. It's like a sandcastle on steroids," Deb said.

Once inside the gates, Phoenix, with the dogged gait of a tracker, her body almost at a diagonal, led Deb through green fields with crumbling, crooked headstones; past engraved benches and rows of simple grave markers; up and down winding paths, until she slowed and stood in front of her destination with what seemed to be a sense of pride.

The angel was on her knees, her head down. Angels, whether benign or avenging, were generally righteous, Deb thought. They could be joyous or solemn, but in any event they tended to hold their heads high. Not this one. Her head was sunk into the crook of her arm, supported by the pedestal. Her other arm hung uselessly, the hand broken off. Deb touched the stony stump, running her fingers over the rough surface. She wanted to see the angel's face but it was hidden. All that was visible was the tight coil of hair atop her head. Sensing that Phoenix was waiting for a response, she managed to force the words out: "She can't even lift her head up."

"Desolate," Phoenix agreed, with a glum smile.

"We expect them to be above it all, but she's down here with us. On her knees, on the ground. I love this angel. How did you find her?"

"One day I took a walk here and then happened on the angel, and there was something about her that spoke to me. When I got home I looked her up—apparently she's known as the Angel of Grief. I guess that's why I connected with her."

Deb let out a breath she didn't realize she'd been holding. "She's not the usual redemptive type of angel. This one is like —yeah—I did everything I could, but I couldn't save this person. Looking at her, I get this sense of relief. She's defeated, just like me, but she's so beautiful. Maybe it's okay to be dejected. You know, instead of strong and moving on and all."

Phoenix nodded slowly. "That's what makes her unique. The despairing angel."

They wandered to a shady spot a respectful distance away from the grave and sat down.

Phoenix turned her piercing eyes on Deb. "It must have been unbelievably hard to lose your brother," she said. "He died so . . . violently."

Yes. The implicit violence. Deb hadn't seen it; it had only played out in her imagination. She nodded, speechless. After a while, she managed to speak, and true to form, she found herself turning the attention away from herself. "It must have been hard for you too."

"I want to ask you something, and if you don't want to talk about it, it's okay," Phoenix said.

"Go ahead—ask."

"The day RJ died. You came to the house. What did you find when you got there?"

She pulled at the grass. She didn't want to talk about it, except that she did—she always wanted to talk about it, and now that she had someone who would truly listen, she held back. Why? Now there was a small pile of grass beside her. Had she yanked it all out in this short time? Stop doing that, she told herself. Jumping to her feet, she went over and touched the Angel's rough, weathered surfaces, then came back and sat down. "It was gone."

"What was gone?" Phoenix looked as if she were waiting for the answer to her question with every pore of her body.

Start at the beginning, Deb told herself. Go ahead. She'll hear you out. "I was at work—I had a work-study job in the campus library. It was around 5:30. My roommate came in and she had Mama Linda with her, and I thought, That's weird, what's Mama L. doing here? My roommate had this weird look on her face, kind of embarrassed and scared. Then

194

Mama L. put her arms around me and told me, she just said, straight-out, that RJ had shot himself. I asked if he was at the hospital and she shook her head so sadly. "He's passed," she said. When she said that, I had this picture in my mind, like one of those big old-fashioned clocks, and me turning the hands back just a few minutes and going back to what she said, except for I'd change what she'd told me. Like it was a movie and I could replay it and edit it—even though I never had made a movie or even thought about it, but I really did want to turn the clock back and have a remake of my reality. When I tell you about it now—it's like I'm remembering a dream. Some of the details are super-clear and some are hazy. This is clear: I was wearing my overalls, with a forest green blouse underneath, and hiking boots. I can see all that in my mind. But the drive to the house is completely fuzzy. When we got there, it was nighttime. The police had come and gone, and they'd taken him away. His body. I went into his room; I had to go in there. He wasn't there anymore and *it* wasn't there, either, and I was so mad. I asked Mama Linda, *Where is it?*"

"What wasn't there anymore?" Phoenix touched her arm lightly. Her voice was so soft it was almost a whisper.

It was quiet in the cemetery except for the distant hum of traffic and the persistent chirping of a solitary bird. "The mattress. It used to be mine—from our house in Grand Rapids. When he moved to San Francisco he got it out of the basement and took it in the U-Haul with a few other things. I kept asking Mama Linda what happened to it, and finally she said the police took it away as evidence. That was my bed."

Phoenix nodded and put her arms around her. The tears rolled down Deb's face. She never got to see him, so there was only what she had imagined. An angry red stain on the mattress, blooming like a malignant hibiscus. It would have been better to look at it than to have it play on and on in her head, in an endless vermilion loop.

That night, over dinner, she told Phoenix about her conversation with Che.

"He thinks it was a murder and cover-up? Yeah, I remember him as being a bit strange. I think, now that I look back on him, he was kind of unbalanced."

She shook her head. That wasn't true. "Really? When you say, 'unbalanced,' do you mean—"

"I mean, I think he was nuts. Wait, are you considering that his story might be right?" Phoenix said.

"Yes. I am," she snapped. What the fuck? Why was Phoenix being so judgy? She was hoping for some under-standing.

Phoenix was silent for a while, then said, out of the blue, "Would you play your guitar? And sing?"

Okay, she thought, Phoenix doesn't want to talk about this. It was annoying, but she decided not to push it. "Are you sure you want me to? I'm not very good."

"You brought your guitar, right? And I remember your voice—so clear like a bell. You used to sing all the time at the House. I would love to hear you sing again."

She took the guitar out of its case and tuned it. Picking a song from a Leonard Cohen album that she and Phoenix used to play at the house, she started strumming the chords to "Suzanne," and Phoenix grinned. When she got to the line *you want to travel with her, and you want to travel blind,* her friend joined in and they sang together.

Chapter 20

Triggered

Nikki woke in the dark to the smell. The crack under the door showed the light was on in the living room. She hated the smell. She got up and opened the bedroom door.

Meadow was on the fold-out bed, smoking a joint and writing in a notebook. Smiling sheepishly, she said, "Sorry if I woke you."

"This place reeks of weed."

"Wow. You seem pissed."

Nikki's chest felt tight. "No, it's—just—yeah, I guess I overreacted. I've never liked marijuana. It's complicated."

Meadow stubbed out the joint, jumped up, and opened a window. "Sorry. Sometimes I need it to sleep." Settling back on the couch, she patted the bed next to her. "I remembered you're not into it, but I didn't realize it actually upsets you. I won't smoke around you anymore. What is it, though?"

She sat down. "The smell. It has this weird effect on me. I guess it reminds me of the House."

"Ah. Is it like a trigger?"

"Trigger," Nikki said and laughed, mirthlessly. "That's a

buzzword now, but yes—that's probably right. Certain rooms in the house, especially RJ's room, smelled like weed. I get this scared feeling when I smell it. Also, my ex-husband was a pothead. He smoked almost every night. He'd be in another world, and I couldn't find him—couldn't connect with him."

Meadow nodded. "I get that."

Nikki bit her lip, thinking, okay, time to change the subject. "What are you writing about?"

Meadow looked down at her notebook and chewed on her lip. "The investigation—what really happened with RJ."

Nikki thought, This again? What the hell? Out loud, she asked, "How's it going?"

Meadow said she was trying to get in touch with the detective who'd been in charge of RJ's case. "What do you think? Do you have any ideas?"

Nikki shook her head. "Not really." She didn't want to say, I think you're nuts. She tried for a smile, hoping her feelings wouldn't show. "I'm going to go back to bed. Good night."

Meadow looked shocked, as if she'd slapped her. "Okay. Sorry, I know it's late, but you *said* I could bounce ideas off you. I thought this was something you cared about too."

"It's just that I'm half-asleep."

"Right. Sorry I woke you. Good night." There was an edge to Meadow's voice.

Nikki got back in bed. Meadow seemed pissed or hurt or both. Maybe she shouldn't have been so abrupt with her, but for god's sake, it was three in the morning. She turned over and went back to sleep.

The morning light fell in slices through the slatted blinds. Rolling out of bed, Nikki cracked open her door softly, not wanting to wake Meadow up. The fold-out couch was all closed up and the quilt and pillows in a neat pile. Meadow wasn't in the kitchen or the bathroom either. Did she go for coffee? Nikki's eyes swept the living room once more "Shit!" Meadow's backpack and guitar were gone. On the coffee table, a piece of notebook paper lay waiting. She picked it up by the edges, like it was evidence from a crime scene.

> Phoenix,
>   I'm sorry, I had to leave. I decided to go back to Philly to spend an extra day with Andy. Please forgive. Thanks for everything.
>   Love,
>   Meadow

She flicked the paper with her thumb and middle finger, hard, and it sailed to the floor. "Love?" she said sarcastically. She'd taken the day off so they could spend it together. Now the hours yawned before her, empty. She pulled on her running clothes and shoes and headed for the park.

Without Ira to slow her down, she ran faster than usual. The more she thought about Meadow abandoning her like that, the faster she ran. A pain shot through her ankle, so fierce it stopped her in her tracks. She bent over and rubbed her ankle, then hobbled over to the side of the path. When the pain subsided, she tested out walking, which was doable, and then tried jogging, which was not. Gingerly, she made her way home.

When she opened the door to her apartment, faint traces of her friend were everywhere: the bedding on the couch, the note lying on the floor where Nikki had left it, and Meadow's sandalwood scent. She picked the note up off the kitchen floor, crumpled it, tried to toss it in the garbage but missed, and then threw it directly in the recycling. "Fuck." Scooping it out of the bin, she laid the note on the table, using her palm to smooth out the wrinkles. After she read it again, she folded it up neatly into a square and put it in her desk.

She sat on the couch, propping up her ankle on the coffee table. Sometimes an injury was a message from the body-mind. Right? What was her body trying to tell her? She just wanted the pain to go away, she didn't want a message or any kind of inner fucking monologue. She hobbled over to her desk to get her sketchbook and then sank back into the couch and started drawing, without thinking, a sketch of Meadow, playing her guitar. As she penciled in the outline, tears came to her eyes. She thought she had made a new friend, more than that—a soulmate from her long-gone family, someone who really understood her. How could Meadow do something so mean? Not even waiting until Nikki was up to say goodbye —leaving her a cowardly note and sneaking out before morning? Obviously, Meadow was hurt and angry, and Nikki knew she shouldn't have cut her off so sharply last night, but still, it just wasn't right. Fuck her. Nikki wasn't going to call and say she was sorry; it was Meadow who should apologize.

Chapter 21

Fear of Flying

Deb and Andy waited for the airport shuttle on the sidewalk. She hugged her daughter again. She wished they lived closer, but she didn't say it aloud. She knew how Andy hated it when she said that.

"Mom—promise me something."

"Maybe. What?"

"Call Phoenix and work it out. You seem really upset, and —there are always two sides to every story, and if you talk to her maybe you'll see she didn't really mean it. Friends are important. You taught me that."

Deb was heartened by her daughter's words. But she shook her head. "True, but sometimes you have to part ways if you feel you can't trust the person."

When she got to the airport, she ate a cannabis cookie. It would only take about a half hour to take effect. It didn't make her phobia go away, but it softened the panicky edges.

She'd tried to get an aisle seat, but they were all taken, so she'd ended up with a window seat. She avoided looking out. If the flight was smooth, she'd be fine. It was the turbulence that got to her. And the takeoff. But the landing was okay. Of course that was irrational; statistically speaking, the landing was more dangerous than when you were in the air, but then nothing about phobia was rational, was it, and there you go.

The extra day with Andy had helped keep Deb's mind off Phoenix, but now it was all coming back to hit her. It was bad enough that she had been judgmental about the weed, but then the way she just dismissed her investigation and said good night so—coldly. Deb realized she didn't really *know* Phoenix if she would do something like that. It wasn't the words she said, it was the way she said them. How she just shut Deb out.

The plane taxied, about to take off. Her insides skittered. She took a deep breath, trying to calm herself, and took out her book, *Love*, by Toni Morrison. She held the book tightly while the plane sped up and her heartbeat quickened. She'd loved flying as a kid; the phobia didn't start until she was in her twenties. When she went into therapy years later, she realized the phobia had started right after Ron's death. But that revelation didn't change anything. She was still afraid of flying. The wheels left the ground, and when the plane rose she thought, as usual, I should not be tilted in this wholly unnatural position. I should not be here. I will never do this again. Her heart pounding, she took some deep breaths and reminded herself that her feet were on the floor and she was grounded. As usual, the affirmations did nothing. She was seized with the certainty that the plane would crash, sometime in the next five hours. At the same time, part of her, aided by the cannabis kicking in, floated up and up, out of the plane, someplace where she didn't have to feel anything.

Chapter 22

Boundaries

Nikki had the TV on while she got ready for work. The aftermath of Hurricane Katrina was a nightmare, worse than the storm itself. Buses that were supposed to take residents to safety dropped them off on a highway instead. People who tried to walk over the Crescent City bridge to Gretna were turned away by police with shotguns. If you didn't have the means to get out of New Orleans in a car or on a plane, you were screwed. She slammed her coffee mug down, and it cracked and fell to pieces. Mopping up the coffee, she thought: if she had been living in New Orleans, would she have been able to leave in time? Yes. Probably. She'd probably have had a friend who had a car. More than anything, it was the class divide that ultimately decided who could and couldn't get out.

The morning walk from the subway to the Fort Greene brownstone was her time to mentally gear up for another day of house painting. It wasn't that she disliked the work; in fact, just the opposite, it was actually kind of grounding. But working with kids was her calling. She was waiting, underwater, until she got the news from the Board and could come back up to the surface. And then she'd get her job back. Probably.

By the late afternoon, she'd finished the trim in the large front room and started on the walls. Interesting, she thought, that she was painting interiors. As a child therapist, she helped her clients integrate their interior and exterior worlds. But now she was painting physical interior walls. What did it mean? Nothing, she told herself. It means nothing. She was brought up to believe it was a good thing to look inward. She remembered the House family singing along to the Joni Mitchell song. The lyrics were something like, if you dig deep, you lose sleep, and that makes you heavy company. As a child, she didn't understand what that meant, but later, in college, when she listened to the song, she got it. The lyrics implied that being a heavy made you no fun at all. But the subtext was that going down deep gave meaning to your world, making your life nuanced and shadowed and poetic. Most of her friends and colleagues would agree about the soul-searching— your life was richer because of it. She did too, of course she did. But really, what had she gained over these last months by digging through the shards of her past, trying to remember what happened? True, there was the occasional memory of the House that would pop into her head, like her flash about RJ and the compost the other day. And she was getting fewer of the panicky sensations she'd had when she first started working with Hannah. But she had a deeply felt sense of some kind of trauma as a kid, and she wasn't convinced that RJ's death was it.

She moved the ladder over to the next section of the wall and was climbing back up when she heard the key in the door. The client was home early. "Hi, Rod. I'll be out of your way soon. One more wall to go."

"You don't have to rush," he said. "I'll be working in my

office down the hall. Let me know if you need anything." He smiled.

No, she didn't need anything. Last time, on her way out the door, they had chatted for a while and Rod had sent out some flirtatious feelers. He was attractive and seemed like a nice guy, but no. She told herself: *Boundaries.*

An hour later, she stuck her head in his office before leaving. "Have a good night."

He got up from his desk. "Would you like to stay for a drink?"

"Thanks, but I'm meeting some friends, so I can't," she lied.

On her way home, passing a bar, she looked in the window and felt a wave of longing. Why couldn't she be like those people—meeting up with friends after work—drinking beer, talking, laughing. The people she saw through the glass were in the present moment: watching the game on the screen, yelling in glee for a win, crying out in anger or sadness at a defeat. But who was she kidding? She would never be like them. It wasn't color—the people in that bar were all different shades. It wasn't a class thing either. It was that sometimes she felt like an alien, from a culture of sharing whatever you had, of endless meetings and consensus, and nonviolence training when you were twelve years old. She would always be on the outside looking in. She laughed and told herself, Of course you wouldn't be happy in a sports bar—you barely know the names of the teams. She moved on from the window and made her way home.

In the month since Meadow abruptly ended their friendship, Nikki had been going over what had happened. She understood, maybe, that Meadow was hurt and had fled, but then, to not answer Nikki's two emails and one voice mail over the last few weeks—that really pissed her off. And it hurt.

She unlocked the door to her building and stopped at her mailbox to collect the usual envelopes and junk mail. When she got upstairs, she threw the mail on the kitchen table, where a few pieces of her coffee mug remained from her morning outburst. Her righteous anger hadn't fixed any of the injustice in New Orleans.

Rummaging through the fridge, she found some tortillas and cheese and started making a quesadilla. Then something caught her eye. It was an actual letter, sticking out of the stack of junk mail. Picking it up, she checked the return address. It was from the Board. With a jumpy sensation in her stomach, she ripped open the envelope. She skimmed the paragraphs until she found what she was looking for:

> Summary: Licensee failed to maintain appropriate personal boundaries and engaged in a dual relationship with a client's family.
>
> Action: Penalty: 2 years stayed suspension; 2 years' probation; $1,000 fine.

She read the action part over a few times. What did it mean? She looked up the legal meaning of *stayed* and it meant *stopped*. If the suspension of her license was stopped, then her license wasn't suspended and she could go back to work! She jumped up from the table and raised her arms in victory.

Chapter 23

Home

Deb took one last look around the campsite she'd called home for the last year. She felt strangely guilty, as if she were leaving a lover, when it was just a job. But no, it wasn't just a job, it was a dream. Being a park ranger hadn't brought her the brand-new life she'd thought it would. A lot of picking up trash and handing out maps. But the sabbatical had given her the time and space to create the memorial website, and that had led her to her search for the truth about Ron's death.

Driving down the dirt road, she took in the dawn sky over the purple haunches of the Panamint Mountains. All that follow-your-bliss thing, surely Joseph Campbell would never have coined the phrase if he'd had any idea people would interpret it as a kind of carte blanche to whatever-land. There was a sense of entitlement in the blisserati, she thought. Did she just make up a new word? She would tell Ming about it, who would understand instantly. Sometimes you follow what you *think* is your bliss. But she'd discovered there was no place like home; it was time to click her heels together three times. She missed the sun coming through the French doors, Duncan lying in a patch of gold light, his tail flicking up and slowly lowering.

When she reached the highway and turned toward Bakersfield, she switched on the radio. The news was the usual bullshit. When were they going to get out of Iraq? Just a month ago Cheney said the "insurgency" was in its "last throes," but now he was backpedaling, saying that *throes* refer to a violent period, not an ending. And yesterday Rumsfeld spun it out even further, saying insurgencies can go on for five to twelve years. History was repeating itself. Had they learned nothing from Vietnam? Or had they just learned lessons in how to spin a story?

She stopped at a gas station. Lifting up the nozzle, she stuck it into the opening with a satisfying clunk and held it in place as the gas pumped. And who was letting Cheney and Rumsfeld run the show? George W. *Fuck him.* She must've said the last sentence aloud, because from the other side of the pump a woman with big hair, filling up her tank, grinned sympathetically. "Honey, men are such jackasses. But you'll get over him. There are good ones out there."

Deb returned the smile. "Thanks. I hope so." She didn't tell the woman she wasn't talking about a boyfriend but about the President of the United States. Or that if she *were* going to be pissed at someone she was in love with, it would be Phoenix, but then she'd have to explain even more that Phoenix was a woman but not her *lover*, but on the other hand she *loved* her so much, and it really fucking hurt, and she was really mad. When the pump stopped, she yanked the handle out and rammed it back in its slot.

Hours later, she pulled into her driveway and heaved her bag to the front door. She was tired from the long drive and couldn't wait to be back in her home. On the door, there was an attempted delivery notice from the post office. She grabbed it and examined it—yes! It was from her mother. The box of Ron's stuff. Once inside, she was greeted by Duncan, meowing angrily at her for being gone so long. Ming had brought him over for her homecoming. Kneeling down, she scratched his ears, and before long he was purring and nuzzling.

The next morning, she went to the post office as soon as it opened. In her truck, she ripped open the box and dug through it, finding photos and papers and mementos, but no journal. The folder the detective had given her wasn't there. An unlabeled file caught her eye. Inside was the police report from Ron's death. The pain of seeing it in all in black and white, in police-speak, made her stomach clench. Cause of death: Suicide. The report was signed and below the signature was typed: Tadhg Murphy. She smiled: Maybe Murphy was a common name in 1975, but Tadhg?

This time, when she called the San Francisco Police Department, the man she talked to said Ty Murphy was retired. He wouldn't give her a phone number, but said he'd contact Murphy, pass on her name and number, and maybe Ty would call her.

She disconnected and slammed the kitchen table in frustration.

That afternoon, she and Ming sat in her backyard with mugs of green tea. Deb rolled a joint and handed it to her friend. "This is really mild."

Ming lit it, inhaled, and passed it back. She blew the smoke out. "Did you talk to Phoenix yet?"

"No."

"Look—she's called and emailed you. She obviously wants

to make amends. Why don't you just talk to her? I know about girlfriend-ship pain. It's the worst. I think it's worse than romantic love problems. I mean it. Just get in touch with her." She raised her eyebrows at Deb.

Deb handed her the joint. "Maybe I should."

Chapter 24

Budget Cuts

Nikki approached the clinic building. Her palms were sweating. Keep your feet on the ground, she told herself. Wiping her hands on her jacket, she started up the steps. For nine years, walking up these same steps had felt like coming home. Her job had been a haven. Before she fucked it all up. But today's meeting might change all that. Bring her back to her true calling. At the door to the building, she tapped in the code on the key pad, but nothing happened. Of course they'd changed it. She pressed the intercom button.

A voice answered—it didn't sound like Bianca, the long-time receptionist. "May I help you?"

"I'm here to see Susan." She cleared her throat. "Dr. Parker. I have a ten o'clock appointment."

"And you are?"

"Nikki Gold."

The door clicked, and she pushed it open. Inside, a new, skinny young receptionist in a crisp white blouse addressed her coolly. "Please have a seat and I'll tell her you're here."

What happened to Bianca, the plump, mother-hen receptionist who'd been there longer than she had, who'd always looked out for her? So much had changed in four months. She sat down in the waiting room, taking some consolation that no one else was seated there; she didn't want to have to face one of her kids' parents. They weren't her kids, though, she reminded herself—they were clients. Former clients. She picked up a copy of *Psychology Today* from the coffee table and pretended to read it.

The hallway door opened and a claw of fear snagged her chest. It was Victor. Fortunately, he didn't notice her. He had a hurried conversation with the receptionist—it sounded like he was freaking out because the internet connection was down. Nikki kept her eyes on the magazine.

Then she heard a voice. "Nikki." She looked up. Vic stood a couple of feet in front of her, a coolly polite expression on his face, his arms full of folders.

Shit. She had hoped to avoid this. She stood up. "How are you?"

He tightened his arms around his files, hugging them to his chest. "Good, and you?"

"Fine."

"Great," he said frostily and turned away. The hallway door shut behind him with a soft click. Without looking, Nikki sensed the receptionist's scrutiny. She went back to pretending to read the magazine. If she got her job back, she would make sure she didn't have to share an office with Vic.

After a few minutes, the security door that led to the therapy offices opened, and there was her friend Imani, all smiles. She came over and gave Nikki a big hug. "Fingers crossed," she whispered, and went back through the door to the offices.

Nikki looked at her watch. She'd been waiting for ten minutes. The receptionist's phone rang and she answered it.

"I'll send her in." Opening the hall door for her with her security card, the receptionist gave her a genuine smile this time. Maybe she knew something. Was she being friendly because Nikki was about to be brought back into the fold? Or was the receptionist sorry for her because she was about to get the axe?

Susan's door was open. She greeted Nikki, standing up and leaning across her desk to shake her hand. Nikki shook her hand and closed the door behind her. Before her supervisor even opened her mouth, Nikki knew. Susan hadn't bothered to come out from behind her desk to greet her, her shoulders were practically up to her ears, and she held a rubber stress ball in her hand, squeezing it for dear life.

"It's nice to see you. Please—sit down."

"Good to see you too." She felt the blood draining from her face.

"So—good news from the Board," Susan said cheerily. "They copied me on the letter to you. You've got the two-year probation, but that won't be any problem. This is a terrific outcome."

"Yes, I was relieved," Nikki said cautiously, waiting for what would come next.

"Unfortunately—" Susan took a deep breath and exhaled noisily. "We've had some budget cuts."

Ah, she thought, budget cuts. So convenient for times like this.

"So," Susan continued, "we won't be able to offer you your position back. I'm sorry it worked out this way. But feel free to use me as a reference, I'll give you a good recommendation."

Nikki attempted to speak but nothing came out. The fury was building inside her. She wanted to say, "After nine fucking years of working my ass off, this is all you have to offer me?" All the times she'd worked late or on the weekends—seeing her clients at the times that served the working parents who wouldn't be able to get their kids to the clinic otherwise. All the difficult clients she'd taken on—"Give the kid to Nikki," her coworkers would say. Susan would ask her if she was willing, but everyone knew Nikki would take the kids who were "challenging"—a euphemism for withdrawn and sullen or even potentially violent. She'd been kicked, scratched, and slapped. But it was okay with her because they were children who were hurt inside, and they needed some kind of connection; sometimes that was the only way they knew how to reach out, and she was there, ready and willing to receive it. But she didn't say all that aloud. Because Susan knew it. Which meant there was only one explanation: behind her semblance of compassion, there was a kind of passive-aggressive payback. Susan was actually firing her but didn't want to cop to it. Budget cuts: what bull-shit. Don't say *fuck you*, she told herself. Don't burn your bridges.

"And since this is technically a layoff," Susan continued brightly, "you'll be able to collect unemployment."

Nikki blurted, "What about if you get more funding in the future? Would you have a place for me then?" Her voice sounded strangled to her ears. Holding on to this last shred of hope, she waited for the answer, even though she knew what it would be.

Susan avoided eye contact and gave the stress ball a reso-lute squeeze. "I can't promise you that."

And then she bolted. Storming through the lobby and past the receptionist, who raised her eyebrows but didn't say anything, Nikki made it out the door, down the steps of the building, and halfway down the block before letting out the breath she'd been holding and yelling, "Fuck, Fuck, Fuck!" The passersby ignored her. What she needed was a drink. In a bar. Maybe she could be like one of those people who sat in a bar and drank to forget their problems.

After stopping at a bar for a whiskey on the way home, she remembered she wasn't one of those people. The alcohol had only dulled her righteous anger and made her feel sad. On the walk home, a recriminating voice started up. If you hadn't gone to the soccer game, or if you'd signed the agreement with Susan early on and worked on having better boundaries, you'd still have your job. Or if you'd realized that Vic was so hurt and angry he'd do something vindictive, you could have tried to make peace with him. In fact, if you hadn't had sex with him at all, this whole mess wouldn't have happened. If, if, if.

Once home, she cast about for something to do. She made a cup of tea and sat at her desk by the window, gazing out at her sycamore tree. Picking up her sketchbook, she began to draw. The familiar feel of the pencil in her hand, the smell of graphite, and the whispery sound of her sketching comforted her.

She woke up coughing, her throat dry and sore. Her head was on the desk, her hand on the sketchbook. She sat up and picked up the pencil from the floor. She got a glass of water and gulped it down. She checked her email, still hoping for something from Meadow, even though it had been over a month since they'd seen each other. Nothing. Okay, she'd been insensitive, and Meadow had been angry and hurt, probably. She freaked out and she fled. Nikki got that. But radio silence? She didn't understand that. Didn't Meadow owe her at least an honest response? Should Nikki write her again? No, she'd already contacted her a few times.

She went to bed and slept restlessly. Something woke her from a dream. She and Meadow were at the kitchen table in her trailer in the desert. Meadow was a teenager, all blond braids and long skirts, and was saying to her tenderly: "When people get hurt, they get scared. But you know what? It's okay to be scared. You can have a physical reaction, like animals or babies do—they tremble. It's the body's way of healing the psyche."

She turned on the light and wrote down the dream, shivering in the warm night. What Nikki had given—to the kids, to the clinic; all dismissed in an instant. She felt betrayed. Exploited. Fucked. Her throat was still sore. She got out of bed, unsteady on her feet, and went to the kitchen for a glass of water. Gulping it down, she looked out the kitchen window. A woman walked quickly down the sidewalk, heading home, her shoulders hunched. The streetlights glowed, and a few leaves, jostled by wind, drifted down. Betrayal. If she felt that about losing her job, maybe that was what Meadow felt, in a friendship kind of way. The kitchen clock said it was a few minutes before midnight, so in California it was just before nine. Not too late to call. She made her way back to her bed and put the glass of water on her nightstand. There was her landline, sitting by her bed. So much nicer than a cell phone for a conversation. The heft of the old-fashioned receiver in her hand felt comforting, reminding her of long talks on the phone with friends before cell phones, the tones of their voices richer and deeper. She called Meadow but of course she didn't answer. That was no surprise; the phone service in Death Valley was spotty. But then her voice mail came on. The husky tone of her voice proclaimed, "Hi, this is Deb. I'm back in town. Please leave a message."

Back in town? Which town? She started to speak but her voice was hoarse and no words came out. She swallowed. "Meadow. This is Nikki. I mean, Phoenix. I was just thinking of you and—I thought I'd call. To say hello."

She turned off the light and slid under the covers. She was

starting to drift off to sleep again when the phone rang. There was no screen on her phone, and she couldn't see who was calling. Half-asleep, she mumbled "Hello," then coughed.

"Hi, Phoenix."

Meadow's voice slid through her like warm honey. She sat up in bed. "You called back. Your voice. So good to hear."

"Yours too. Are you all right? You sound sick."

"I'm fine. Your voice mail message said you're back. Back where?"

"Oakland."

"Wow. What made you move back?"

"There's no place like home."

Nikki shivered and pulled the covers up around her shoulders. "I'm picturing you there in your little cottage with your cat." Meadow laughed and Nikki relaxed. Maybe it was all okay now. "Like I said in my email, I apologize. I know it was harsh—cutting you off, not hearing you out about your investigation. And maybe I was a bit judgmental about the weed thing too. But it wasn't personal, it was really just my issues."

Meadow sighed. Or maybe, Nikki thought, she was blowing out the smoke from a joint.

"It seemed like you thought I was nuts," Meadow said. "Like I was some kind of crazy conspiracy theorist. But I think I'm onto something. And I have to know the truth."

"I know what you mean."

"You do?"

Nikki coughed, then took a drink of water, soothing her sore throat. "You can't live with a lie. And you want to pursue justice for RJ. That's admirable. I think when you started talking about it, I just got scared."

Meadow said, "Oh, I didn't think of that. That makes sense. Because it's part of your history too. And then I ran away. I'm sorry for disappearing on you like that."

"I understand, though. I've done that. Run away. I always assume people will leave because . . ." Nikki said.

"Because?"

"Not sure where I was going with that." She felt feverish and threw the covers back. "Because I'm too fucked up. Not on the surface, but underneath."

"That's how I see myself, in a way. Too messed up for love," Meadow said, with a hollow laugh.

Nikki was surprised. "I don't see you that way. Not at all."

Silence on the other end of the line, and then she heard Meadow sigh.

Maybe, Nikki thought, she could make amends. "How is your investigation going?" she asked.

"Are you sure you want to hear about it?"

"Yes, I really do."

Meadow filled her in on what she'd done so far, and said she was waiting to hear back from the detective who'd been in charge of RJ's case. "And I need to talk to Che again. I left a message for him, but he hasn't called back."

"What if I call him?"

"Would you?" Meadow said, a note of excitement in her voice.

"Yes. I want to know the truth too."

Chapter 25

Detective Murphy

The fall quarter hadn't started yet, and the courtyard outside the UC Berkeley library was quiet. Deb, taking her morning break, sat on a cement bench and dug through her bag to check her phone. A new voice mail—probably spam, she thought. It was an older man's voice, gravelly and clipped. "This is Ty Murphy. I got a message from the precinct to call you. Here's my home number."

"Yes!" She couldn't believe it. This was it. Detective Murphy had been so kind all those years ago, and maybe he would help her now. She called back right away. A harried-sounding woman answered. Deb introduced herself and said she was returning Ty Murphy's call.

The woman sighed. "This is Mrs. Murphy. Are you from the Senior Center?"

"No, I'm actually calling about a case Mr. Murphy worked on in the 1970s that involved my brother."

"The 1970s?" the woman said. "Oh, dear. I doubt if you'll have any luck, but you can go ahead and try. I'll put him on."

She called out to her husband, and he got on the phone. When Deb told him about Ron, giving him dates and places, he said, "Oh, yeah. The Zebra killings."

"I don't think," she started to say, and he interrupted her.

"Yes, the Death Angels. Serial murders. There was that one on . . . on . . . Divisadero Street."

"This wasn't on Divisadero," Deb said. "It was in a house in the Haight-Ashbury, and it was ruled a suicide. In 1975. Are you saying it was a murder?"

"Oh no, honey, the Zebra killings stopped in . . . in . . ."

"I'm talking about my brother's death, which was ruled a suicide. His name was Ron Travis. I'm looking into his case because there might be new evidence that it was a murder."

There was silence. Was he still on the line? "Mr. Murphy?"

"What's your name again?"

"Deb Travis. You came and met me at school when I was at San Francisco State and gave me my brother's journal."

"Are you from the school? Is little Bobby in trouble again? Are you his teacher?"

Deb heard a voice in the background talking to him—his wife. "Give me the phone. Give me the phone."

Then her voice. "Miss, my husband is not well. I don't think he'll be able to help you."

Shit. Of course—the pauses, the confusion. Dementia. "Thank you, Mrs. Murphy. I'm so sorry to have bothered you."

That night, she went over her notes. Phoenix reached Che, but he'd told her the exact same thing he'd told Deb. Phoenix said he was broken up about Willow's death, even though he hadn't seen her in years.

Deb went down her list of people to call: her mother, Mama Linda, and Matt. She called her brother first, even though she didn't expect him to be supportive. When she told him everything she'd found out about Ron's death so far in her search, there was an ominous silence.

"Deb."

"Yes."

"I would think you would have asked me, a law enforcement professional, what I thought *before* you went off on some wild goose chase. Do I think Ron was an informant? No. Do I think the police were involved in a cover-up? No. Where is this coming from? After you put so much into your memorial website project, putting it out there that Ron committed suicide because of the war, after all that—now you're saying it's murder?"

"I'm not *saying* it is, I'm looking into it."

"Well, look no further. They had it all, forensics and fingerprinting and interviews with neighbors who heard the shot but saw no one coming in and out of the house. Just let it go. Ron had mental health problems. That's it. He was bipolar."

"What? That's so out of left field!"

"You don't have to yell. I'm not saying he was diagnosed, I'm saying that back then we didn't know how common it was or what it looked like. But I'm pretty sure that's what he had."

"No, that's not right. I mean, yeah, I know he would get depressed sometimes, and he would sort of withdraw and shut off. But that never lasted. Before long, he'd start joking around, and he'd get everyone laughing, and his whole mood would change."

"Yeah," Matt said. "Right. That jokester thing was his cover. Look, Mom and I agree on this. You should talk to her."

"About my investigation? I'm not sure that's a good idea."

221

"No, I mean ask Mom about Ron's mental health. She'll tell you."

"I guess I can't count on you to look into this new development, then."

"Deb," he snapped, "there is no new development. Look, just call Mom. I gotta go." And he disconnected.

"Fuck you," she said to the empty cottage. Duncan climbed into her lap. She stroked his fur. It was probably too late to call her mom—10:00 p.m. in Grand Rapids. But Mom loved email, treating it exactly like it was the postal mail, writing articulate, fully realized letters that were just like the ones she used to write on paper. Deb wrote a carefully worded email saying she had talked to Matt and asking whether her mom thought Ron was bipolar.

Before bed, she checked her email, just in case her mom had been up late. There was already a response:

Dear Deb,

Last year, I read an article in the *Oprah Magazine* about bipolar disorder. When I read it, I got chills. I thought it sounded so much like our Ron.

I took him to the doctor when he was thirteen because he was so moody; he'd be so happy and then so sad, and then so angry, like a roller coaster. But Dr. Ivers said it was just puberty.

I never brought it up because you were always so sure he did what he did because of the war.

Deb, after I read that article, I talked about it with Pastor Ken, and he said something that really helped: no matter why our Ron took his life, it doesn't matter—we still love him, and God still loves him.

I hope that will give you some peace.

Love,
Mom

Deb sighed. Of course it won't give me some peace, Mom. I'm not a Christian, and I haven't been for thirty years.

Chapter 26

Che

1975

D rinking coffee at the breakfast table just after dawn, he thumbed through his well-worn copy of *Blood in My Eye.* "You want to know what it means to be a Black man in America? Read George Jackson's book. He finished it *days* before the San Quentin prison guards fucking murdered him," Cinque had said, back when Che was a volunteer tutor at the Vacaville prison. That was before Cin escaped from Vacaville. Before they formed the Symbionese Liberation Army. Before everything blew up.

The morning light slanted in the window and lit the table, warming him. Che liked this house. He hoped he wouldn't have to pick up and run, leave everything at a moment's notice. Looking out the window to the garden below, he couldn't help but see RJ, doing his goddamn composting and weeding and whatever-the-fuck. Doesn't he ever stop? What a motherfucker. Everyone thinks he's such a saint. Don't they get it? For Chrissake, he was a *Marine.* A hired killer. He says he was never in combat, he just fixed generators on the base or some shit. Any way you look at it, he's the enemy. He sold out to the military-industrial complex. *Once a Marine, always a Marine*, that was the saying. Right. Che still didn't understand why Mama Linda even let RJ into the collective.

And then there was the way Willow looked at RJ. Anybody could see she was fucking hung up on him. It's not like Che and Willow were in a *relationship*. More like friends who sometimes fucked and sometimes fought and sometimes even liked each other. But Stretch was hot for RJ, too—what was it with that guy? She wasn't in love with him or anything, but she seriously wanted to ball him, that was clear. And why was it that RJ never had a girlfriend or someone he fucked? Because, Che thought, he's a homo. In the closet. He'd asked him once, point-blank, if he was gay, and RJ had laughed grimly and said he wished he was, that would make things easier. Whatever that meant. Yeah, he's probably a homo, and that's why he's never even brought someone home for a one-night stand. He did have that friend from the food co-op who came over for dinner sometimes, but she was probably gay too. Che didn't have a problem with that. Mama Linda was a lesbian, and that was cool. She made them all swear not to tell anyone outside the house, and as far as he knew, no one ever had. But, she always said, *inside* the house, we're open, we don't keep secrets from each other. Okay, he'd love to be open and honest and all that shit. But he couldn't and wouldn't tell anyone in the collective about the SLA. If they knew, and if the FBI ever came for him, they could be considered coconspirators. He didn't want any of them to be hurt by his stupid past. He should never have put up the Che Guevara poster in his room—once the collective started with the house name, it stuck. But maybe the FBI wouldn't find him here; he'd covered his tracks, and the place was like a safe house without meaning to be. Plus the rent was cheap, and even with all the fucking rules it was a cool place to live. It was a short walk to All You Knead, and he only had to work two shifts to make enough bread for the rent. The diner was a far-out place to work because no one hassled you, the chicks were fine, and you got a free meal at the end of your shift.

He was hoping to be upstairs by the time RJ came back inside, but no such luck. The sounds of RJ's boots on the deck and the squeaky kitchen door were enough to piss him off.

"Hey, man," RJ said. "What's happening? You going to work?"

"I'm off today. Gonna reinforce the railing. Get ready for the big shindig tomorrow. You?"

"Just got off the night shift. Did some gardening. Going to sleep now." RJ's eyes were bloodshot and he had a strange look. He started to say something but then headed down the hall and up the stairs.

That was weird, Che thought. He hadn't ever seen RJ look freaked.

A while later, someone came into the room. He kept his eyes on his book. Out of the corner of his eye he saw her. As long as he didn't make eye contact, she wouldn't bug him. But she stayed put, staring at him. He couldn't help it, he looked up. Those dark-as-night eyes, so wide and fierce. How could such a little person pack so much into her gaze? She was going to ask him for something, and most likely he wouldn't be able to say no.

"Knock Knock," she said.

He knew what was coming. The joke she'd made up a couple of years ago was how she got her house name. "Who's there?"

"Nik-Knock!" She giggled, as if it were a brand-new joke. "Che. I want to hear the box song."

He put the book down. "I don't know. It's early. People might be sleeping."

"No. Mama Linda is at work and everyone else is awake 'cept RJ, but he sleeps like the dead. Ha ha! He sleeps like the dead, and I want to hear the Dead on the record player!" Nik-Knock put her hands on her hips.

It was funny how she was more like a miniature Mama Linda, the way she talked and her gestures, than she was like her mother. Sighing, he put the book down and stood up. She grinned and ran to the record shelves, pulling out the Grateful Dead album *American Beauty*.

He put the record on and gently lowered the needle to the groove for the kid's favorite song. They sang along, and at the chorus, Nik-Knock belted out the lyric: "Just a box of rain . . ." For some reason, she loved that line.

When the song was over, she said, "Flip me, please."

"I think you might be getting too old for that."

She shook her head. "Please?"

He lifted her up and hung her upside down over one shoulder.

She yelped with glee. "Again!"

Willow came into the room and put a bowl of granola on the table. "Nik-Knock. Breakfast. We have to get to the bus on time." She gave Che one of her mixed-message looks—slightly annoyed, which meant *You're getting in the way of our morning routine*, with a flicker of an amused smirk that meant *I dig it when you horse around with my daughter*.

After they left, he went out to the front steps to get the paper. The *San Francisco Chronicle* was a fascist pig publication, but Mama Linda subscribed to it, so he figured he might as well read it, just to see what the Man was up to. He took the paper with him back to the dining room. There was another front page story about the SLA bank robbery in

Carmichael last week and the hunt for Tania and the others. He shook his head. *Fuck.* The robbery didn't bother him, but that they'd killed a bank customer in the process was so fucked up. He'd split with them two years ago when they murdered Foster. Killing a Black man, even if he was superintendent of schools and they disagreed with his fascist policies, was wrong. It was against everything they stood for. *Had* stood for. He hated what the SLA had become, the kidnapping and murder. He still believed in their original vision, to end racism, monogamy, and the prison system. To establish a homeland in the United States for people of color. *Death to the fascist insect that preys upon the people.* He didn't have any regrets about breaking with them, but still, they'd been his comrades, and in a weird way he missed them.

Every night, he reminded himself of his new identity and history. Joshua Brown had a driver's license and passport and social security number. "My name is Joshua," he would say, before he went to sleep and first thing in the morning. The FBI was on a manhunt for the remaining SLA members, and Tania/Patty Hearst was the prize. What would happen if they caught her and she decided to make a deal? What if she made him a scapegoat? She knew his real name, so the FBI would be looking for Daniel Schwartz. That was good. But they might, somehow, connect the dots from Daniel Schwartz to Joshua Brown.

He heard someone coming down the stairs, laughing—it was Stretch and Orchid. They came into the dining room, Stretch in a see-through blouse, braless as usual; Orchid teetering on high heels in a vintage cocktail dress, padded to the hilt with falsies.

"Darling," Orchid said. "You're so sexy, with your wire-rimmed glasses, reading the paper. You have this kind of *je-ne-sais-quoi* Jewish intellectual look. Oh my. That curly hair.

And that man-of-the-people thing with your blue work shirt. Are you sure you don't want to take a walk on the wild side, straight boy?"

He grinned and put the paper down. Orchid was the only homosexual he really liked. "No way," Che said. "But your shows are far fucking out. When's the next one?"

"Funny you should ask that," Orchid said.

Stretch cut in, "Would you be a sweetheart, Che, and run lights for us Monday night? We're doing a joint show: Working Women Dance Collective and Angels of Light. It's a fundraiser for the Haight-Ashbury Free Clinic."

"Sure, I'll run lights," Che said.

"Outta sight!" Stretch climbed in his lap, hugging him. He squeezed her ass. It was probably a good thing they weren't balling anymore. Things were already complicated enough with Willow.

Stretch spotted the article he was reading. "Jesus, the SLA are some weird fuckers. And Patty Hearst—the heiress turned revolutionary. That's wild. She could've escaped by now if she really wanted to, right? She must be into it."

Tania, he corrected her, silently. *Not Patty*. Aloud, he said, "Yeah, it's bizarre."

Stretch shook her head. "I'm all for revolution, but this is some fucking terrorist shit. Come on, Orchid, let's split; we gotta get to rehearsal." On her way out the door, she called back to Che, "Don't forget to fix the railing!"

"Yeah, I'm taking care of it." Jesus, the women in this house. Was she nagging him now too?

He finished the paper, ate some toast, and headed down to the basement. Making a series of trips back and forth, he brought up the sawhorses, lumber, and tools and set them up on the deck.

Starting up the circular saw, he made the first cut and

blew the sawdust away. The clean smell of pine cleared his head, and for the first time in months he actually felt good about what he was doing. He was making something with his hands, working out in the open air. He had all day to do the job, so he didn't have to rush. He'd told Willow he'd check on Nik-Knock when she got home from school, see that she got settled in and all, make her a snack.

It was a good thing RJ was asleep. If he was around, he'd be hovering and saying how *he* would do it differently, in other words, better than Che. Or he would keep offering to help until Che would snap. They'd tried working together before, and it just didn't fly. He snorted. Why did the house-mates like RJ so much? What if they found out the real story, like, that RJ sold pot, when it was a house rule not to deal drugs out of the house? Then there was the other thing. One day he was crossing the Panhandle on his way to the food co-op, and he saw RJ there in the park, talking to a guy who had narc written all over him. The narc handed RJ a piece of paper, and he looked at it and shrugged his shoulders. Okay, maybe Che was paranoid and the guy was a Jehovah's Witness or a Scientologist. Or maybe he was right, and RJ was a police informant.

A couple of hours later, he was making one more cut when the back door banged open. It was Nik-Knock, her face drained of color, her small body shaking. He turned off the saw. She opened her mouth like she was trying to say something, but no words came out. He scooped her up and sped into the house. Surveying the downstairs and finding nothing, he ran up the stairs with the child in his arms.

They reached the second floor. And nothing was ever the same after that.

Chapter 27

Santa Fe

2005

Airline seats were not made for tall, big-boned people like Nikki. Squirming in her seat, she tried to put a bit more distance between her and the man seated next to her. When Meadow had suggested they visit Mama Linda together, she'd jumped at the opportunity. She had waited too long to see Mama Linda.

She was excited about seeing Meadow again, but nervous. Was the rift between them truly resolved? She didn't want to feel like she was walking on eggshells around her.

She tried to concentrate on her book—*Twilight*—a young adult novel that was all the rage. Her new job at the foster care agency was starting in October, in a couple of weeks, and she was reading a YA book to get into the teen mindset. After reading a few chapters, she gave up on the paranormal romance and stared out the window.

When she got off the plane in Santa Fe, there was a voice mail on her phone from a number she didn't recognize. "This is Petro. I hope you don't mind I am calling you. I hear from my sister you are no longer therapist of my niece. So I am thinking. Maybe there is no problem and we see each other now. I invite you to soft opening of my restaurant, Pan-Brooklyn, next Saturday. I hope you will come." He gave her the address and said if she couldn't make it, maybe they could meet for coffee sometime. Listening to his voice, she got a buzz, a delicious sort of wave of excitement she hadn't felt for so long. She'd be back in town next Saturday. She would go and check out the gentlemanly Petro.

The shuttle pulled up to the adobe house, and Mama Linda came out the door and down the path, her face lit with a broad smile. She moved more carefully than Nikki remembered, planting each foot on the path with concentration. Her salt-and-pepper hair was no longer in a puffy Afro, but she still wore it natural. The orange of her dress set off her umber-brown skin.

"Nik-Knock!" She reached out her arms, tears in her eyes. "Meadow just called; she'll be here soon."

After a brief struggle over who would carry her bag, which Nikki won, they stepped into the house. The living room, kitchen, and dining area were connected in an airy, open space, terracotta-tiled and furnished in a southwestern style, with hand-woven rugs, the soft glow of lamplight, and the curved adobe walls. "This is breathtaking," Nikki said.

They sat on the patio, sipping margaritas from salt-rimmed glasses. It was dusk, and the lights of neighboring houses winked on the sloping hills.

"How is your health?" Nikki asked. "Soon you'll be done with the Tamoxifen, right?"

"Yes—almost at the five-year point. My markers have been way down for three years now, so it's looking good."

"That's a relief. But it must've been difficult."

Mama Linda pursed her lips and didn't answer right away. "It was, but mostly—it was a healing journey. It got me back into making art."

"Listen, you have to promise me something. If you ever— and I'm not saying this will happen, but if you're ever sick again, please let me know. I could come stay with you for a while. Take you to treatments or whatever. Spend some time with you."

"Thank you, sugar. I don't think it will come back, though."

The door to the patio slid open, and there was Meadow, her cheeks flushed with excitement.

After a boisterous reunion, Mama Linda went and got Meadow a margarita and then disappeared into the kitchen to warm up the food she'd prepared. Meadow right away started talking about her investigation and Nikki listened closely, determined to show her friend she would be there for her.

Mama Linda brought out green chile stew—a traditional New Mexican dish—plus rice and beans and salad. Nikki ate too much of the delicious stew, which had just the right bit of tartness and heat.

She and Meadow washed the dishes, and when they came back to the patio, Mama Linda had lit lanterns. In the soft night air, the desert stretched around them like a warm embrace. Nikki took a big breath. "Mama Linda. You said some things have to be discussed in person. Here we are. What happened the day RJ died?"

Mama Linda nodded her head slowly and began. "Your mother had a new, full-time job, and so she was free to walk you to the school bus but not to pick you up in the afternoon. You were seven years old, and in those days, it was acceptable for children to walk around on their own. Not like it is now. That day," she paused, and when she started again, her voice was shaking, "That day, after school, you let yourself in with your key and—well, you must've gone upstairs to RJ's room first thing. And you found him. His body. There was a lot of blood. Maybe you looked for me or your mom, I don't know, because we weren't there, but Che was on the back deck and he said you banged out the back door, trembling and unable to speak." Mama Linda's voice broke.

Nikki started to say something but her throat was closed. She tried again. "I *found* his body?" She could barely breathe. A shiver ran through her.

Meadow had had her face in her hands, but now she lifted her head, and she and Mama Linda both moved toward Nikki and put their arms around her.

"Yes," Mama Linda whispered. "I'm so sorry. We shouldn't have let that happen."

"But how can you be sure I found him, if you weren't there?" Nikki asked, her voice escalating to a shout.

"It's what Che said, but also the police dusted the floor, and they found your little footprints," Mama Linda said softly, her eyes tearing.

"Why didn't you tell me?" They had been lying to her, all this time. A bolt of anger shot through her, and she started to stand up but then sat back down. "And you," she said to Meadow, "when we reconnected, you knew I was trying to remember something. Why didn't you tell me then?"

"I had no idea," Meadow said, shaking her head. "I swear. I—"

Mama Linda cut in, "Willow, Stretch, Che, and I decided not to tell anyone Phoenix found the body. I mean, we told the police—we had to. But aside from that, we made a pact not to tell anyone else. Meadow, it was almost like if we didn't tell you, then it didn't happen. Phoenix, when you made up the story that RJ moved to Oregon, at first we would remind you that he'd died, but you continued to insist he'd moved away. After a while we went along with your fictional version. We really thought it was for the best."

Meadow, her face drained of color, asked, "What else do we not know? Che thinks RJ was murdered. Is that what happened? Did he tell the police?"

"I know what Che thought. But RJ wasn't murdered," Mama Linda said. "Che didn't tell the police his theory. He was scared to death of the cops. I have a feeling he was running from something, I don't know what. But his police informant story—that was crazy, because RJ was so anti-police. He hated the military after his time in the Marines, and he put law enforcement in the same bag. He wouldn't have wanted anything to do with the cops."

Nikki folded back into herself and watched her two friends. Why were they talking about all this stuff? What about her, what she'd just found out?

"But what if that was just an act—what if Che is right?" Meadow said.

Mama Linda shook her head. "There was so much evidence. Even though he didn't leave a note, the police found enough to prove it was suicide."

"In a way, his journal was like a suicide note," Meadow said. "I thought I packed it with his other stuff and stored it in my mom's basement, but she just sent me the box, and the journal wasn't there. Did I ever show it to you?"

Mama Linda didn't answer at first. Then she put her hand gently on Meadow's shoulder. "Sugar, you gave it to me. You said it was too painful to have around, but you didn't want to throw it away, either, and I offered to keep it for you."

"What? I don't remember that. Wait, do you still have it?"

"I do. You want to see it?"

"Yes."

"I'll be right back." Mama Linda disappeared into the dark house.

Meadow turned to Nikki and, with a sharp intake of breath, said, "Oh, Nik-Knock. How terrifying it must've been for you. No wonder you couldn't remember it." She put her arms around her friend, and something broke inside Nikki. She put her head on Meadow's shoulder and sobbed. Soon she felt Mama Linda's comforting touch as well, and that brought on another burst. After a while, she sniffed and wiped her eyes, moving out of the hug. "Wow. Thank you both. All those tears just waiting to come." Mama Linda brought her a box of tissues, and Nikki blew her nose. She offered a weak smile, then, "I'm okay. Really."

Mama Linda switched on the patio lights and handed a brown accordion folder to Meadow, who opened it, pulled out a sheaf of papers with typewritten text, and started leafing through it. Nikki watched her friend closely.

"This isn't how I remember it," Meadow said, her voice tight. Dividing the stack equally, she handed out the three piles. "The pages aren't numbered, so keep them in the same order, please. When we're done with these, we can switch."

The paper was cool and crinkly under Nikki's fingers. It was the same type of paper her mother used to roll into her typewriter to write poems. Onionskin. And the same kind of typewritten print. Courier font. As she read through the pages, Nikki felt like she had slipped into Ron's mind. This was not the RJ she knew, but a different man. It was like when you dream about someone you know well, but instead of that familiar person, their doppelganger says and does things your friend never would.

236

One page was full of a rant about how women were bad, and you should never trust them. But there were many more tirades about how men are inherently evil. And then she saw her house name.

```
I have to protect Nik-Knock and Deb
from males. All men are predators.
```

Nikki's belly clenched. Don't take it on, she told herself. Don't take his fears into your body.

When each of them had finished her first stack, Meadow, with a sigh, shook her head slowly and thumbed through her pages until she found one passage. "Maybe Matt and my mom were right about Ron after all. Listen to this:

```
The whole Watergate break-in was actu-
ally a power trip by Johnson to over-
throw Nixon. Charles Manson was behind
it too, and behind them were the inter-
planetary aliens in the top ranks of
the military-industrial complex. They
manipulate the government like puppets
on a string."
```

Meadow set down the page and swallowed hard.

"What do you mean, your mom and Matt were right? About what?" Mama Linda asked.

"They think Ron was bipolar or—mentally ill, anyway. Phoenix, you're a therapist. What do you think?"

Nikki hated you're-a-therapist questions. "I wouldn't make a diagnosis just from reading this. It seems like he was delusional, and yes, it was likely he had some sort of mental illness. Some of the stuff here is a mystery, though, like the two articles from a church newsletter in Grand Rapids—he'd cut them out and pasted them onto his journal pages."

"They're probably from our church newsletter," Meadow said. "My mom always read through it faithfully, and she used to send us copies of it after we moved away." She rolled her eyes. "I'm surprised he would clip anything from it, though."

"There are newspaper article clippings in what I read too," Mama Linda said. "About the fall of Saigon and Operation Babylift. I remember how upset he was when that all went down—it was like he held himself personally responsible. Those are from April 1975, not that long before he died."

Meadow nodded. "Okay, let's read the rest and we can talk when we're done."

The night air was chilly, and they all moved inside to the living room, settling on the couch, taking another section of the journal to read.

As she pored over the pages, Nikki kept getting a funny feeling in her chest. It was the vibe she sometimes got when she had a client who was holding something back.

An hour later, they'd each combed through the entire journal. They spread out the pages on the coffee table and compared notes about chronology, agreeing on a sequence and numbering the pages in that order.

When that was done, Mama Linda brought out a bottle of wine and poured three glasses. "Meadow," she said, "you start. What do you think?"

Meadow took a sip of wine. Looking down at the neatly stacked pages and back up at her friends, she sighed. "He doesn't come out and say he's going to commit suicide, but . . . he is so out of touch with reality and so despondent. So. I believe it now, that he killed himself." She stopped and brushed away tears. "As far as Che's weird-ass theories, there's nothing here to confirm them. Not a hint of working with the police or dealing drugs or anything like that." She placed her hand on the pile of papers, bound together with a binder clip, and rested it there. "There are so many strands here—the war, diatribes about religion, rants about men as sexual predators. I don't know what to think. My stomach hurts."

Nikki reached out at the same moment as Mama Linda, and each placed her hand lightly on Meadow's. After a while, Nikki said, "Those passages about religion and Jesus and sin. I wonder *why*."

Deb shrugged. "Starting when he was around fifteen, he had—I guess you could call it a crisis of faith. I stopped going to church as soon as I left home, but I was never conflicted like Ron was. For his whole life, it was like a love-hate relationship. He had so much fury about Christianity, and our church in particular, but he never gave up on God and Christ."

A question had been tickling the back of Nikki's mind ever since she finished reading the journal. "Did something happen at your church?"

"Like what?"

"Did he have a bad experience?

"Nothing that I can think of."

"Whenever he writes something about being attracted to or interested in a woman, he says it's not possible because he's 'damaged goods,'" Nikki said. "I hate to open this can of worms, but is it possible he was molested?"

Meadow's eyes widened. "God, I don't think so. I never even thought of that. I didn't see anything like that in the journal, did you?"

"No. It's just that my clients who were sexually abused often use that same word, they say they're 'damaged.' But I don't want to read something into it that isn't there," Nikki said.

Mama Linda spoke up. "I think his whole thing about

239

being damaged is his shame about the war. It was a crime how this country treated Vietnam Vets when they came home, disgracing them. That's what he's talking about." She crossed her arms. "Why aren't we talking about the good parts of the journal? Like the one about his first Christmas at the house, how he and I picked out a tree and decorated it and made a nice dinner. How excited he was to get presents for Nik-Knock. Those are nice memories for me too. He and I were the only ones at the house who celebrated."

"I saw that, and yes, it was sweet. There were a few positive things in there, but they were kind of the exceptions," Meadow said. "What do you think about his religion issues, Linda?"

"Honestly, so many of my friends rejected their religious upbringing and had mixed feelings about it, so I didn't find RJ unusual in that way. I'm the weird one—I still go to church, after all these years."

"You're not weird; you're at peace with your faith," Nikki said. "So you think it was the war and its aftermath—that's why he killed himself?"

"I'm not saying it was the *only* reason. So many things led to his hopelessness."

"It's weird to me that he didn't have a girlfriend. He was so attractive and so sweet," Nikki said. "Occasionally, in the journal, he made a reference to a woman, like 'she' or 'her,' but he never called her by name."

Mama Linda stood abruptly, gathering up the wine bottle and glasses. Nikki tried to help, but she waved her away and took everything into the kitchen.

"I noticed that too," Meadow said. "I wonder why it was such a big secret. It was his private journal, after all."

Mama Linda came back from the kitchen. "My dears, it's

1:00 a.m. I'm going to turn in. Your beds are made up and towels are laid out. I'll see you in the morning. Sleep well."

Nikki stayed up with Meadow for a while, going back and forth about the mystery woman, but they got nowhere. Finally, she put her arm around her friend. "Time for sleep. Let's let it rest for now."

Meadow smiled sadly. "How can it rest?"

Chapter 28

Arroyo Walk

Deb dreamed she was living with a bunch of roommates in a mansion—not the house on Ashbury, but a ramshackle place in Death Valley. She was trying to call someone to get a ride home to Oakland, but she couldn't fit her fingers in the holes of the rotary dial phone.

After a fitful night's sleep, she got up, showered, and dressed. The smell of coffee and something sweet drew her into the kitchen. Linda and Phoenix were already at the table, drinking coffee and eating muffins.

"Oh! Amazing. Morning Glory muffins!"

Linda smiled proudly.

Deb took a bite and moaned. It was just as she remembered—a hippie delight, full of carrots, apples, raisins, coconut, and honey.

After breakfast, they headed out for a walk through a nearby arroyo. As they trekked in silence in the cool morning air, thoughts about the journal circled though Deb's mind. Ron mentioned the May Day ritual, so that must have been right before he died. But he didn't say anything that sounded suicidal, and it didn't sound like there was a different tone to his last entry. Did it? She stumbled on the rocky trail and then found her footing again. "We never did have that May Day ritual. Did we?"

"Right, we canceled it. There was no way we were going to celebrate anything," Linda said. "The house was so grim in those days."

The stony texture of the path under Deb's feet reminded her of Death Valley. This was a different kind of desert, the colors redder, the air cooler, with a predominant smell of sage. She was wondering about animal life in the New Mexico desert versus the Mojave when Phoenix interrupted her thoughts.

"Meadow, how are you doing with all this? Must be hard."

"Trying to absorb it. Didn't get much sleep."

"I'm sorry, sugar," Linda said.

Deb swallowed. She was wired and tired. "Everything in those pages—so much fear and anger and regret. I don't know what to think. He kept blaming himself for some mysterious sin. What sin?" She sighed. "Maybe I have to accept that I won't ever completely understand why he killed himself."

"That's true. But we know so much more now than we did before," Linda said.

"I guess so." Deb took a deep breath and blew it out. "I'm going to leave the journal with you, Linda, if that's okay. I got what I needed from it. I think it's time for me to stop obsessing over this stuff."

"Of course it's okay."

They walked in silence for a while. "Was there ever a funeral?" Phoenix asked.

"Yes, at our church in Grand Rapids. And a graveside service too."

"And as soon as you got back to town, we had a memorial in Golden Gate Park," Linda said.

"Right," Deb said. "I remember I was pissed off at Stretch because I didn't like how she was leading the ritual." She snickered. "Those were strange times." She recalled the memorial—a saltwater cleansing, tears and laughter, and a serpentine dance through the trees.

"I don't remember it at all," Phoenix said. "One more fucking thing I blocked out."

"You didn't forget," Mama Linda said, "You weren't there. By then you had already started imagining that RJ had moved away, and so your mother decided to keep you home with her. She said she did it to protect you, but I always wondered if it gave her a good excuse to bow out because the memorial would be just too painful. She was devastated—we all were—but the rest of us wanted a ritual for some kind of closure. She didn't want that. It kind of worked for her to go along with the story you made up, Phoenix, so she could pretend he'd moved away."

"All those grieving traditions—the Irish wake, the Jewish sitting shiva, the reception with tons of food—people think they're about honoring the dead, but really they're for the living," Phoenix said. "For the mourners. I wish my mom had taken me to RJ's memorial." Her voice, which had started out level, escalated to a heated pitch.

"Believe me, I argued with your mom that it was important to take you to the ritual for healing," Mama Linda said. "But she wasn't having it. She said *she* was the one to decide. She played the mother card."

Okay, Deb thought, I'm the only one here who's a mom. "It was her right to play the mother card," she said.

The trail gradually sloped upward, and as they climbed, the flow of their talk ebbed.

The more Deb thought about the ceremony in Golden Gate Park thirty years ago, the more an idea took shape. Yes, she would create a re-memorial for Ron. A reimagining. A ceremony for all who loved and mourned him, but especially for Phoenix, who never had a chance to remember.

Chapter 29

Deuteronomy

Nikki and Mama Linda waved goodbye to Meadow, who was hanging out the window of the shuttle bus, miming her sadness at leaving. At the last minute, Nikki gave a raised fist salute and mouthed the words *yoni power*. Meadow burst out laughing and raised her fist as the shuttle pulled away.

"What was that? A Black Power salute to our white friend?" Mama Linda smiled.

"Me and Meadow realized we'd each gotten our real sex education from Stretch. She taught us the Sanskrit word for vagina and kind of indoctrinated us into yoni power."

Mama Linda nodded. "Meadow and *I*."

"What?"

"You said 'me and Meadow.' You should say 'Meadow and I.'"

"Oh my god, you're still correcting my grammar?" Nikki snickered. "You were constantly on me about that. The only difference is that now it doesn't make me mad." They went inside, and Nikki put a kettle on for tea.

The kitchen was open to the dining area, and Mama

Linda sat at the table, watching her. "I call mine a vagina," she said.

"Right on. Tell it like it is." Nikki measured out hibiscus flowers into the teapot. "On that note, did you see *The Vagina Monologues?*"

"Of course. My friend Janice was in the Santa Fe production. The playwright is a lesbian."

"And?"

"So. You know."

"No, I don't know."

"She's an expert on the subject."

"Ha, so true." Nikki brought the tea things to the table. "Hibiscus tea. You always made it for me, remember?"

"I do."

"I can't believe you finally let me in your kitchen." Nikki put her hands on her hips. "You know what? I'm cooking dinner tonight. No argument."

"All right. I grok that."

Nikki laughed. "I haven't heard that word in a long time. I grok you too." Waiting for the tea to steep, they lapsed into silence. She looked around Mama Linda's house, reflecting on how different it was from Ashbury House. The room they sat in opened out into the living room, with its rust-colored walls and worn leather chairs. Everywhere she looked had a desert patina, from the sun-bleached cow skull on the shelf to the sage-hued rugs covering the terracotta tiles. Even though it was different from the House, it had the same comforting vibe. She turned her gaze to the window and saw the Sangre de Cristo Mountains, maternal and enfolding.

Mama Linda cleared her throat. "Except for that one phone call, we haven't really talked about your discovery. That you're biracial." She opened her hands, palms up. "What's it like?"

Nikki had been looking forward to having this conversation, but now that it was here, she was nervous. She realized how much she wanted Mama Linda's approval. Almost like she was still a little kid. Except she wasn't. "It's so important to me to talk it over with you—you're family."

Mama Linda's eyes teared up and she smiled. "It's true, Nik-Knock, we *are* family. So. I'm listening."

"When I first found out, it was disorienting. I thought, okay, I'm not Black and I'm not white. I was afraid I'd always be in-between. But after a while, getting to know Charles, talking it over with Black friends and white friends, reading about it, I understood more about being mixed. People have always asked me that stupid question, 'What are you?'—and sometimes they'd try to guess my ethnicity or color, and I'd say I didn't know. Now I do know. Regardless of how other people see me, there's a deeper place inside me that knows where I came from now. I'm Jewish from my European ancestors, and I'm Black from my African ancestors. Both are integral parts of me." She paused, thinking over the last year of revelations. "It's lucky, really, that I like Charles. I mean, we *get* each other." She laughed. "He would say we 'dig' each other. Because if we didn't, it could've been, like, 'Hi, I'm Charles, your dad,' and I would've been like, 'Hi, so what, I have nothing in common with you.' Charles and Bernice have totally welcomed me into their family. It's so amazing. It's made it easier to know where to put my new self—how to process it."

"Charles is good people. You know, when your mom moved the two of you up to Petaluma, she demanded that we never let Charles know where you lived and never give him your phone number. I almost did, though, so many times, over the years. He always kept in touch with me, to find out how

248

you were doing. He never gave up." She sipped her tea. "So. Pray tell. Do you identify as Black or mixed, or what?"

Nikki smiled. She'd thought about it a lot over the last year. "Black. Regardless of how I was brought up, that's who I am now, and that's how I identify." She nodded slowly. "I'm still getting used to it."

Mama Linda looked down and bit her lower lip. She brought her gaze back up. "I'm sorry I never told you—I always wanted to, but your mother would say to wait, because *she* was going to tell you. But then she never did. The last time I saw her was in New York, at your graduation for your master's program. Eleven years ago, right? You were twenty-six. I confronted her about it, saying the time to tell you was way overdue. We had a big fight about it, and I broke off our friendship. You know how there's a thing you argue about with someone and then there's the thing underneath that you're really fighting about?"

"Yes."

"That underneath thing was I always suspected the real reason Willow kept the secret from you was that she'd just rather you be white. But when I look back on it now, I think she was telling the truth after all, that the reason she didn't tell you was she wanted to protect you from Charles. Her dad was an alcoholic—did you know that?"

"Yes, that was one thing she *did* disclose."

"Your mom knew what it meant to be the adult child of an alcoholic. It had screwed her up, and she was adamant that wouldn't happen to you, with Charles."

Nikki shook her head in wonder. How did she not see that until now? Of course that's why her mom kept her from seeing her dad. "You and my mother got back together, though, as friends, right? When did you reconnect?"

"A few years ago. She called and apologized, said she

wanted to let bygones be bygones. She was sorry for keeping such a big secret from you, but by then, she said, she'd waited too long, and she thought if she finally told you you'd be furious with her. She asked if we could be friends again. And I knew if I wanted that friendship back, I was going to have to let it go—my anger and my sense of righteousness about what she *should* do as the mother of a biracial child."

Nikki nodded slowly. She poured tea for Mama Linda and herself and tried to process what she was hearing. Her mother was right—Nikki had been furious with her when she found out about Charles. But by then her mom was gone, and in that field of loss, Nikki's anger had gradually drained away, into the earth. "What you're saying about her—I see that now. And for your part, Mama Linda, I know what it's like to have to keep a secret so you don't betray a trust or hurt someone you care about. I have to do it all the time with my clients. Their parents tell me something in confidence, and, even if I think it would be good for the child, I don't tell them because it might hurt them and because I made a promise. That's a professional thing, and I know it's different, but still, I'm saying I understand how it was for you. And maybe I'm starting to get it about my mother too."

"I'm glad you do, sugar. You know what, I'm going to get us a little something to nibble on. I'll be right back."

Nikki took a sip of tea. The tart, sweet taste stirred up an image. She was in the kitchen of the House, terrified and shaking, and someone was scooping her up in their arms.

Mama Linda came back with a plate of cookies. "Oh my, you're shivering. What's wrong?"

"I just had a weird flash." She told her about the shadowy images that had surfaced. "I guess that was like a flashback. Just that flicker, and it was gone."

Mama Linda placed a hand on her shoulder. "What you

described—it's exactly how Che told us it happened. He was the one who scooped you up."

Nikki shook her head. "So strange." She picked up a cookie and set it down. Then she reached for it again and took a bite. It was chewy and sweet. "I remember these cookies. Snickerdoodles. So good. Did you used to make them?"

"Actually, it was Stretch. She gave me the recipe when she moved."

"When was that? I vaguely remember her leaving."

"It was only a few months after RJ died. She was devastated by his suicide, and she didn't want to live at the house anymore. Che was freaked out too. But he stayed on anyway for a few years, just like you and your mom, and then, not long after you two moved, he did too. It was like when you pull one loose strand and the whole sweater unravels. The collective fell apart. But the timing worked out okay because Consuelo's divorce was final by then, and we were both willing to make a go of it, so she and her kids moved in."

"Right. I remember. We still used to visit you at the House back then." Nikki got up from the table and stretched. Then she thought, why not? Ask her. "I keep having this strange feeling about RJ's journal."

Mama Linda's eyes widened and she sat back in her chair, her shoulders tense.

Nikki paced the room as she put into words what had been bothering her ever since she woke up that morning. "When we were putting the pages in order, there were still a few that didn't seem to go anywhere. Like, the text at the bottom of the page didn't continue on any other page. And we noticed that, but we just kind of blew it off, right? It keeps popping into my mind, and I have sort of a creepy feeling about it."

"*Creepy?*"

"I know. It's crazy."

"Oh no, it isn't." Mama Linda smiled sadly. "Not at all. You picked it up on your radar. I'm just glad Meadow didn't notice."

Nikki felt a chill run through her body. So her instinct was right. "Okay, then. What's missing?"

Mama Linda went still. She gazed out the window silently. Then she turned to Nikki. "I pulled out a few pages before I brought it out last night." She straightened her spine and stood up. "I'll go get them."

When she came back, she held a couple of pages close to her chest. "Give me your word you will never tell Meadow about this."

Nikki balked. "I'm not sure I can do that."

Mama Linda gripped the papers tightly, her knuckles showing pale through her skin. "There is nothing here that would help her make sense of things. I'm showing it to you because you're a part of this, too, and—truth be told—I don't want to carry this weight on my own anymore. But believe me, if I thought it would help Meadow resolve things, I would've shown it to her."

Nikki sighed. "Okay. I believe you. I promise."

Mama Linda handed her two sheets of the familiar onion-skin paper. Nikki took a deep breath and started reading. When she finished, she laid the pages down on the table and looked at her friend. "Okay, he was obsessed with someone. She was off limits—maybe she was married or underage or something inappropriate, but god, the way he talked about it, like it was some huge sin? What's the big deal? And why did you make me promise not to tell Meadow?"

Mama Linda shook her head, sorrow in her eyes. She went to the adjoining living room, pulled a book off the shelf, and came back to the table.

Of course, Nikki thought, the King James Bible. RJ cited a chapter and verse on the first page—she'd wondered why. She leaned forward.

Thumbing through the pages, Mama Linda found what she was looking for and marked the spot with her finger. "Deuteronomy 27:22," she read aloud. "Cursed be he that lieth with his sister, the daughter of his father, or the daughter of his mother. And all the people shall say, Amen." She looked up, her gaze piercing.

"What?" Nikki tugged the book away from Linda and read the passage to herself. Then she read it over a few more times. Sitting back in her chair, she picked up the two pages from RJ's journal, looking at the words at the top of the first page, words she thought she had understood just a few minutes ago. But now they had a whole different meaning.

```
right there in Deuteronomy 27:22. I sin
by thinking about it even if I've never
done it.
She is the only one I feel safe with
She is the only one I can save
She is the only one I love
She is the only one I fantasize about
My feelings are lethal
as deadly as the weapon in my hand
```

Nikki shivered and looked up from the page, meeting Mama Linda's eyes. "Man, oh man. He's talking about Meadow, isn't he?"

"Yes." Linda inhaled and blew out her breath in resignation. "When I read that part, all those years ago, and I checked the Bible, I was stunned. At first I didn't believe it, but then something clicked. How overprotective he was with his sister.

How he kept her at arm's length. How he never dated or even had a one-night stand. It was horrible to realize what he felt, but also deeply sad. I just put that accordion folder in a box and stored it away in the basement of the house. Years later, when I was packing to move out here, I came across it and decided I should hold onto it, just in case Meadow wanted it someday. That box has been sitting in my garage all this time. I pulled it out a few days ago, knowing you and Meadow were going to want answers. I wasn't sure what I'd do if she asked to see the journal. I prayed about it, and it came to me—all I had to do was remove those two pages. I just hoped Meadow wouldn't notice anything was missing."

Nikki jumped up and paced restlessly from the breakfast room to the living room and back again. "Poor RJ. How awful for him. It must've held him back in so many ways. From love, sexuality, even friendship. He was so vigilant about her boyfriends, always guarding her, and maybe he was protecting her from himself too." She shuddered and rubbed her arms, thinking the whole thing was fucking creepy. But was it, really? she asked herself. "His feelings weren't inherently horrible. Only acting on them would have been. But he never did. Act on them."

Mama Linda nodded. "Right. That's where I arrived, too, once I got over the shock. I came to another place with it. What he felt was a kind of love. And love comes from God."

Nikki usually didn't understood it when people talked about God that way, but with Mama Linda, it made sense. She nodded in agreement. She hadn't reread the second page, and now she turned to look at it. It was all about how he'd tried to fix himself but couldn't stop fantasizing, couldn't stop thinking about her, couldn't stop imagining it.

They lapsed into silence, each retreating into her own thoughts.

Finally, Mama Linda said, "Do you think this is why he killed himself?"

"I don't know. He was full of anguish about so many different things. So I guess I would say no. What about you?"

"Yeah, I don't think it was the reason, but more like it was part of the whole picture."

Nikki thought about her clients who'd been devastated by incest. But that was always with an older relative who took advantage of her or his trust. Just thinking about it made her furious. She took a deep breath and blew it out. With siblings, it was different. Or was it? There was still a power dynamic, still a setup for exploitation. "The incest taboo is kind of a sacred boundary," she said.

"I like that." Mama Linda smiled.

It was quiet, with only the faint hum of the refrigerator. Nikki ran her fingers over the wrinkled surface of the paper. A coyote yipping nearby broke the silence.

Mama Linda nodded slowly and said, "Okay." She went into the kitchen and came back with a castiron pot and a lighter. She put the two pages in the pot and handed Nikki the lighter.

Nikki went still, her breath caught in her throat. Was this right? She exhaled. Yes. Do it. She flicked the lighter and held the flame to the papers. The two friends watched as the onionskin caught and burned to ash.

Chapter 30

Cool Gray City of Love

T hey held the ritual in early December at Peacock Meadow in Golden Gate Park. Deb had driven into the City, bringing Linda, Andy, and Matt. They got there early to prepare, and while her brother and daughter unloaded the car, Deb and Linda set up an altar.

A couple of months earlier, when Deb and Phoenix had decided to collaboratively create a memorial ritual for Ron, they came up with a list of friends and family to invite. She wasn't sure who would respond to the invitation, but right away the two locals, Ming and Stretch, said they'd be there. It turned out almost everyone from out of town agreed to come to San Francisco. The only two who couldn't make it were Che (he never responded to her messages) and her mom. Okay, her mother just wasn't a ritual kind of person. She said she had a church event to organize, and Deb didn't question her about it, even though she guessed it was only partly true. But her brother wasn't a ritual kind of person either, so she was surprised and pleased when Matt said he'd booked his tickets. He was on the foldout couch, Linda was in the guest room, and Andy was staying with Deb in her room.

Looking around the park, Linda said, "I've missed the fog."

Deb snorted. "I haven't. It's so damp. It was sunny when we left Oakland, remember?"

"Lightweights! Sixty degrees is *warm*. It's snowing in Evanston," Matt said.

A car pulled up and parked across the street. Phoenix got out of the driver's seat and opened the passenger doors for an older Black couple—of course, that was her father and step-mother. Phoenix and her dad carried a large picnic cooler between them, and even from far away, it was clear that Phoenix was nervous. They crossed the street, and, after intro-ductions, Deb gave her friend a big hug. Phoenix, her shoul-ders tense, smiled distantly.

A short, chunky man with curly black hair, dressed in slacks and a sports coat and carrying a backpack, emerged from a taxi. Phoenix introduced him around as her friend Ira.

From down the road, Ming approached at a fast clip, carrying several plastic bags of food. When she arrived there were more introductions, along with nervous laughter. Okay, Deb thought, she wasn't the only one who was anxious. Conversations were starting up, and soon there was a steady exchange that kept getting louder.

The sound of a Tibetan bell, sweet and clear, broke through the chatter. "Shall we make a circle?" Phoenix asked.

Matt gave Deb a pained look, and she whispered, "Don't worry, we're not going to hold hands."

As the circle formed, a rounded woman in a purple dress draped with scarves appeared out of the fog. She joined the circle. Everyone stared until Linda said, "Stretch?" and the woman smiled and nodded. Wow, Deb thought, how we've all changed.

Phoenix began: "Thank you for coming." Lighting a stick

of sage, she walked around the circle, spreading the fragrant smoke. "We borrow from the Native American tradition of smudging, to clear the air and cleanse the spirit. And now, Deb will close the circle, to begin the ritual."

Deb called the four directions, invoking the elements of air, fire, water, and earth. Each time she called a new direction, she made a quarter turn, and everyone followed. When she got to the last one, she said, "Now we turn to the North. Welcome, Earth, element of the North. Bring to our ceremony the comfort of dark caves, the solidity of stone, and the acceptance of death as part of the circle of life. May we find through this ritual the fertile field of grieving and beneath it, the bedrock of love." When she said the word *love*, she glanced over at Phoenix, but her friend was gazing down. Deb made the final turn, and everyone pivoted with her, back to where they started. "The circle is cast."

It was Phoenix's turn to lead, and she took over. She began: "We are gathered here to remember RJ, or Ron, by acknowledging his life and death, in a ceremony of our own. Even though thirty-one years have gone by since he passed, each of us still carries him within us." She looked down and tears dropped on her index cards, smearing the ink. She wiped her face and continued. "We are here today to honor and remember this special man, Ron Travis. I was a young child when he died, but I remember him as a nurturing person. He was a father of sorts for me, and taught me how to grow vegetables, how to compost, how to pace myself while hiking, and how to sew." Everyone except Deb laughed in surprise about the sewing. It was no news to her. Ron had asked her to teach him to sew back when they were kids and had sworn her to secrecy, in fear of being called a sissy.

Phoenix continued, "There is a ritual tradition that involves the drinking of spirits, holding it in one's mouth, and spitting it on the other person." A hush descended on the circle. "But we're not going to do that."

More laughter.

"I am going to pour a libation to honor our ancestral spirits. This is a religious tradition across Africa." She opened a bottle of whiskey and, pouring some on the ground, said, "For our ancestors. And for you, RJ." She put the bottle back on the altar. "Anyone who wants can now make a tribute. You can say or do something to remember RJ. Deb will close the ritual at the end. After that we'll have the traditional feasting."

Deb picked up her guitar. "Ron came back from Vietnam a changed man who was passionately against war. We're going to sing an anti-war song in his honor." She and Andy sang Bob Dylan's "Blowin' in the Wind." After they finished, Meadow cleared her throat. "When I was little, a toddler, I used to . . ." She stopped, her voice breaking. Tears rolled down her face, and she struggled to speak. "I used to stand at the window in my room upstairs and watch Ron leave for school. When he'd get to the sidewalk, he would look up at me and wave goodbye, with his big-brother smile and his laughing brown eyes, and I would cry because I wanted to go with him. But then he always came back, every afternoon." She paused and sniffed a couple of times. "So now. I'm finally getting to a place where I accept that he's not coming back. And that I can't go with him. At least, not until my time comes." She looked down and said softly, "That's all I want to say." When she glanced up, Phoenix was gazing at her from across the circle with so much compassion, it was like a healing balm.

After that, Charles said a short prayer, Bernice scattered rose petals, Ira passed around black armbands, Stretch led a movement meditation, and Linda brought out a bowl-shaped sculpture woven in forest green wool and laid it in the center of the circle.

Silence. Then Matt cleared his throat. "I wasn't sure about coming to this event. My family had a funeral for my brother in our church. Frankly, I thought this ritual idea was kind of weird, but I knew how important it was to Deb, so I showed up for her. That's what I thought I was doing, but now that I'm here, I think maybe . . ." His voice broke, and he swallowed and blinked his eyes. "Maybe this sort of ceremony is a good thing for me too. I always regretted that I didn't talk to Ron about—whatever it was that he felt so much guilt about. Like he was taking the weight of the world on his shoulders. I don't know."

Deb noticed Phoenix and Linda exchanging a charged look across the circle. It reminded her of the loaded glances that used to pass between Phoenix's mom and Linda. Interesting. She turned her attention back to Matt.

"Ron was always thinking of how to help people. But he wasn't—I guess—he wasn't so good at helping himself." From his jacket pocket, Matt pulled out a can of beer and popped it open. Raising the can, he said, "Speaking of libation, I brought this for you. Your favorite. Rolling Rock. Big brother, you have nothing to feel guilty about. Rest in peace." He took a swig and passed it on, and the beer made its way around the circle.

Everyone had taken their turn, so Deb recited the incantation to open the sacred circle. Finally, she chanted, "Merry meet, and merry part, and merry meet again. Blessed be." Linda called out "Amen!" and everyone laughed and clapped. Noisemaking instruments were passed around, and the sounds of drumming, clanging, and hooting broke the ceremonial spell.

They all spread out blankets and unpacked the feast. There was no shortage of food. Along with Deb's carrot sticks and hummus, there was Andy's potato salad, roasted chicken with tarragon from Linda, dim sum from Ming, and bagels and lox from Ira. Charles and Bernice brought deviled eggs, Matt provided drinks, Phoenix brought RJ's specialty— eggplant parmesan—and Stretch contributed a chocolate cake. Toasts were made and food was devoured. As the conversations became more animated, the volume got louder and louder, each person raising their voice to be heard.

After lunch, Deb lay on her back, staring up at the sycamore tree above. The leaves had turned yellow and brown, but, unlike December in Michigan, when a tree like this would be bare, this one still had most of its leaves. She tuned in and out of Linda and Ira's conversation. They'd met today for the first time, yet they coasted effortlessly into a blend of chitchat and heart-to-heart: "Can I get your recipe for the tarragon chicken?" or "How did you meet Javier?" or "It sounds like you're ready to start dating again." On the other side of the field, Matt, Ming, and Andy had joined a group of strangers in a game of Frisbee. Charles, Bernice, and Stretch had gone for a walk. Where was Phoenix? Deb sat up.

Setting off in search of her friend, she crossed a lane and headed to the next meadow. In the distance was the regal Conservatory of Flowers. A lacy, gazebo-like building, it was from a grand era of public works, built by people who actually cared about cultivating parks for the masses. Everything looked and felt so clear, as if she'd received a brand-new consciousness, bright and shiny. A sense of ease spread through her, and she thought: Is it possible? Did the ritual somehow free me?

She didn't see Phoenix, so she looped back and headed toward a row of cypress trees. One tree stood out. She checked the ground beneath it—yes, it was dry enough—and sat down, her back against the sinewy trunk. The roots were magnificent, some plunging down into the earth and some stretching out along the surface, pushing farther, seeking sustenance. Across the way, she saw Phoenix in the distance, emerging from behind the Conservatory of Flowers. She was strolling back in Deb's direction, glancing around dreamily. Phoenix spotted her, and a smile lit her face. She sped up, closing the distance in long strides.

Phoenix arrived, giving off a scent of ritual sage. "Here you are, Meadow in a meadow. Under a tree. Are you all right?"

"More than all right. I am amazed. What about you?"

"My mind has been blown. A gentle blowout." Phoenix reached out and touched the trunk. "What a magnificent cypress." She leaned back against the tree, gazing up.

Deb pushed herself to her feet and joined her friend, feeling the support of the gnarled trunk against her spine. They stayed that way for a while, heads back, staring up at the kaleidoscope of branches against the silvered sky. A dog ran up to them, panting, and, getting no promise of play, ran away. The sounds of passing cars, a bird alight on a branch above, voices of children playing nearby—nothing interrupted their vigil. In time, Deb sensed something had shifted. She brought her gaze down from the sky and into the world. She turned to Phoenix.

The End

Acknowledgments

Thank you to Ragdale Foundation, In Cahoots Residency, and Virginia Center for the Creative Arts, where portions of this novel were written. Many thanks to my wonderful writers' communities: to Janet Ference, Elizabeth Gjelten, Lori Habige, and Christine Rodgers; to Castro Writers' Cooperative; to Page Street Writers; and to Boat at the Watercooler Project.

To the friends and editors who read and commented on various drafts, my gratitude: Donna Levreault, Libbie Stephenson, Borys Procak, Mike Karpa, Michelle Richmond, Shana Mahaffey, Melina Selverston, Natacha Ruck, Tracy Guzeman, Gabriella West, Maureen Brady, Sulay Hernandez, Beret Olsen, and Sarah Branham.

Thank you to my location scouts: Lisa Chess, Isabella Marriott, Jen Senn, and Desi Stitt.

For insights into the psychotherapy profession, big thanks to Sara Gifford, Lynn Rosenfeld, and Michael Tyson. For reflections on the life of a park ranger, thank you to Anna Gilay and Sushawn Robb. Any errors or misconceptions regarding these two professions are mine.

Much gratitude to Mike Karpa and Mumblers Press.

Big thanks to Sara Gifford for everything. To Rowena Richie, my partner in crime, thank you for conspiring. Finally, ten bears' gratitude to Borys for sparkle, kindness, and laughter.

About the Author

Susie Hara's first novel, *Finder of Lost Objects*, was a finalist for a Lambda Literary Award and recipient of an International Latino Book Award. She has worked in theater as a performer, director, and writer. Her stories appear in several anthologies, including *Fast Girls* and *Stirring up a Storm*. She lives and writes in San Francisco.

Also by Susie Hara

Finder of Lost Objects

CPSIA information can be obtained
at www.ICGtesting.com
Printed in the USA
JSHW022310120323
38849JS00003B/16

9 781736 244494